# What people are saying about
## *The Devil's Breath* . . .

"Hogan takes you inside Auschwitz—its workings and its people—in a manner that is fresh and compelling."

    –JIM GOETZ, top-ranked Venture Capitalist by FORBES

"A compelling story that illuminates the horror of the Final Solution and the dignity and courage of both the victims and survivors."

    –JOHN AND AMY ISRAEL PREGULMAN, Co-Founders of KAVOD,
    Ensuring Dignity for Holocaust Survivors

"A murder mystery set within the murderous organized violence of Auschwitz. Fast paced, chilling, and informative about the Nazi death machine."

    –LINELL CADY, PH.D; Professor emerita and founding director,
    Center for the Study of Religion and Conflict, Arizona State University

"A riveting read, from opening lines to memorable conclusion. Tom Hogan has illuminated one of history's darkest times."

    –JAMES FALLOWS, best-selling NYTimes author.

# THE
# DEVIL'S BREATH

# THE
# DEVIL'S BREATH

"A riveting read, from opening lines to memorable conclusion. Tom Hogan has illuminated one of history's darkest times."

*James Fallows, best-selling NYTimes author*

## TOM HOGAN

LAUGHING DOG PUBLISHING • AUSTIN, TEXAS

*The Devil's Breath*
Tom Hogan
Copyright ©2021 by Tom Hogan



ISBN: 978-1-7369436-5-6 Paperback
ISBN: 978-1-7369436-0-1 eBook
Library of Congress Control Number: 2021912088

Published by
Laughing Dog Publishing LLC

Editing by Melanie Mulhall, Dragonheart
www.DragonheartWritingandEditing.com
Cover design by Maya Hogan, Annika Kalac
Interior design by Bob Schram
www.BookendsDesign.com

First Edition
Printed in the United States of America

# Author Note

*The Devil's Breath* takes place in Auschwitz in 1943–1944. All of the characters, save Rudolf Höss, the Auschwitz Kommandant, are fictional.

A note on terms and ranks contained in this book: Germans capitalize nouns, wherever they occur in a sentence. As a result, nouns such as "Kommandant" and "Kapo" are capitalized appropriately throughout the novel, even when they are not used as proper nouns. Also, no German words have been placed in italics, as is commonly the practice when they (or words in other foreign languages) are used in writing that is otherwise in English

Finally, to keep the action as true to the reality on which it's based, I've chosen to use German military titles rather than their American counterparts, as well as a number of German terms, some of which are listed below.

| German Title | US Military Counterpart |
| --- | --- |
| Reichsführer | Commander of the SS |
| Generalmajor | General (top-tier) |
| Kommandant | Base Commander |
| Obersturmführer | Lieutenant Colonel |
| Sturmbannführer | Major |

| German Title | US Military Counterpart |
| --- | --- |
| Hauptsturmführer | Captain |
| Oberscharführer | Senior Squadron Leader |
| Truppführer | Squadron Leader |
| Sturmscharführer | Master Sergeant |
| Scharführer | Sergeant |
| Truppführer | Sergeant First Class |
| Sturmmann | Corporal |
| Unterscharführer | Corporal |

| German Term | Translation |
| --- | --- |
| Kapos | *A prisoner guard* |
| Einsatzgruppen | *Mobile killing unit* |
| Kübelwagen | *A jeep-like vehicle* |
| Judenrat | *An administration imposed by the Nazis* |
| Lebensraum | *"Living Room" (room to expand)* |
| Untermensch | *A racially inferior person* |
| Vernichtungslager | *Extermination camp* |
| Wehrmacht | *Germany's unified armed forces* |
| Organisierung | *A system of bartering* |
| Sonderkommando | *Prisoners forced to work in the gas chambers* |
| Kanada | *The warehouse system at Auschwitz* |

# Prologue

HER FACE CARVED by hunger and pain, the woman hefted the gold ingot, her thumb partially covering the swastika in its center, and displayed it to the four men. Forehead pebbling from the furnace heat, she raised her voice above the harsh metallic chorus issuing from the adjoining room. "So this is it," she said, her voice half statement, half question. "The thing that could end your careers." Her eyes took in the three men in uniform. "And our lives." Her gesture took in herself and the fourth man, also clad in stripes.

She dabbed impatiently with her ragged sleeve at the sweat that had pooled at her eyebrows and snaked its way into her eyes before she gestured at the river of gold sluicing its way along the floor, disappearing beneath a heavy grey canvas curtain. "So let's explore, gentlemen. Let's trace this gorgeous river back to its source and see what we learn along the way."

The three stiff men—starched grey and black, lightning bolts on their collars—didn't return her gaze or acknowledge her at first. They weren't used to being talked to that way by a woman, much less a Jew. But they had no choice, at least for now. They would restore the balance and take their revenge after the woman and her partner had served their purpose.

As she turned from the soldiers, the woman chanced a quick gaze at her striped cohort. He was her age, mid-thirties, and as drained and beaten down physically as her. But his posture was almost as erect as those of the men in grey and black, and his eyes were alert. Catching his eye, the woman winked and saw him smile slightly before he dipped his head.

She placed the bar on the table with a deliberate thud, bringing the men's attention back to the item and her, and turned her eyes to the oldest and smallest of the three, the one with a bar and leaf next to his lightning bolt. "Herr Kommandant, if you would."

The Kommandant strode across the spotless cement floor, the harsh staccato of his heels cutting through the sweltering air, and led the group to a heavily polished steel door that mirrored the image of the approaching group in silver and grey tones. The group waited, eyes fixed on the door, until the Kommandant broke the silence. "I don't think it's going to open itself, Fritzsch."

As if slapped, the man to his right snapped to attention. Narrow faced with a grey complexion and deep-set eyes, he stepped forward crisply and placed one hand on the large, numbered wheel, the other on the thick steel bar that bisected it. He turned the wheel twice to his left, listening for the click, then repeated the process in the opposite direction. At the second click, he pulled down on the bar.

The door opened silently on well-oiled hinges, the only sound the whispering of the rubbery seal at its bottom gliding along the floor. A blast of heat rushed out, causing the woman's short, butchered hair to stand to attention. The men blinked once collectively at the heat before their eyes tightened and focused on the room that emerged before them.

With the Kommandant again leading the way, the group stepped into a large warehouse, its expanse cordoned off into separate areas by heavy canvas curtains that felt more like walls than dividers. The interior landscape was a study in grey: floors, curtains, walls, even the air.

A new wave of flamed air swamped the group, bringing a wet sparkle to their faces. As the Kommandant reached for his coat pocket, Fritzsch stepped forward with a handkerchief and moved to dry his glistening skin. But the Kommandant snatched the square cloth and dabbed at his own growing sweat. The other two SS officers stood silent and still, the sweat running down their temples, pooling along their jaws, and dropping to the floor. The striped pair put their sleeves to use, the thin cloth drying before they lowered their arms.

The first area contained two tables bowing under the weight of the ingots that were putting forth a drying heat as they congealed in their cooling forms. As the ingots neared their final state, a prisoner moved down the line, impressing a small swastika into the soft gold. When the group approached the table, the worker snatched off his striped cap and snapped to attention.

The Kommandant looked expectantly at Fritzsch, who again stepped forward. "Take your water break now," he ordered, "and don't return until we're gone." The man hastened off, his stride stiff from standing at his post for the past four hours.

The Kommandant walked to the table and picked up a still-warm ingot from a stack and examined it idly, turning it over in his hands. As if to regain his authority and control of the moment, he tossed the gold bar at the woman. Expecting the move, or something like it, she caught the brick cleanly with both hands and placed it back in its place on the stack.

Squaring his shoulders, the Kommandant took a deep breath and surveyed the small group. The two uniformed men, schooled in the Reich's ways, looked at him without meeting his eyes. The two prisoners, reflecting their new roles and the self-confidence that came with them, held his gaze, though there was nothing challenging in their eyes.

Letting his breath out slowly, the Kommandant looked first at the woman, then at her partner. "You're correct, my Jewess, both about my career and your lives. We have one week before Reichsführer Himmler and his accountant arrive for their audit and subsequent share of . . ." He motioned roughly at the table of gold. "Which brings us to our discrepancy. One that could prove fatal to all of us." He shook his head slightly, as if he couldn't believe it had come to this.

"These ingots," he continued, "are now regarded as a critical Reich asset, a major contributor to the war effort. So they are treated as such, meaning that we record and track them with diligence. There is one slight caveat. As creators and administrators of this prized asset—one that is unique to Auschwitz—both Reichsführer Himmler and I take a small portion as recompense for our initiative."

The man in stripes spoke for the first time. "I'm assuming, then, that this ingot has a twin. One without a stamp."

"Correct. At the end of each shift, the workers introduce a separate form, one that lacks the swastika. Those ingots, once cooled, are stored and counted separately from their swastika compatriots." He motioned to a separate area, partially hidden by a smaller canvas curtain, behind which the group could see a small stack of ingots cooling on a metal table.

"Now a significant percentage of these ingots—to be clear, *my* ingots—have gone missing, along with the means of accounting for them. Finding those missing ingots and ledger, and the murderer who stole them, is your assignment. And as you correctly surmised," he said, nodding at the woman, "your only hope of survival."

The Kommandant led them alongside the sluice of gold until it disappeared under the canvas, a piece of which had been cut to allow the river's flow. Fritzsch parted the curtain and motioned the group forward.

The next area was dominated by a head-high cauldron of yet another shade of grey, this one the hard tone of a gun barrel. Its top issued a steady hissing sound, interrupted occasionally by the belch of dissolving gold. Haphazard wooden stairs in need of repair and additional support led up one side of the cauldron, culminating in a small platform, a precarious perch at the cauldron's lip with no railings. The workers up there strained against two objectives: emptying their wheelbarrows as quickly as possible and avoiding the ten-foot drop to the concrete, knowing that even a sprained ankle would be grounds for immediate replacement and subsequent execution.

A prisoner clad in only pants and heavy gloves stirred the liquid with a large oar-like object, his ropy muscles tensing and straining. In the gloom of the large room, he was a man of two colors, a fierce yellow on the front from the sweat and the ingredients of the cauldron and a dull grey on the back. On the far side of the room, a gradually escalating ramp made its way from the warehouse floor to the platform. The ramp was wide enough to contain two wheelbarrows, one ascending and the other descending. As the incoming wheelbarrow arrived, another worker stripped to the waist dug his shovel into the wheelbarrow bed and emptied its contents into the cauldron.

At the Kommandant's nod, the group moved as one to the next curtain, stopping to let the empty descending wheelbarrow pass. Fritzsch walked on ahead, put his hand on the curtain opening, and looked at the Kommandant, who shook his head, gesturing to keep the curtain closed.

"Last stop, the source of our gold," the Kommandant said. His eyes fastened on the prisoners. "And spare me your moral outrage, my Jews. As you'll see, the contributors of this gold are making no such objections." He nodded at Fritzsch, who parted the curtain.

This section of the warehouse was draped in darkness that was only interrupted by three high-intensity lamps, each of which hovered over a gleaming metal table. Halos illuminated the tables with harsh clarity, the strength of the light dimming with each meter away from the table and the body it held. It took a moment for the group's collective eyes to adjust to the dark and make out the pile of corpses stacked against the far wall. Two men, their arms and shoulders muscled, the rest of their bodies emaciated, hauled a corpse by the wrists and ankles to a waiting table where a striped worker opened the corpse's mouth, peered in, and then either shook his head—at which time the corpse was taken away—or went to work with his hammer and pliers, extracting the gold. Whatever he extracted, he dropped into the wheelbarrow next to his table, the sound of its landing softened by the teeth already harvested.

Then, with his right hand, which was clad in a thin surgical glove, he inserted a finger into the corpse's anus and felt around. If he discovered anything of interest, he reached for a large carving knife that sat on a stool next to him. Otherwise he motioned for the corpse to be taken away.

The woman held her face steady as she looked at the operation and the pile of teeth. She felt the eyes of the group, especially those of the Kommandant, on her. Her jaw tremored slightly, but she controlled it. Then she spoke. "I've seen what I needed."

The Kommandant nodded and turned to the striped man. "And you, my detective? Have you seen enough?"

"More than enough," the man said, his eyes fixed on the Kommandant. "It's an impressive operation that you and the Reichsführer have built here. I'm sure history will be kind to you both."

Fritzsch took a step toward the man, but the Kommandant placed a single restraining finger on his chest. "I like your sense of irony, Jew. And your gallows humor." He smiled slightly. "Unless you and your wife would like to join that pile of corpses, you'll find me my killer, my ledger, and my gold. Now get the hell out of my sight."

# One

*May 1943*
*Six months earlier*

THE HUNDRED OR SO INHABITANTS of the dank, fetid car had been standing meekly for the past four hours, ever since the train whistle sliced the late-morning air and the train lumbered from the Warsaw platform. Now the late spring light eased through the cracks in the rail car siding, dressing them in horizontal bands. The car was packed so tightly that sitting down was next to impossible. The elderly who had slumped to the floor stayed there, the space above them filling as they fell. The air was heavy with the excretions from bowels and bladders from the very young and very old. And though the train was moving at a brisk pace, not enough air made it through the thin slats to dissipate the odors.

Every rider wore a heavy garment with the yellow star somewhere on its upper left quadrant. Most men wore a cap or a hat. Their faces slack with helplessness and shame, they avoided each other's eyes. The women, clad in scarves and dresses with heavy folds of cloth that came to their ankles, held their children close to their hips and thighs, talking to them in low tones that had lost any assurance or hope in the past few hours. Long past the point of bewilderment, the children were now settled into exhaustion.

In the middle section of the cattle car and pressed up against the far wall, a couple stood, the woman's head resting on the man's shoulder. In contrast to the majority of the car, their postures were still erect, their eyes alert.

They had been attractive once, but three years of ghetto life had leeched most of the vitality from their faces, aging them at least a decade. The man had the remains of a military bearing, both in posture and appearance. His short hair was cut unevenly, and because it had been a week since he had last shaved, his facial hair partially hid a mole on his upper lip. The remainder of his face was heavily lined and scarred. He scanned the car and its sea of heads and shoulders with unblinking grey eyes.

The woman was light-skinned and light-haired, setting her apart from most of the women in the car. Her slim, patrician nose and cheeks had been sharpened by hunger and the daily trauma of ghetto life, her limp hair was pulled back and tied with a piece of torn cloth, and her green eyes were alert but brittle. Unlike the rest of the women, who wore overcoats, she had chosen a heavy wool man's suit coat as her one outer garment.

As the train passed through the open countryside, the woman sniffed at the air. She looked at her partner to see if he had noticed the new aroma that had entered the car, but his watchful attention was on the inhabitants of the car. His eyes were better than hers, she acknowledged, but she was stronger in the other senses, especially when it came to smell and taste.

Frowning, she took a deeper inhalation and held it. The smell was stronger now. She looked out the railcar slats, hoping to see a farm with a large open fire where they might be cooking their animals in bulk, laying in a store of winter meat. But she knew better. The smell was too reminiscent of when the Nazis used flame throwers on the tunnels in the ghetto, burning out the resistance.

The final evacuation of the ghetto had begun the previous day with the resistance's last gasp. At the city's peak, the couple had been able to look down from their apartment and see neither road nor pavement, just an ocean of hats and shoulders. But the activities of the past few months had turned Warsaw into a charred ghost town. The skyline was nothing but remnants, jagged and smoking, some still glowing from the most recent German attack. The Warsaw skyline had shrunk dramatically over the past month, constricting along with the stomachs of the remaining residents.

Recently, the population had been reduced dramatically with over three hundred thousand deported to Treblinka and Auschwitz. Like a snake coiling its prey, the Nazis had forced the remaining sixty thousand, an amalgam of city center dwellers and resistance fighters, toward the center, where they took shelter in a system of tunnels and the few remaining apartment buildings.

Now, after a heroic but ultimately futile resistance—including one glorious day in which they had ambushed the Nazis with Molotov cocktails, grenades, and cobblestones, sending the Germans fleeing for the first time in the war—the die was cast. A new Generalmajor, one driven by discipline rather than hubris, had taken charge, and working from the outside in, he had destroyed building after building, sending his flamethrowers into the ruins to either burn the resisters alive in the tunnels or drive them deeper toward the city center.

The following day would certainly be the ghetto's last. Acknowledging this fact, the rabbis and resistance leaders had met and discussed options. All agreed that this would not be another Masada, where the remaining Jewish resistance fighters and their families had committed mass suicide rather than surrender to the Roman army. Each person, or each family, could choose between surrender and deportation or stay and fight, with death a certainty.

Those who argued for surrender talked of the letters they had received from friends and family who had preceded them during previous deportations. The letters talked of hard work, to be sure, but also of healthy meals and of families being allowed to stay together as long as they fulfilled their work obligations. Those who wanted to stay and fight rebutted this optimism with the recent testimony of Jacob Grojanowski, who had escaped the Chelmno extermination camp and returned to the ghetto to sound the alarm. He had explained that one of the requirements the Nazis made of arriving prisoners was that they write letters or postcards back to friends and families, explaining that they'd arrived safely and had just received their work detail. This task, for most of the arrivals, was their last act before being herded into the gas chamber.

Shimon and Perla Divko, he a former chief detective and she an investigative reporter, had been leading members of the resistance and the Jewish Council, a loose confederation of ghetto leaders that served as an alternative to the Judenrat, the Nazi-installed government that administered daily life in the ghetto. While the Judenrat spent the majority of its time carrying out Nazi dictates, the council led an underground culture that did everything from running soup kitchens and schools to resolving housing issues and disputes between neighbors. On the legal front, it worked with an informal police force to enforce the laws that the Nazis and Judenrat ignored, including the trials and executions of collaborators.

With evening falling on their final night in Warsaw, the Divkos had huddled in a stairwell, cleaning their weapons as they talked. "I know we've had this conversation before," Shimon said, "but this time it's for real. What's your vote: stay or go?"

Perla smiled crookedly and nodded at the street below. "I gather it's too late to convert?"

He smiled back and held his thumb and index finger apart. "A little."

Her face hardened. "If I thought we could help our people in the camps the same way we've done in the ghetto, I'd get on the train tomorrow. But you know the Nazis. They're going to find out who the leaders are and execute us on day one. And I'll be damned if my last moment on this earth is going to be spent breathing those bastards' gas." She took out the German luger from her suit coat. "Let's take out as many of them as we can tomorrow. And when they start with the flamethrowers, we save a bullet for ourselves."

He put an arm around her shoulder and drew her to him. "I love it when you talk dirty."

That afternoon, those who had chosen to stay and fight gathered to say their good-byes to those who were surrendering. In a final gesture of support, the remaining fighters had pooled their valuables, given them to the rabbis for distribution to the neediest on the train platform, and hugged their departing comrades, who then went out into the street where the Germans met them with food, water, and blankets, making sure their largesse was visible to those remaining.

The Generalmajor stood to the side as his famished prisoners ate what they could of the fare, pocketing what they couldn't. Unlike his predecessors, there was no bluster or swagger to him, just tight precision. He surveyed the group and selected five of their number. Trembling, the group gathered before him, expecting some form of punishment, but he gave them a slight smile, one that lacked the nastiness of the smiles they'd seen on German faces for the past four years.

"All I want to know," he began in a low, calm voice, "is how many of your compatriots are left behind." He looked first at a heavy-boned woman he had chosen for the practical way she had herded her children during the feeding.

"I'm not good with numbers, sir," she said in a surprisingly strong voice.

He gestured at the group that had just left the building. "More than these?"

She nodded.

He then turned to a rabbi. "And you, sir. Your estimate?"

"More than I can count. Beyond that I could not say."

He gathered estimates from the other three, but even with gentle prodding to his questions, a rough estimate eluded him. Nodding his thanks to the five, he motioned for them to rejoin their group, which they did hastily.

He picked up a bullhorn and stepped into the street, clear of his troops and their prisoners. "I appreciate your bravery, men and women of Warsaw. But I believe your decision to remain behind was made without considering all the facts. To that end, I have one final demonstration."

He nodded to a nearby truck, which had backed up next to where he was standing. A soldier reached into the truck and pulled out a child, a little girl who looked to be six or seven years old. The commander steadied the frail figure and whispered something to her that caused her to stand up taller, a small, hopeful smile at the corner of her mouth. He motioned for her to look up at the top of the apartment building. As she did so, he pulled out his Luger and shot her in the back of her head.

He let the lifeless body slip through his arms and lie curled at his feet, a bundle of wool and cooling flesh. Stepping away from the body, he nodded at the truck, where two other soldiers parted the canvas curtain, revealing a group of children, roughly a dozen in number, seated on the benches. The soldiers used soft voices and gentle hands to extract the children. When they had all exited the transport, they were lined up next to the commander.

"The next child," he said, placing a calming hand on a four-year-old boy's head, "will not meet such an immediate and painless demise. I have brought Sergeant Gruber from our kitchen. He is our specialist in meats, specifically dismembering the farm animals that have been part of our liberation of your country. In thirty minutes, Gruber will visit the same treatment on young . . ." He bent forward and talked soothingly to the boy, then brought the bullhorn next to the boy's mouth.

"Shmuel," the boy said in a quivering voice.

"On young Shmuel here," the commander continued. "And from prior experience, I can attest that master Shmuel will lose at least four limbs before he passes on to your Jewish afterlife." He nodded at two other soldiers, who lifted and brought forward a rough wooden table. Sergeant Gruber then stepped forward and placed a hatchet and a large knife, its blade slick with oil, on the table's scarred surface, which included drainage channels.

"You have thirty minutes to reconsider your decision," the commander said before motioning the children back into the truck. "Oh, and one last thing. If our young Shmuel should survive the loss of the first four appendages, there is a fifth appendage. And Sergeant Gruber assures me that the neck of a child is far softer, far less sinewy than its adult counterpart. He likens it to the difference between veal and a tough steak." He looked back at his watch. "Twenty-nine minutes."

With five minutes to spare, Shimon Divko exited the apartment building and told the commander that the majority of the group would surrender. But they wanted an extra hour to gather their belongings and say their good-byes to those who had chosen to remain. "You and I both know what will happen to those belongings and to their owners," he said. "But I ask you not to deprive them of this final hope."

The Generalmajor nodded, assuring Divko that he would guarantee the hour as well as safe transport to all who exited. Divko looked three meters to his left, where the little girl's body still lay, and then looked back at the commander with a raised eyebrow.

The Generalmajor nodded. "Point taken. But it worked. Not only in getting your attention but in saving needless bloodshed."

"Only to be shed in Treblinka?"

"It's Auschwitz now. Treblinka is being shut down." He noted Divko's surprise at his candor. "I'm speaking soldier to soldier now, not German to Jew." He looked over Divko's shoulder and nodded. "I respect the battle that you and your people have fought. But it ends tomorrow. You know that, right?"

As Divko nodded, the Generalmajor continued. "Look, I don't know what's at the end of the railroad line for your people. I hear the same rumors you do. But whatever is there has to be better than being roasted alive, which is the fate awaiting anyone who stays behind." He put a hand on Divko's arm. "I take no pleasure in tomorrow." He nodded at the little girl's corpse. "Nor that. But I'm a soldier, and I have my duty. Tomorrow this city will be both charcoal and free of Jewish inhabitants. Please relay that to your troops, Herr Divko."

As Divko's head cocked in surprise, the Generalmajor nodded again. "Yes, we know of you. And your wife. A formidable pair, we're told. And again, one soldier to another, I know that even though some will come out with their belongings and their hands up, some of you will choose the soldier's route and fight us to the death." His hand closed over Divko's arm, strong but not enough to inflict pain. "And I'm telling you right now that you and your wife will not be among their number."

Divko kept his eyes steady on the German. "And you're confident of that how? Soldier to soldier."

"Because, as a commanding officer, I want to lose as few of my troops as possible. And based on what I've heard of you, I have a better chance of achieving that objective if you're on tomorrow's transport rather than up in that apartment building." His grip tightened. "So let me make you this promise: If you and your wife are not among the group that exits that building in one hour, I will revert to my original plan, and the death of those twelve children will be on your head, not mine."

He offered his hand to Divko, who looked at it without reaction. But the Nazi kept his hand extended, his eyes level on Divko. Soldier to soldier. Divko nodded and shook the proffered hand.

# Two

THE LANDSCAPE COULDN'T make up its mind what it wanted to be, Perla thought as the train hustled along in a droning rhythm. The trip had begun with the familiar grim Warsaw palette: the grey of damage and decay, the black of soot, and the brown of recently disturbed dirt. But an hour free of the Warsaw char, the train entered a brightly verdant landscape of farmlands and fields of wildflowers. It was like that American film she'd read about—something about a wizard—where it started in black-and-white and then burst into color.

Eyes pressed to the slats, she watched the countryside roll by, every now and then raising her eyes to check on her husband. Leaving the ghetto and resistance behind had sapped him of his self-worth, even if they both knew he had no choice. They had sat in the stairwell and discussed the situation, looking for alternatives, both knowing that the Nazi commander had them boxed. Rationally, they knew they were probably buying the children at most another day of life if the rumors about the camps were to be believed. But they also knew that the Nazi commander would follow through on his threat if Shimon didn't show, if only to live up to his word. And the effect this would have on the recently surrendered Jews would be catastrophic. And they knew that the Nazis would make sure the Jews knew who was responsible for the slaughter, even as they conducted it. The commander knew his business, she had to admit—and his opponent. And from Shimon's face and the slight slump in his normally military-erect posture, she could see that he knew it too.

Now she watched as Shimon tried to use the train ride to perform a metamorphosis she knew to be impossible. She could see him eating his dignity, trying to round his shoulders, and attempting to shuffle even though he was still capable of striding. The rest of the transport was going to look to him for guidance, and he had to communicate to them by his posture that submission was the only path to survival.

Grojanowski had given the council elders the lay of the land in the camps: The only chance to survive was to be a nobody. The somebodies, those who were recognized or respected by the others at arrival, were deemed possible threats and eliminated early, usually on day one. Now Divko was trying to make the transition from ghetto commander to camp nobody in the course of a train ride. Worse, he would have to stay in character twenty-four hours a day. She had serious doubts that he would survive beyond the first day.

Four hours into the journey, the landscape began to lose its vibrancy, the colors reducing in both number and intensity as the train began to slow. What little green left was scarred, as if it had been recently assaulted. Green gave way to brown, then to grey. Buildings started to appear, at first occasionally and in disrepair, then newer constructions with fences around them. As the newer buildings increased in number, the train slowed proportionately. For the first time in hours, the riders stirred. No one spoke, but the railroad car was now on collective alert.

As the train slowed further, Shimon pressed his eyes to the slat. A series of empty poles passed. With the final slowing, a sign came into view: Oscwiecim. Underneath it, in all caps, read "AUSCHWITZ." He pulled back and gestured with his chin for Perla to look. She squinted, read the sign, and pulled back, her face hardening.

From the back of the car a voice rose. "Where are we, Inspector?"

Shimon looked at Perla, who shrugged and gestured with her head at the expectant faces. "Tell them the truth. But in stages."

"Oscwiecim. The Germans call it Auschwitz. It's a labor camp."

"Is it our final stop? What should we do, Inspector?"

Shimon pressed his face against the slat. As he breathed in the smell of the approaching camp, his face froze. "If you have money, use it now," he said loudly, his voice carrying to the back of the car.

"We were told to save our money to get the better jobs, the better housing. The Nazis told us this morning—"

"They lied. Your only job now is to make it through the next twenty-four hours. Do anything you can to survive. Anything."

The crowd in front of him parted slightly, allowing a woman to squeeze through. She carried a baby in her arms and used her thighs to usher a small boy, four years old at the most, before her. "What can I do, Inspector? I have no money. And the Nazis will see these little ones as burdens."

Shimon looked down at the woman, her face empty of any resolve or hope. Her clothing, and that of her children, was far too large for them and in multiple layers. It was the look of those who no longer had housing and were sleeping in the street. Divko reached into his pocket and pulled out some money. At the sight of the cash, the front of the crowd almost involuntarily surged forward.

Perla grabbed his arm and spun him to face the slats, grabbed the money from his hand, and hid it in the folds of her dress. Then she placed her face next to his. "Damn it, Divko. We agreed. You're not the law here." She looked over at the mother. "Or the bank."

His eyes followed hers. "Perla, these people need more—"

"Than we can provide." She looked back at the mother and sighed, reached into her dress, extracted some bills, and pressed the bills into the grateful woman's hands. Then she divided the remaining money into two handfuls, one of which she pressed on Shimon. "We're not in the ghetto anymore, Shimon. It's just the two of us now. And if we're going to make it through this, we're going to need to harden our hearts. And lower our profiles."

As Shimon's eyes left hers and strayed over the crowd, she grabbed his face between her palms and pulled it down until he focused on her. "Yesterday, when we agreed to join this group, what did we promise each other?"

"That we'd get through this," he replied. "Together. Whatever it took."

"Which means we need to play our new roles, starting now. From here on in, we're nobodies. And we need to start acting the part. Especially you." She kept her hands on his face, not letting him look away. "Which means . . ."

"Don't look them in the eyes. Hunch my shoulders. Play the beaten dog."

"Thank you," she said, her hands softening on his cheek.

His response was lost in the simultaneous jolt of the car's halt and scrape of the door opening. Men garbed in fading stripes, their arms brandishing armbands that held purple triangles and read *"KAPO,"* began to shout at them in Yiddish and Polish even before the doors were fully open. Over their shoulders, lined up along the exterior of the platform in loose groupings, black-clad soldiers stood, a bored look set on most of their faces. Some of them sat and barked directions at the Kapos. Others just watched with eyes that held neither sympathy nor interest.

The smoke from the engine had drifted back to the platform, enveloping and confusing both hunters and prey. As it cleared, the Kapos sprang to life, grabbing the passengers closest to the door and pulling them down roughly, causing them to spill out onto the platform. As the fallen tried to stand and reach back into the car for their luggage, a second group of Kapos pulled the suitcases and valises out indiscriminately and passed them down to another group of Kapos who tossed them up into a large idling flatbed truck.

The initial arrivals, many of whom had just regained their feet, were herded forward by truncheon-wielding Kapos and SS soldiers barely containing snarling dogs who seemed to have more animosity for the new arrivals than their human handlers did. Urged forward by the disembarking passengers behind them, the group encountered a funnel of Kapos and other prisoners who forced them to narrow from a confused amoeba into an orderly group of no more than two across within the space of a hundred meters.

As the confusion and violence on the platform increased, many of the passengers looked to Divko for guidance. Ashamed of his passive behavior during the train ride, he pulled a cloth cap from inside his jacket and jerked it onto his head, pulling the brim down to shield his eyes and avoid those of others.

The young mother from the train, a child in each arm and her hand clutching the money Perla had given her, watched hopefully as a Kapo led her to the side of the crowd where it was quieter. He took the proffered money, then grabbed her older child and handed him to a compatriot, who hoisted the startled child onto another waiting flatbed. The first to populate the truck bed, the boy looked around at the emptiness, too confused to cry. The Kapo then grabbed the infant from the mother's arms, ignoring her pleas, and tossed it idly up to the truck bed, where there was no one to receive it. The mother gasped and tried to climb up the truck ladder after her child, but with an almost careless flick of his leaded truncheon, the Kapo clubbed her into unconsciousness.

Muttering under his breath, Divko started to move forward, but Perla restrained him with a tight hand on his elbow before turning him away from the fallen woman and into the surging, funneling crowd. "I'm not ready to be a widow, Shimon. You've got to get ahold of yourself. Starting right now." She nodded toward the front of the line. "It looks like they're going to separate us, and I don't know when I'll see you again. So promise me this one last thing. Don't fight battles you've got no chance of winning." She looked up at him, her eyes imploring. "Promise me that."

Divko seemed not to hear her, his head swiveling, taking in the surroundings. Then his eyes came to rest on her face. He nodded at the chimneys. "You recognize that smell?"

"I do. But that won't be us."

As they shuffled forward, a heavy hand fell on Divko's shoulder. He wheeled and faced a scar-faced Kapo whose face was devoid of emotion, his eyes darting from Divko to the front of the queue.

"Inspector Divko? You are Divko, the detective?"

Shimon took the man's measure quickly. His face, though drawn, was alert. His uniform fit better and was in better shape than those of his compatriots. "And you are?"

"Chernov. Father of Anna Chernov. My family is forever in your debt."

When Divko had sought to join the Warsaw police, there were no Jews among its ranks. To show their egalitarian principles, the officials admitted him into their training program. Despite the constant harassment and slurs, he persisted, and when his scores for both the physical and psychological tests ranked consistently at the top of his class, the Warsaw police had their first Jewish detective.

The news of his joining the ranks of the oppressor was met with suspicion and disdain by the Jewish population. While not going so far as to make him a pariah, they kept their distance and refused to assist him with his cases, even when it was to their direct benefit to do so.

That all changed with the Chernov case. Anna Chernov was a twelve-year-old girl who simply vanished one afternoon. The Warsaw police told the parents they would open the case after three days, but Divko, working after hours, initiated his own search that day. He knew the official reaction would be to come down hard on the Roma population, so he went to visit their chief, with whom he had developed a collegial working relationship in his first year on the force. The Roma chief swore that his community had nothing to do with the girl's disappearance, and Divko believed him.

With one of their own missing, the Jewish community changed its tune about cooperating with Divko. But despite three days of investigation, Divko had nothing to show for his efforts. Then a shopkeeper who had been away when Anna had gone missing returned from his sourcing trip and remembered a police sergeant—the kind who came into the store and took what he wanted, never paying—had been eyeing Anna and her friends in a manner that he termed "disgusting." Perhaps it was nothing, but he wanted to report it.

Of course, Divko knew the sergeant. Nowak was a legend within the police force for his conviction rate, though it was acknowledged that many of these convictions had been achieved at the end of a baton.

Divko had taken two days off and followed Nowak on his rounds. It was true that he took some liberties with shop owners and their merchandise, but he also had a network of informers he cultivated and rewarded. At the same time, he clearly had a thing for young girls, flirting with them inappropriately—sometimes in front of their parents, even, knowing they had no recourse.

On the second night of his reconnaissance, Divko had continued his pursuit of Nowak after Nowak signed off from his shift. Divko followed him to a popular police bar and waited outside for two hours. When Nowak came out, Divko expected him to turn right, toward his apartment. Instead, he turned left and careened his way three blocks into the sketchy part of Warsaw, where he buzzed his way into an apartment complex.

Realizing Nowak was drunk beyond the point of being careful, Divko had sprinted ahead and caught the door before it locked. He gave Nowak a minute before following him up the stairs. He caught up to the sergeant on the third floor as he weaved down the corridor and then stopped in front of number 31. Nowak knocked loudly on the door and waited. Divko slowed his walk down the corridor but upped his pace as he heard the door open and walked beyond the door before it closed, looking past Nowak and the policeman who opened the door as he passed by. Beyond the men he saw two young girls dressed in peignoirs, neither of them Anna.

Divko returned to the station and grabbed three sets of handcuffs and a sap that he kept in his top drawer. Then he returned to the apartment complex, made his way to apartment

31, and knocked loudly. He identified himself in a drunken slur and waited for the door to open.

Nowak opened the door. His face was just beginning to show its surprise at Divko's presence when the sap struck him behind the ear, sending him to his knee. Divko walked briskly into the living room where two other cops had two distraught underage girls on their laps. He employed the sap again, handcuffed the two staggering cops, and returned to Nowak, who was struggling to recover, and tapped him again with the sap. Then he handcuffed him as well, hands behind his back.

In the bedroom he found Anna, naked, face-down, and drugged. He went back into the living room and told the two girls there to put their clothes on and dress Anna. Then he took the three girls to the head rabbi's house and headed back to the police station, where he told the captain where he could find Nowak and the other two men.

The Chernov case had multiple repercussions. Divko, who was already a fish out of water in the department, was now a figure of disdain. No one would partner with him or share any information. He was also reassigned from his day shift to graveyard. On the other hand, the Jewish community regarded him as a hero and funneled all of its information to him, some of which he used himself, leading to an unparalleled conviction rate. Some he funneled to his captain, increasing his captain's conviction rate as well and guaranteeing Divko's continued place within the department.

—⁓—

Perla placed a hand on Chernov's arm and nodded toward the end of the queue. "What's going on up there, sir?"

"A Selektion. They'll separate you first by sex, then prune out the unproductive, keeping only the strongest and most useful. Stay to the right, whatever it takes. To the left is death."

Whistles sounded, and the Kapos waved to their partners at the front of the line, indicating that the boxcar was now empty. With that, the shouts and the intensity of passenger herding on the platform increased. As Perla and Divko were pushed forward, Chernov accompanied them.

"One last thing," he said as he produced a handmade knife, its blade honed and lethal. Divko quickly grabbed Chernov at the wrist, but released it once he realized there was no threat in the action. As Divko released his wrist, Chernov sliced open his own palm. Returning the blade to his pants, he took two fingers and dipped them in his bloody palm. Then he smeared the blood on their cheeks, first on Perla and then on Divko, and rubbed the makeshift rouge in.

"For a healthier look. It's the least I can do for my Anna."

Perla nodded her gratitude. "Your Anna. Is she here?"

Chernov looked to the row of chimneys on his left, and his eyes watered. "In a way."

The funnel of clubs and dogs had done their job, forcing the arrivals into two orderly lines. Chernov stayed with the Divkos until the separation point, about fifty meters from where the SS was conducting its Selektion, at which point the men were pushed to the right and the women to the left. Shimon was able to grab Perla's hand for one last squeeze. Then their fingers separated and they queued up, single file.

Perla shifted her attention from Divko to the activity at the front of the line. Mindful of Chernov's advice, she focused on the decision process and the common factors. There were two different selections, it seemed. The Nazis guards and Kapos did the initial pruning, sending the very young—often with their mothers, who refused to part with them—the elderly, and the disabled to the left before they even reached the desk with the SS personnel. The majority of those who made it to the desk were sent to the right. But the SS officer at the desk was accompanied by an officer Perla assumed was a doctor by the way he scrutinized the arrivals, asking them questions, having them take off their coats to display their arms, and even making them open their mouths for examination. The process reminded Perla of the summer she had spent on her uncle's farm and how he and potential buyers inspected horses at auction.

One other item caught her eye. Well-dressed women of her age made it to the front of the line, but after a cursory examination, including an inspection of their hands, they were pushed to the left. Seeing this, she disheveled her clothing even more than they already were, ripping them slightly around the collar. She wasn't sure what the inspection of the hands was all about, but she was determined not to be mistaken for a woman of privilege, one who would bridle at the work ahead.

Ten minutes later, she reached the front of the queue. The SS officer's eyes captured her in a single glance, and he motioned her forward with a wave of his riding crop. Perla strode forward with as determined a gait as she could muster.

"Empty your pockets," the SS officer said.

Perla pulled the money from the folds of her dress and held the bunch of paper in one hand, hoping that this was what they were after. But the two men stared at her until a female Kapo stepped forward, reached into the pockets of her overcoat, and produced a notebook.

"Occupation?" the doctor said.

"Journalist."

The doctor took her empty hand and pulled it to him. He kneaded the flesh for a moment. "Soft hands. We need workers, not scribes."

When he started to motion her to the left, Perla placed the stack of money on the table and took a slight step back. "Soft hands that can type ninety words a minute."

The SS doctor pocketed the money. "To Kanada, then. Incoming. Let's see if your fingers can keep up with our little operation there."

Shimon had gone through the same mental preparation as Perla, trying to discern what factors other than age and physical fitness went into the life-or-death decision. It seemed that more men than women were being guided to the right, which was encouraging. He was relatively sure he would be joining their number.

Surprisingly, some of the younger boys were being taken to the right after the examination of their hands. Chernov, who had rejoined Divko as he approached the front of the line, saw his confusion. "Trigger assemblage. The wiring and switches require the smallest hands possible."

And then there was no line, just the two waiting SS figures.

"Name and age."

"Shimon Divko. Thirty-eight."

"Occupation?"

"Detective. Warsaw."

"And now here you are, just another race criminal. Ironic, no?"

"As you say."

Before the SS man could respond, Chernov leaned in. "I know him from the ghetto. He's strong, a hard worker. I'll vouch for him."

"Very well. Krupp Metallwerke." His eyes left Divko, a finality to them. "Next."

Divko placed a hand on Chernov's arm. "Thank you."

"Don't thank me yet. Munitions is the hardest work here. The longest I've seen anyone last there is six months."

# Three

*December 1943*

IT WAS NEARING EIGHT IN THE MORNING, and the wispy fog that had hugged the prisoners' ankles during roll call was in the process of burning off. A young soldier moved briskly between the buildings, his step fresh and precise, as if he were aware of being watched. The uniform was crisp and complemented his physique. His hair was blonde and beginning to thin, his chin tight and small-boned. Bland lines defined a face that was pleasant but unmemorable.

The barracks were empty and would remain so until evening roll call. Anyone caught inside during the day without permission was subject to public punishment, including death. The only prisoners left inside the fence were those who tended the grounds and the fortunate few with inside jobs running errands between the buildings.

The camp was in the grips of a harsh winter. The sky was empty and weak, and the ground was a frozen mix of exposed dirt and packed snow hardening to ice. Soldiers were swathed in their heaviest coats. The Kapos had extorted multiple layers of clothing from their charges and from the Kanada stores. The winter was taking its toll on the prisoner population, with the prisoners trying to supplement their issued year-round clothing with stuffed rags, leaves, and paper. Despite these efforts, the attrition rate was still high, with prisoners dying in their sleep in the frigid barracks, at work, and at roll call, where any slight infraction or irregular count translated into hours-long recounts or punishments. The only respite was that the cold sapped the tempers of the Kapos, making most days punishment-free.

Intense cold also brought a significant decision for the prisoners. The old guard, when pressed or paid for advice, advocated maintaining a semblance of cleanliness at any cost. Sunday showers were critical, as was morning time at the sink in the latrine. Let your hygiene go, they cautioned, and you became a breeding ground for disease. But in the harsh, windy cold of the camp, the lack of towels translated into wet, exposed skin, resulting in a choice between disease and frostbite. And so the infirmary—and later the morgue—were filled with the sufferers of typhus and meningitis, as well as infected open sores and their more serious cousin, gangrene.

The most recent snow, earlier and harsher than normal, was on its last legs, its remnants striating the grounds between the barracks. The gathering areas in front of the barracks were completely free of foreign elements, including snow, having been tamped down and scuffed by thousands of feet every morning and night until they had, like archaeologists, taken their site down to bedrock—in this case, tamped earth. There was no need for the camp custodians to rake or sweep these yards because the odd leaf or paper was quickly picked up and used as insulation for either shoes or coats.

Normally the grounds would have been long empty. Five o'clock reveilles—four o'clock once the spring sun enabled an earlier work start time—were normally followed by a brief breakfast and then roll call, which meant the prisoners were on their way to work by six if the count was correct. But that morning's departure had been delayed twice, first by a miscount, then by the resulting public punishment.

Public punishments normally consisted of flogging, with the prisoner stripped to the waist and bent over a rounded block of wood. Lash count depended on the infraction or the whim of the SS man, Kapo, or senior prisoner administering the lash. The prisoner was forced to call out the number of each lash in German, and if he forgot, the count began anew.

That morning's punishment, though, had been different. In an incredible show of either bravery or stupidity, a nameless prisoner had refused to exit his bunk. His stunned barracks-mates had not reported him and hoped for a hurried count. But the count had been accurate, which reflected poorly on the Kapo, who quickly extracted the story from a nearby prisoner and disappeared into the barracks, returning moments later, dragging the missing prisoner by his collar, which ripped in his grasp.

Because of the Kapo's mood, and perhaps to lessen his own consequences, the resulting punishment was more severe than normal, with the prisoner subjected to The Post. His hands were tied behind him and he was hung from a vertical post, his feet unable to touch the ground. The assembled prisoners were then forced to walk past the dangling prisoner, his cries quickly growing hoarse in the bitter cold. Every head turned to view the prisoner, knowing that the price of looking away was their own flogging at day's end.

The young German soldier looked up briefly at the prisoner, long since passed out from the pain, but didn't break his stride. He exited the gathering yard and walked quickly past the more recently constructed barracks, distinguished by their prefabricated thin wooden walls, and then past the earlier solid brick barracks. Every third building or so had one or two corpses sitting up next to the main exit, awaiting the collection wagon.

He walked past Block 24, which was in the process of being converted into a brothel. At first, no one believed the rumors. Then one of the higher-ups confirmed that, in fact, most of the other camps already had one. Auschwitz was behind the times.

"Who's it for?" one of the soldiers had asked the officer.

"Everyone except Jews."

"And where will they get the women from?"

"From the inmates, of course. The other camps bring them in from the German cities and don't seem to have any trouble recruiting, due to the promise of both food and money. But given the size and diversity of our population here, the decision was to select from the prisoners."

"Including Jewish women? You clean some of them up, put some meat on those ribs, and . . ." He raised his eyebrows.

The captain had shaken his head. "Please. Remember the race crimes? If we jailed Germans for sleeping with Jews before the war, we can't be changing the rules now. No, it will be Slavic women for the few prisoners who earn the right to visit Block 24 and German women, most of them Communists, for our soldiers."

The young soldier had listened to the officer but had no intention of availing himself of the bordello's services. When he voiced that opinion at the dinner table, the captain had looked at him with mild amusement. "That's because you've only been here six months, Feuer. Let's see if your opinion changes once you've been here a year."

The soldier nodded at a uniformed sentry as he walked through a gate, an opening in a heavy fence that was electrified and topped with barbed wire, a sign of Kanada's importance to the camp and to the Reich. No other camp in the Nazi's vast complex of camps—labor, concentration, transit, and death—had an operation like Kanada, both in terms of size and function.

Whistling softly, the soldier walked across a small courtyard, a haphazard combination of brick and tamped clay, then stopped in front of a standard brick building. Taking out a set of keys, he opened a side door and entered.

The offices were just coming to life, and the hallway was empty. There was a stillness and a hint of dust in the air. The soldier stopped before one more set of doors, that one with a desk and sentry.

"Sturmmann Feuer," the sentry said, barely looking up and not saluting.

Feuer nodded curtly and signed in, looking briefly at the small list of names before his. The sentry opened the door with an electronic click and motioned him in. Feuer took a quick right and bounded up the stairs, humming as he went.

He stopped in front of a pebble-glassed door with the words "Chief Accountant" lettered in white on it because a ghost of light trickled from the bottom of the door. Frowning, Feuer began to knock, but as he touched the door, it eased open slightly. His frown deepening, he pushed the door open and leaned in. There, his head resting on the desk, was his boss, Obersturmführer Elster.

"Herr Obersturmführer," he said, a forced lightness to his tone. "You're in early this morning." When there was no answer, he continued. "Or did you work through the night? If I'd known, I could have . . ." As he moved around the desk, the pool of blood on the desktop came into view. He stepped back and uttered a high-pitched sound that caught in his throat. Then he turned and fled.

Two hours later, Feuer was back in the office, again staring at Obersturmführer Elster, whose head had been raised off the desk. The body now sat back in his chair in an almost relaxed posture, as if he were lounging or napping. His mouth was agape, his eyes empty, and his grey uniform shirt covered with blood issuing from multiple slits in his chest and stomach. Feuer was held at the elbow by Sturmbannführer Frankel, a bulldog soldier, his hair tight to his scalp, his chest tight in his uniform shirt. His grip on Feuer was relaxed but firm, holding him upright and giving him nowhere to go.

Feuer's voice skittered. "The door was slightly open, which it never is, so I—"

Frankel tightened his grip with just the thumb and forefinger, causing Feuer to wince and close his mouth. "You'll get a chance to tell your story when the Kommandant arrives. Until then, I suggest you shut up."

Outside in the hall there was the sound of the guards' clicking heels. "Herr Kommandant," one of them said.

Ignoring the guards' salutes, Rudolf Höss strode into the room and surveyed it, his face betraying nothing. His uniform was beautifully tailored, his posture was composed but not rigid, and the slightest touch of oil held his freshly cut, brushed back hair in place. Trailing in his wake was Hauptsturmführer Fritzsch, his face tight, his uniform askew. As the Kommandant's longstanding adjutant, he was an expert in both anticipation and fulfillment. His eyes darted around the room, staying an uncomfortable length of time on the inhabitants, each of whom looked away under his gaze.

Fritzsch and Höss had been a team since Dachau, the first of the Nazi concentration camps, which opened in 1933, just months after Hitler came to power. Originally intended for political prisoners, the camp had grown in size and purpose with each year of Nazi rule, becoming a brutal holding pen for Jews of every political or social stripe. As early SS enlistees, Höss and Fritzsch had joined Dachau in its infancy and helped develop the camp procedures and laws, with Höss on the administrative side and Fritzsch on the discipline side.

Without much precedent to guide him, Fritzsch had used his imagination to come up with such punishments as the standing cell, the flogging bench, and the pole, all of which had become standards in the growing network of camps. Höss had been less dramatic in his proficiencies, but he had emerged as one of the foremost experts in camp administration by the onset of the war.

So it was no surprise to Höss or the other camp commanders that he was chosen to build Auschwitz from the ground up. And it was no surprise to Fritzsch that he had been summoned by Höss to be his right-hand man in that endeavor.

"Heil Hitler!" Frankel said, snapping to attention while still holding Feuer's arm. Feuer attempted to click his heels, but Frankel's grip had thrown him off-balance. Höss ignored both men, walked over to the desk, and stared down at the body. His eyes then slid up the wall, which held a safe that appeared to be closed. Höss's eyes twitched and the muscles in his neck tightened. Reaching the wall in three strides, he took out a pen, eased the safe door open, and extracted a small ledger similar to a child's homework book. After thumbing through it for a moment, he looked deeper into the safe, felt around in it, and pulled out an empty hand.

"Who found him?" the Kommandant asked.

"Feuer here, Kommandant," Frankel said.

Fritzsch walked over and stopped in front of Feuer, who now seemed to be held up only by Frankel's pinched grip. "Did you touch the body?"

"Only to see if . . . I mean—"

"The safe," Höss interrupted. "You found it like this?"

"No, Herr Kommandant." Feuer's eyes moved to the safe and stayed there. "I mean, I don't know. Once I saw the body, I . . ."

Fritzsch nodded to Frankel. "Take him to interrogation. Let's see if our friends there can make him more articulate."

Frankel began to turn Feuer but was halted by the Kommandant's raised hand. "Let him go. He's got nothing to do with this." He took in the room with a single sweep of his hand. "Clean this place up. Then secure the premises. No one is to enter without my approval." Taking in all three men in a single glance, he lowered his voice. "Speak to anyone of this and you're dead men. Do I make myself clear?"

The men nodded without looking at the Kommandant, who pocketed the ledger, locked the safe with a violent twist of his wrist, and exited the room without another word.

# Four

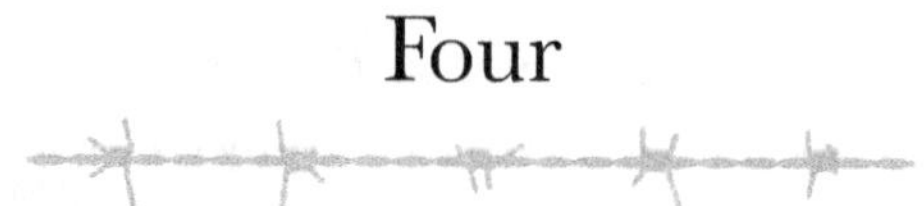

THE NEXT MORNING, Höss was in his office early with an unshaven face and a uniform lacking the previous day's crisp lines. It had been a long night and a short, uneven morning. His wife had been asleep when he arrived home that night but had been up having breakfast when he walked through the kitchen.

"You look like hell, dear," she had said, cocking her head as she took his measure. "Woman or camp problems?"

"Yesterday was a long day, and today looks like it's going to be worse. Don't wait up."

"I never do, darling. Have Ruth press your uniform before you leave. You're not going to command any authority looking like one of the prisoners."

He waved her off and walked out the back door, where his driver was waiting. Höss could have easily walked to the camp. His villa was just outside the camp fence. But he liked arriving in the chauffeured vehicle and having the car at his disposal throughout the day should he have to visit any of the forty sub-camps under his command.

The house was one of the major benefits of the job and the reason his wife Hedwig had agreed to join him for what she called "our Polish sojourn." The house was a stylish square villa like the ones they'd seen while vacationing in northern Italy. It came with a full staff of prisoners—a combination of German Jehovah's Witnesses and Jews, making for ease of communication and because Hedwig found Polish cooking abominable and the Poles' social skills lacking.

During their time at Auschwitz, the relationship between Rudolf and Hedwig had undergone a metamorphosis, one that in some ways tracked the evolution of the camp. In the early days, when the focus was on building a model camp for new regions that came under Nazi control, she took an active interest in the designs, including the town square, theater, and public buildings. When the plan shifted to detention and labor, she lamented her loss of stature. Still, knowing that the new duties elevated Rudolf's status in Berlin, she showed interest in his new responsibilities, asking how his day had gone, what the problems were, and whether there was anything she could do to help. But as the camp's primary purpose shifted from labor to death, the mood at home shifted dramatically. Sensing more than knowing the camp's transition, Hedwig quit asking and Rudolf quit volunteering.

In the summer of 1943, while working in the garden, she had overheard two of his junior officers discussing the gassings. Later that day she confirmed their accounts with the nanny, Hannah, the prisoner who had been with her the longest and whom she trusted the most. That night, when she confronted Rudolf about the camp and his role, he had denied it at first. But when she persisted, his voice had become steel-like and he had given her a brief but harsh accounting of the camp's new function and his own role. By mutual agreement, he slept in the guest bedroom after that night.

Initially, Hedwig had resolved to quit the camp immediately and return to Berlin with the children. But when friends apprised her of the toll the war was taking on the city and on their lifestyle, as well as the state of their children's schools, she chose to remain at Auschwitz, her new goals being to distance herself from any association with the camp while devoting herself to the children's upbringing. She and her husband came together only at official functions, of which there were few. Auschwitz was now a twenty-four-hour factory with no time or need for ceremonies.

The ledger from the safe was open on his desktop, the numbers staring back at him in tight, mocking lines. He lit a cigarette and peered through the smoke at the seemingly endless list of figures, neatly arrayed, marching down the page from the operation's start date. Totals would grow, then dip with every visit of either the Reichsführer or his accountant, which had ended with their returning to Berlin with sealed boxes of ingots. He looked at the latest entry and wondered yet again how fatal it was. How far off from Himmler's expectations would the actual yield be, and what explanation could he provide to buy himself more time? Time to either find the murderer and thief or engage a replacement for Elster, the accountant, someone who could help him right the ship or at least muddy the waters while they looked for a more permanent solution.

Höss had sat up most of the night going through his options, but the list that stared back at him through the morning light was small and lacking. He could pin the missing gold on Elster, saying that he had gone rogue with a partner, which had led to his demise. But both Himmler and his accountant were acquainted with Elster and would immediately reject that scenario out of hand.

Or he could melt down some of his bars without swastikas, recast them with the swastika, and add them to Himmler's total.

Perhaps that windfall, which Himmler would most likely siphon off into his own vault, would buy him time until the next audit. But Höss had been a Nazi long enough to know that a one-time windfall wasn't enough to allay the concerns of both Himmler and his accountant that such a critical part of their contributions to Hitler's efforts was suddenly, to use one of the Reichsführer's favorite expressions, "out of alignment"—a seemingly innocent phrase that held fatal overtones. Himmler might accept and pocket the gold this time, but he would leave his accountant behind, and the operation would be revealed and documented within days.

The third option was to destroy the remaining ledger, the one on the table staring up at him, which might buy him time. But three men had seen him remove it from the safe, and they would volunteer that information readily, aware of the distinction in rank between Himmler and Höss and the ramifications of holding back.

After reviewing all of his options, he decided that the best one was to concentrate all his efforts on finding the murdering thief, regaining the missing ledger, and sending the murderer up the chimney. While it was a major endeavor, it was entirely under his control. What he needed was the right team.

He looked up at the sound of the door opening. Fritzsch entered the room, bowed a good morning, and placed a crisp sheet of paper before him, which Höss read quickly. Then he balled the paper and threw it at Fritzsch, hitting him in the chest.

"These are all Gestapo, idiot. We've got ten days until Himmler arrives, and you waste one of them assembling this list of flunkies?"

"Four of these men are in your private guard, sir. They report to you, not—"

"*Everyone* in the SS reports to Himmler, you moron. Any of these men would betray us at the drop of a hat. And be nicely rewarded for it."

"But Herr Kommandant, you need people with investigation and interrogation skills if you're to solve this crime before Reichsführer Himmler arrives. These men are your best hope. When Reichsführer Himmler comes for his audit, if you can't account for—"

"*We*, Fritzsch. *We*. If *we* can't account for the missing gold." He looked at Fritzsch and cocked his head. "Fritzsch, Fritzsch. Please. Don't think for a minute I don't know how much you skim from Kanada. Elster documented your operation as thoroughly as mine. I just had no need to speak of it. Until now. Am I making myself clear?"

Fritzsch looked down at the floor. "How may I best be of assistance, Herr Kommandant?"

"You can find me a goddamn detective. One whose loyalty is not in doubt."

"Enter," Fritzsch said, in response to a soft knock on the door. A prisoner came in, removed his cap, bowed, and presented a piece of paper to Fritzsch. "The yield from the last transport."

The prisoner left quickly, and Fritzsch held out the document for the Kommandant's review, but Höss's eyes remained fixed on the door. "What about the prisoners? Surely one of them was a policeman or detective."

"But, Herr Kommandant, this is a sensitive issue."

"What is the prison population today?" Höss asked.

"At any moment, eighty thousand, give or take."

"So you have eighty thousand opportunities to show your initiative. Find me my investigator. Today."

# Five

STILL IN HER SS UNIFORM, Oberaufseherin Gisela Brandt reclined on the leather chaise, letting the shoe from her exposed foot dangle. She reached behind and released her white-blonde hair, which had been pinned up all day beneath her cap, and took out a compact from her jacket pocket to examine herself with a critical eye. She liked what she saw: a sculptured, intelligent face that looked a few years younger than her thirty years but not that much younger. And she was fine with that.

Turning from the mirror, she looked at the leg dangling over the edge of the chaise. It was lean and taut, the kind that drew the attention of most men, and the Kommandant was no exception. She had been one of the few girls in the Hitler Youth who actually liked the required physical exercise, which she had kept up since joining the SS, hiking on her days off. It was tougher to keep up the regime at Auschwitz, but she walked the perimeters of the camp whenever possible. At other times, she hiked from one camp to the next, cadging a ride back with one of the transports.

Her eyes looked tired and strained when she returned her gaze to the mirror. They were a reflection of the length and demands of her day, she thought as she stifled a yawn. The day had started earlier than usual, with her block secretary rousing her with the news that one of the prisoners had attacked the head Kapo at reveille. That was an unheard-of offense, and it required an immediate, forceful response. Brandt had gotten dressed and headed down to Block 14, where the prisoners, having been denied their morning meal as collective punishment, waited at attention.

Knowing the Kapo in question and her notoriously quick temper, Brandt stopped at her own office for a briefing by her lieutenant. Questioning a guard's account or considering a prisoner's point of view were both out of character with the rest of Auschwitz—the entire camp system, actually—where the Reich and its emissaries could do no wrong. But Gisela prided herself on keeping an open mind, even when it came to Untermensch.

Even though she used the term like every other SS officer, if she was honest with herself, she found the whole concept of Untermensch a bit dubious, if not laughable. The Slavs, to be sure, were the definition of a lower-class human: slow in both movement and thought; heavy in both. For once, Goebbels and his propaganda machine had gotten it right: The life purpose of these people was to increase the capabilities of those who conquered them. And as the Reich expanded, they would need the Untermensch as slave labor—both utilitarian and expendable.

The Jews were another story. Coming from Heidelberg and an academic family, Gisela had been exposed to Jews all her life. Many of her father's closest friends, as well as the professors admired most at the university, had been Jews. She'd had Jewish friends most of her life, the majority of them being more intelligent, more fun, and more involved than her Aryan friends. She had even dated Jewish men and thought nothing of it.

But when the Nazis had implemented their anti-Jewish laws, she had divested herself of those friends, actions based on practicality, not conviction. The part of her that respected and missed her father, who had moved to Paris as the Nazis took over Heidelberg and most academic institutions, resented Hitler's campaign against the Jews and the resulting loss of people who mattered to her.

In the earliest stages of Goebbels' program, during which he associated Jews with rats and other vermin, she joined her Jewish friends in rolling their eyes at the imagery and utterly ridiculous logic that a group constituting less than one percent of Germany's population could be the source of all of the country's economic and political woes. Her Aryan friends shared her contempt at Goebbels' ham-handed propaganda, since it was so obviously targeted at the masses with their Brown Shirts and spit-filled rallies.

When the campaign against the Jews showed no sign of abating and the laws and attitudes gnawed at the Jews' place in virtually every segment of German life, Gisela's attitude toward them changed. As she recognized Nazism's staying power, her sneering and eye rolls dissipated, then disappeared. She didn't attend the rallies, but she listened to Hitler on the radio. He was a bully, it was clear, and the Jews were his target and path to power. In her mind, the only way to respond to a bully was to fight back. And when most Jews simply rolled over and showed their throats, she lost all respect for them. Maybe they didn't deserve all the contempt and treatment thrown their way, but she was damned if she was going to defend people who wouldn't defend themselves.

Still, when it came to Auschwitz, her old memories of Jews asserted themselves at times. True, most of her Polish Jews were from the country and were nowhere as sophisticated as her former Heidelberg friends. But they were still appreciably better than their Slavic counterparts in almost every way. Slavs made excellent Kapos, and they worked like dogs at any manual labor she assigned them. But for anything requiring thought and judgment, she always used a Jew.

By all accounts, the Kapo in question was blameless. The prisoner had reacted to the clanging wake-up bell like a racehorse, and a rabid one at that. When the Kapo walked down the aisle, her truncheon banging loudly on the wooden bunks, the prisoner sprang up and clawed her face. It was an unheard-of assault: The Kapo would have been well within her rights to kill the prisoner there and then. Surprising herself, Gisela wound up admiring her restraint.

"Who was the prisoner?"

Her lieutenant looked down at her clipboard. "Number 174828."

"Let's try it again, Truppführer," Brandt replied, clearly frustrated. "In German this time. Who was the prisoner?"

"The big girl from Minsk. The one who works in the rubber factory."

"Really? I wouldn't have expected it from her."

"I was surprised as well. But one look in her eyes and you can see she's gone around the bend. And she's not coming back."

"That's a shame. She was a good worker. And popular with the rest of the girls." Brandt stood up. "Well, let's go have a look for ourselves.

When Brandt entered the barracks, the wounded Kapo was standing at attention in front of the assembled two hundred women, equally rigid in their posture. With tempers running high, it was one of those moments when calling attention to oneself, even for the slightest infraction, could prove fatal. Seated against a wall, hunched and talking to herself in a low, guttural voice with two prisoners standing over her, was the big girl from Minsk. The SS officer walked over and motioned for her to stand up. When the girl remained seated and kept her face averted, Brandt motioned to the two prisoners to raise her up and took out her whip. The girl from Minsk was not so far gone that the sight of the whip went unnoticed and unappreciated. She shrank, as if trying to burrow into the wall. But Brandt simply used the side of the whip to turn the girl's head so their eyes met. One look into the eyes confirmed her lieutenant's diagnosis.

"Take her to my office," she said to her lieutenant, who took the unresisting girl into her charge and led her away.

Brandt turned to face the assembled women. "Ladies, we have a dilemma here. And by 'we,' I mean all of us. According to the camp disciplinary manual, our friend from Minsk should hang at this evening's assembly. But it's clear that her mind has left her, hopefully temporarily, so even though she committed a capital crime by attacking a representative of the Reich, I don't think we gain anything by going by the book. Do you agree?"

She expected no reply, and when she received none, she continued. "So here's what I propose we do. Our friend will stay in the hospital until she's back to herself, at which point she'll spend a day in Block 11, our disciplinary block, for the attack. But she won't be returning to this unit. Seeing what life is like in a less humane environment will be part of her punishment. So any of you who want to take the time to say good-bye to her, do so now." She waited, even though she knew no one would step forward. Then she turned and left the room.

Her lieutenant met her in the hall. "You rarely talk to the girls, especially like that."

"Well, she was popular with the girls. And besides, it's good to be unpredictable. Those who think I've gone soft will reveal themselves by taking more initiative. And their reward for this growing courage will be a trip to the gas."

"What do you want to do with our prisoner?"

"She goes to the gas chamber with this afternoon's transport."

---

She watched as Rudolf stood in front of his liquor cabinet, pouring two glasses of scotch. His hand was steady, but the pour was heavier than usual. Taking in the unshaven face and wrinkled uniform, she recognized she had some work ahead of her that evening as both mistress and confidante.

With leaden steps, he crossed the room, handed her one of the drinks, and lowered himself next to her on the chaise, issuing a long sigh as he settled in. Normally, at this point he would lean back and she would cuddle into the crook of his arm. But both hands stayed around his glass and he looked straight ahead, as if she weren't in the room. He put his feet up on the elegant table in front of the chaise and let out another heavy sigh.

"That bad?" she asked.

"It's hard to see how it could get worse."

"What I can't figure out is why he didn't take both ledgers."

"Because then it's a simple theft. I'd look like a fool for not securing my materials, but not a criminal. Whoever did this wants Himmler to know the other ledger is missing, which will lead to a more thorough audit than normal and the discovery of the discrepancies."

"Can't the other ledger disappear as well?"

"It could have, had I been thinking on the spot. But due to my own idiocy, three witnesses saw me go straight to the safe and pull out a ledger." He shook his head. "If I'd only waited until the office was clear. I'm a goddamn fool."

"Couldn't another accountant fix the discrepancies?"

"He wouldn't know where to begin. Nor would I. Only Himmler's man and Elster knew the final totals from the last review. That will be the starting point for the next audit, and if we're off by even a little bit, that Berlin prick will sound the alarm. Any fabricated numbers would be disproven in a matter of minutes. And then the fun would begin."

He took a large sip and patted his uniform pocket. "Fortunately, all senior staff have a cyanide capsule for just such an emergency. I'll see if I can get one for you, my love."

"For me? I'm not a part of this."

"We haven't been as discreet as we should have been, Gisela. And the Gestapo don't make distinctions. I'd love to tell you that I'll be brave and hold out, but I've been on the torturing side enough to know that I'd fold within the first ten minutes. As would you, my love."

They sat together in silence, their frustration almost a third person in the room. Gisela knew that she was in a position to help the investigation, but her involvement would have to come at Rudolf's initiative. Otherwise, he would resent both her presumption and the pity beneath it. As the supervisor of all units staffing the different functions and departments of Kanada, she was intimately aware of most of the operations, including the "underground Kanada" operations of both Rudolf and Fritzsch, as well as a few clandestine operations that thus far had escaped even Fritzsch's watchful eye.

As she sat quietly next to the Kommandant, letting the Scotch take hold and his self-pity ebb, she did a mental inventory of the variety of Kanada operations, from Incoming to Recording and distribution. But they were all silos, with no overlap of operations. Each operation had its own Elster, its keeper of records. And in true Nazi fashion, there were overseers of each operation who reported directly to Berlin.

She sat up abruptly and planted her feet on the floor. "We're forgetting something, Rudi. *We* know that another accountant wouldn't be able to recapture your complete operation. But the thief doesn't. What if we replace Elster and you're seen working closely with him, as if reconstructing the gold yield that has gone missing ? It might force the thief's hand."

"Make it look like I'm creating a new ledger, one that renders the thief's book worthless? It might force his hand at that. Draw him out."

"One last thing, Rudolf. Fritzsch. Are you sure you can trust him? After all, the man has been skimming from you since the camp opened."

"Which means he has as much to lose as the two of us. Fritzsch's balls are in the same vise as mine."

"Perhaps. But all the same, may I suggest that you don't let him know that the new accountant isn't the real thing?"

He nodded and looked at her, his eyes appreciative, no longer tired or tipsy. She looked away, feigning modesty, but he put a finger under her chin and turned her back toward him. "Thank you, my love. Seriously."

# Six

FRITZSCH GATHERED his top lieutenants that evening and told them that Auschwitz was projected to expand during 1944 at a rate that would eventually eclipse current management and policing resources. With other camps reporting disturbances, and in rare cases, even riots, he and the Kommandant wanted to anticipate and prevent those kinds of administrative black eyes. To that end, he wanted them to scour their ranks and come up with someone—a former policeman or detective, preferably—who could help them design and recruit for a pilot program.

"Are you looking more for enforcement or detection?" one of his lieutenants asked.

"The latter. With the support of this new group, I believe the Kapos can handle the disciplinary part of our future growth, especially if they are forewarned by this new shadow organization." Detection would include identifying and preventing uprisings before they occur as well as determining the leaders and possible participants in such disturbances.

"I recognize that this task is made even more difficult by the fact that we have already done our own identification and culling of potential leaders during Selektion or shortly thereafter, so we're looking for someone crafty enough to anticipate and evade our efforts. In short, we're looking for someone smarter than us, at least smarter than us in this area."

He paused, making sure he had everyone's attention. "One week of extra vacation to the man who identifies our Jew detective. I know most of you have little knowledge about your prisoners, so I invite you to enlist the help of your key Kapos. Promise them an extra week of provisions should they find our man." He paused. "Let me sweeten the pot: An extra week of vacation and provisions if you find this person within the next twenty-four hours."

---

The next morning, in an open warehouse three kilometers from Fritzsch's gathering, two men struggling under the weight of a thick missile casing stumbled their way to the assembly area where a small group of men waited, tools at the ready. With a grunt, the men hoisted the dull-grey, freezing cold rocket onto the table and stood back, exhausted.

As the rest of the prisoners bent to their tasks, applying their tools to the different parts of the rocket, one of them looked around, his face a mask of fear and frustration. A grinder in his hand, he continued to smooth an area near the firing pin, but the motor kept quitting mid-task. The fear on his face spread to his hands, and he looked over at the SS guard, fearful that the guard would spot his shaking hands and take immediate corrective action, which usually consisted of a beating. But the guard was lighting a cigarette and focused on that task.

"What's the problem?" Divko asked, suddenly appearing at the man's side.

"I'm never going to make my numbers with this damn thing," the prisoner said, gesturing at the grinder.

"Do something, Divko," a man across the table said. "He's holding up the whole operation. I'm not losing my rations tonight because of him."

Divko gave the complaining man an angry glance and motioned him back to his own task. "Let me show you a couple of tricks," he said to the man with shaking hands, picking up the grinder.

In the six months since arriving at Auschwitz, Divko had lost an additional fifteen pounds from his Warsaw-emaciated frame. His head was shaven and his neck showed the infected flea bites that plagued the majority of his crew. He hadn't seen his image in most of that time, but it was clear from his wrists and the new holes in his handmade belt that he was in danger of slipping below the line. "The line" was what the veterans in the camp called that point when a prisoner's physical condition had fallen to the point they were becoming a "Musselman." No one could tell him why or how the German term for "Moslem" had become shorthand for "the walking dead." But as Divko's mentor—whom he had continued to pay in bread for his orientation to Auschwitz—had told him, "You'll know a Musselman when you see him. They shuffle, and their eyes don't focus. They eat, but it seems like their body has lost its memory on how to turn it into fuel. They fall behind in their work; they fall behind in the marches back to the barriers. We see it, the Kapos see it, and within the week, they're on their way to the gas."

Even with the mental and emotional preparations he had made, both in the ghetto and on the train journey to the camp, Divko's introduction to Auschwitz had been a harsh one. He wasn't surprised to survive the Selektion, watching helplessly as so many of his Warsaw compatriots—people who had looked to him for justice and guidance for the past three years—were led toward the Disinfektion facility. After all, the Nazis needed labor to support their war effort. What had surprised him was the treatment and fate of those who survived the initial Selektions. He had thought that the survivors of the initial sorting process would be viewed as having sufficient value to the Reich that they would receive enough sustenance and protection against the elements to keep them productive and contributing to the war effort indefinitely. After all, experience in any effort was an irreplaceable component.

It took him less than a week to realize his error and see that he had just traded an immediate death for a living one. That awakening began with the disinfection process, a harsh procedure that left Divko and his fellow survivors strangers to each other and to themselves. The first step had been the quick and brutal shaving of their heads, a process that never took more than a minute and left scalps raw and bleeding.

Then the prisoners—nearly six hundred men in Divko's group—were herded onto trucks and driven past a seemingly endless line of barracks, finally stopping in front of a large, industrial-looking building. Prompted by the truncheons and shouts of the Kapos, the prisoners exited quickly, fast-walking to a line of barracks in front of which were rows of barrels, from which emanated a foul, metallic smell that crept up the nostrils and caused their eyes to water. The men were told to sit in a barrel for ten minutes. "You are vermin to the core," one of the SS men said, to the amusement of his peers. "This procedure will at least rid you of your smaller relatives."

Then came the shower, which was hot to the point of scalding and lasted less than a minute, causing the skin to stretch and pinken. The men who had their wits about them grabbed a bar of the harsh soap and applied it to the accumulated grime from the ghetto. But the majority stood there, stunned by the sequence of events, their hands folded reflexively over their genitals. When the water suddenly quit, the Kapos moved in, herding the prisoners with words and whips down a long corridor. As they passed, other prisoners haphazardly threw delousing powder at them, much of it clumped from moisture.

Their skin morphing from pink back to grey, their bodies blotchy with heat and powder, and their heads freshly shorn, the men exited into a large courtyard where another group of prisoners walked in front of them, throwing uniforms at them. As the naked prisoners unfolded the garments, they found them to be of all sizes. Anyone mismatched looked around and quickly exchanged his garments for those of another mismatched prisoner. Then they donned the uniforms and, unbidden, stood at attention.

The newly assembled crew bore little resemblance to the men who had formed a line to the right earlier that afternoon. Divko had to look twice—and then again in some cases—to recognize some of his Warsaw compatriots. He assumed they had the same problem identifying him.

The last stop was the tattooist, with speed again the order of the day. A group of prisoners sat at tables with a set of wooden blocks in front of them. Numbered metal stamps made up of a forest of small needles were then inserted into the form to create a unique number taken from a large ledger. The stamp was then pushed into the flesh of the incoming prisoner's left forearm, with blue ink then rubbed into the bleeding flesh, creating the tattoo.

The men were then herded into a barracks, the right half of which was packed with the new arrivals, the left side empty. Divko found out later that the left half had been occupied by a group of workers who had finished their assignment the day before and been sent to the gas chamber. The Kapos shouted and swung at them aimlessly, telling them to grab a sleeping spot and organize themselves four to a bunk. Divko looked at the three-layered wooden sleeping structure and halted at the end of a row of bunks, stepping aside as if he were a Kapo facilitating the process and motioning eleven prisoners in. Then he inserted himself in as the twelfth and final person in that bunk area, ensuring himself the outside berth.

The next morning began the routine that he and his group were to follow with only the slightest of deviations for the next seven months. The wake-up bell was at 5:30, changing to 4:30 when spring came and the sun was up earlier. They had a few minutes to relieve themselves and do what little washup they could before breakfast, which consisted of ersatz coffee and whatever bread he had saved from the evening before. That was followed by roll call, which could extend to hours at the whim of the guards or if the numbers didn't tally correctly. They then hiked to the day's assignment, where the normal workday was between eleven and twelve hours.

The first night in the barracks had been a cacophony of languages, the air rich with fear and confusion. After dinner, the previously empty half of the barracks was filled with a new set of prisoners. From the numbers on their arms, it was clear that these were veterans being transferred to accommodations nearer their new assignment. Divko looked the group over, picked out the most grizzled of the group, and sidled over to him at dinnertime. When he sat down, the man didn't acknowledge him.

"Can you give me some advice, Father?" Divko asked in Polish. When the man didn't stir, he tried the question in German. Again, no response. Divko started to get up and seek another partner when the man spoke Polish in a low, hoarse voice, nodding at the crust in Divko's hand. "Your bread."

"It's all I have for dinner."

"Nothing is free at Auschwitz. Especially my advice. You're new. Newcomers go up the chimney here unless they learn to survive. You want advice. I want your bread. There will be more bread tomorrow if you last that long."

Divko considered, then he took a small bite of the bread before handing it over. The man nodded and put the bread inside his coat. "What do you want to know?"

"How to survive here."

The man nodded and leaned forward slightly. "First off, as you just discovered, nothing is free here. Nothing. And if you live long enough to become someone others come to for advice, don't mess up our marketplace by giving things away. Everything here has a price—especially advice." His eyes bored in. "If you try to be the nice guy who doesn't charge for his services, those who do charge—and that's everyone else—will beat you the first time as a warning and kill you the second. Got it?"

Divko nodded.

"Second, possession is everything. Nothing is yours except what's in your possession. It could have been someone else's a moment ago, but if it's now in your possession, it's yours." He snatched Divko's cup, which was between them. "Now it's mine. And I'm not joking." He handed it back. "That's for the bread, but now we're even. Next time I won't be returning it. So you can either go hungry or find some other schmuck and take his cup." He motioned over Divko's shoulder. "So wherever you go, even to the latrine—especially to the latrine—take your clothes, your dish, and your spoon with you."

He motioned at his arm. "Finally, check the numbers. The lower the number, the longer they've been here. They deserve respect—and fear. Either stay away from them or become one of them. Higher numbers are newcomers like you. Take full advantage of these people. Like I just did with you." He stood up. "That's what you get for a single piece of bread. You want more advice, bring me more bread."

—⁓—

"It just needs some encouragement," Divko said to the new prisoner, striking the grinder's on-off switch against the side of the steel table. The machine leapt to life, this time holding the spark. Divko leaned over the shell and completed the original task. The prisoner nodded gratefully and reached for the tool.

"There's one more trick I need to show you," Divko said. "Whether you apply it or not is up to you." He pulled aside a small metal flange, revealing multicolored wiring. "The firing pin here," he said, motioning, "is both very fragile and essentially invisible once we complete assemblage. Which gives us the opportunity to . . ." He took a small screwdriver and reached in. Turning the screwdriver slightly, he looked over at the prisoner. "Now we have a misfire."

"What if they find out and trace it back to here?"

"They haven't yet. And we've been doing it for the six months I've been here. And I was trained by someone who'd been doing it for six months before that." He motioned over his shoulder. "The soldiers using these shells are at the front, just trying to survive. And they're just artillery grunts. The last thing they have time or authority for is an investigation." He smiled crookedly. "But even if they do trace it back to us, we'll both be dead by then." He looked at the man's fallen face. "I'm joking. Maybe. But you take your small victories where you can." He nodded at the shell. "Such as this one."

# Seven

THE NEXT MORNING Fritzsch called his top five reports together. Trying to keep his voice casual, he asked about the progress of their search. "I'd like to present this to the Kommandant today so he can flesh out the plan and present it to Reichsführer Himmler next week. It would be a feather in all our caps. If it's one of you, my inner circle, who discovers this individual, I will invite you to join the Kommandant and myself in developing this pilot program."

The group saluted and dispersed. One of their number, Sturmscharführer Horst Lehman, hustled back to the barracks. Disbelieving that Fritzsch would introduce him to the Kommandant, he saw an opportunity for advancement nonetheless and found what he was looking for in moments when he checked the list of work details for his group of prisoners. Commissioning a Kübelwagen, he drove four kilometers to where a crew was building a new set of barracks. Spotting the man he wanted, he shouted, "Kapo Chernov! Get over here. Now."

—m—

In their six months in Auschwitz, the Divkos had not seen each other once, not even in passing. Given both Auschwitz's policies and size, it was hardly surprising. The sexes were strictly segregated. The opportunity for an encounter with the opposite sex occurred only if your camp—one of forty at Auschwitz—bordered a camp of theirs. And then it was only through the fence and only on Sunday.

Employing her investigative skills and bribing one of the Kapos, it had taken Perla two weeks to even confirm that Shimon was alive and another week after that to get a message to him. After that, they were able to exchange brief messages, though they kept their communications to a minimum, mindful that the punishment, if caught, was flogging at a minimum and death the more likely sentence.

Perla's initial assignment was as a recording clerk. Twice a day she was given handwritten records from that day's transports and told to break them down into preestablished categories and enter them into the large ledgers that lined the walls of her workroom—a living, ever-expanding library of death. At first the numbers and their significance had overwhelmed her because she realized that each entry marked the end of a life. And in rare cases, it was someone she knew. Initially, she had sat there, numb, her fingers unable to perform any of her tasks. She resolved not to cry, since that might result in discipline and an immediate transfer. Looking around her desk, she saw the others at work and wondered how they were able to do it.

At lunch during that first week, she had tentatively broached the subject with one of her office mates. The woman explained that she'd adopted one cardinal rule early on: At Auschwitz, numbers were everything. Anything else—discipline, meals, fights among other prisoners, a friend going up the chimney—was a distraction. And distractions often proved fatal. The sooner Perla realized that and incorporated it into her work, the better it would be for her and everyone else since they had both individual and collective quotas to meet. Perla had nodded, but inside, she had resolved to remember the lives behind the numbers in some small way. It was a resolution that lasted the better part of a month before the numbers overwhelmed her intentions.

The numbers possessed both patterns and parameters. It was rare that she entered the name and number of a child under twelve in the "living" category because any child, except the ones who could pass for older, went immediately to the left. The only exceptions came when the Germans needed small fingers for the intricate electronics work on their missile assemblages. She had yet to enter any prisoner under the age of eight. It was the same for anyone, male or female, over the age of sixty. And she was required to keep a list of percentages of how many in each transport had gone to their death and how many had survived and been put to work. No transport to date had exceeded a thirty percent survival rate.

Once the Kapos saw her work ethic and facility with numbers, she had been given more complex assignments. The most recent was a project conducted by the medical staff. A group of physicians under directions from Reichsführer Himmler had been assigned the task of determining "optimal productive longevity." Or as one of the doctors said to one of his underlings in a note, "Basically, we're quantifying and testing the most efficient way to work these Jews to death."

The experiment began by tracking three components: assignment, diet, and length of imprisonment. The doctors had examined the camp diet for the past year and now were working with the quartermaster and kitchen staff to determine how the current diet could be, as the quartermaster joked, skinnied down, the idea being that every Deutsche Mark saved in feeding the prisoners could go to the war effort. But with breakfast consisting of a liter of diluted coffee and a nub of bread, lunch a thin soup, and dinner a repeat of breakfast, there was little hope that this component would yield promising areas of cuts. "We cut the diet any further—it's at eight hundred calories now—we might as well just send everyone to the left on day one," Dr. Mengele had said after the first review meeting.

The next two components were related. The date of each prisoner's death was recorded, that number subtracted from his or her arrival date, and the resultant number entered in the ledger. Next to that number was the job, or jobs, the prisoner had worked during that period. From what Perla could gather, the current thinking was that any form of arduous work, coupled with the current diet, meant a lifespan of no more than six months. With the constant arrival of new workers who could be worked to death under the new mathematical formula, this was ideal for the camp administrators. They could maintain both their mortality and productivity goals by optimizing the six months of veteran work effort as fresh prisoners came up to speed. Prisoners who overstayed their welcome at Auschwitz were marked for future investigation, the thinking being that they would have to justify their longevity or be gassed.

That last piece of information had caught Perla by surprise. Like her husband, she had assumed that those who survived the Selektion and worked hard would at least be kept alive, if not rewarded. After all, the Kommandant had a camp to run and the Germans a war to win. Why eliminate a person or group who could contribute to both efforts?

It took her a long time to realize that common sense had no place in Auschwitz's arithmetic when it came to Jews. She watched the most productive workers sent to the gas chambers for a variety of reasons, from Kapo whim to barracks commanders' quota goals. And in times of numeric stress, she saw entire trainloads of arrivals go to the left without even the artifice of a

Selektion. Anything to make their ever-changing quotas from Himmler's office.

"It makes no sense," she said one evening to a German Jew who had lived through the rise of Hitler, the Nazi empowerment in 1933, and the restrictive laws and Kristallnacht. "We could be such a resource to them if they didn't hate us so."

"You're missing the point," the Berlin Jew told her. "Most of these Germans, from Höss on down, don't hate us at all. They couldn't care less about us. That may be different for you Polish Jews, but my guess is that only a handful of the guards have much of an anti-Semitic bent."

"How can you say that? Every SS soldier here looks at me with cold eyes. Dead eyes with a hint of violence."

"That's because they're soldiers, not because they're anti-Semitic. Soldiers are taught to hate their enemy, and they've been taught that you're their enemy. Simple as that." The Berlin woman reached over and patted her condescendingly on the knee. "Look, honey, here's how it is. Hitler hates us. Pure and simple. And it's a blind hate that has no limits. And the Brown Shirts, the trash that put him in power, hate us too. But the rest of Germany grew up with us and *used* to see us, if not as friends, at least as neighbors. Now they see us as something new, something it's dangerous to be around. They liked—or tolerated—us before. Now they don't. That's it. And for the soldiers, even the SS, we're just a job to do."

"That's hard to believe, given what's going on here."

"I'm telling you, if Hitler had a revelation tomorrow and decided that we Jews were the salvation of Germany, we'd be in charge of the army and other institutions by the end of the month. No one would ask why the vermin were running the show. They would say Heil Hitler and tell us they were big fans of us all along."

Perla looked at the woman, gauging how serious she was. "You're a more forgiving person than I am, then."

The woman shook her head. "Listen, I'm not saying I forgive my German captors and executioners. I hate the bastards. I'm saying you've got to understand your enemy. And these bastards just see themselves as having a job to do. That's all."

"To kill us."

"Exactly. But just remember this: It's not personal. Nothing here is."

Once Perla realized how transitory and tenuous her situation at Auschwitz was, she resolved to make her days there as productive as possible, whether they ended the next day or when the war was over. That meant transferring her Oneg Shabbat responsibilities from the ghetto to the camp.

Oneg Shabbat—literally, "the joy of the Sabbath"—was the code name for the Warsaw Coordinating Committee's actions to document and preserve the history and culture of the Warsaw ghetto for future generations. And should the Nazis lose the war, it would provide evidence for future trials. From the documentation of the destruction of smaller ghettos to the vague reports from death camps like Sobibor, Chelmno, and Treblinka, her team collected and preserved every account and document they could, providing evidence for future prosecution, whether they survived to present it or not.

The team also sought to preserve accounts of life in the ghetto, from court documents and census rolls to children's drawings and religious scrolls. On the night before the Germans' final push against the ghetto, the group buried milk cans and metal boxes crammed with almost twenty-five thousand documents. Perla was one of twenty who knew the location. Along with nineteen others, she had vowed to do everything she could to survive and return to Warsaw to unearth and publicize the archives.

Once Perla decided to conduct her own Oneg Shabbat at Auschwitz, she encountered an immediate logistics problem. Even if she were able to collect documentation of the Nazi slaughtering of her people, where and how would she be able to bury the evidence? The ghetto may have been occupied, but the Nazis maintained an administrative distance from its daily operations, leaving that to the Judenrat and its spies. So the actual burial of the assembled documents had been quite easy. But as her archive grew beyond a single shoebox at Auschwitz, she would need to find a way to gather and hide her evidence, both while she was conducting her investigation and when it was to be buried. She needed a partner who shared her hatred and her goals. It needed to be someone who had been at Auschwitz long enough to know the ropes, had a certain freedom, and had outside responsibilities.

It took her a month to find the right person. Magda Wolfowitz had been at Auschwitz for nearly two years, rising to the position of foreman for the prisoners who were building the supporting buildings for the Farben factory. Since Magda was housed in the next barracks over from Perla's, communication was possible only on Sundays, when the prisoners were free to gather, repair their clothing for the coming week, and shower. Perla first approached Magda for advice on long-term survival, which cost her two uniform buttons and that day's bread. Then she expanded the conversation into their personal histories. Over the course of four Sundays, Perla determined that she had found her partner in crime.

Magda was a country girl whose husband had been killed during the Nazi blitzkrieg and who had seen her parents and two children sent to the left upon their arrival at Auschwitz. Unlike Perla's experiences with anti-Semitism, which had been veiled at times in the urban sophistication of Warsaw, Magda had seen Polish anti-Semitism at its rawest.

"I like you, Perla," she said on the third Sunday they were together, "but I must tell you, it pisses me off when you say 'We Poles,' like 'We Poles need to stick together.' Or 'When the war is over, we Poles need to do this or that.' Get this straight, honey. We're Jews. Not Poles. Jews. And the Poles will never let us forget that. You shouldn't forget it either."

"Look, Magda," Perla had replied, "I'm not naïve enough to think my experiences in Warsaw extend to the whole country. I'm just saying that I haven't experienced the depths of hatred that you're talking about. In Warsaw, there was discrimination and slights, but we coexisted. So for me, if this war ends and the Nazis are defeated, I'm hoping that Poles and Jews will be united by our common suffering and our common enemy, that we'll come together to—"

"Honey, you big city Jews wouldn't last a day in my shtetl. You'd be put in your place or driven out of town the first time you went into a goyische store and expected to be waited on."

"Come on. It can't be that bad." Perla looked at Magda's face. "Or is it?"

"How do you think we wound up here and I wound up a widow? The Nazis marched into my town, and the first thing the Poles did was take off their hats in respect. The second thing they did was point out every Jew in town. They did the Nazis' work for them." She took a last drag of her cigarette, smoking it down to her fingertips, flicked it away, and looked at Perla. "They herded all our men into a barn and set it afire. The townspeople surrounded the barn with pitchforks, and anyone who tried to escape the flames was driven back into the barn. By their neighbors."

Her eyes fixed on Perla's. "You see how good this camp is at mass murder. And I will bet you it's not the only one." She shook her head. "So, no. When this is over, the number of Jews who survive this thing is gonna be so small that the Poles will be able to finish off what the Nazis started."

That conversation had nailed it for Perla. The next Sunday she told Magda about her project and requested her help. Magda agreed to help on one condition: that Perla—and Divko, if he survived—would do everything they could to help her emigrate to the United States. They had shaken hands and set to work.

# Eight

"OKAY, CHERNOV," said Sturmscharführer Lehman, "here's how it is. I'm taking you over to see Fritzsch. You're the one who's going to vouch for this Divko. If he's the guy you say he is, you'll be a week's rations richer and I'll move you up in the rotations chart. So don't fuck this up."

---

"Life has changed, for both of us," Scharführer Müller said to Divko as they huddled over their ersatz coffee and looked out at the factory, whose cement floor seemed to almost shimmer in the cold. "The Oberscharführer put me on notice last night, in front of my peers, no less."

"Came down on you for what? Our production numbers are higher than any other part of Munitions."

"A new number that was unofficial initially, meaning I could ignore it without being punished. But now that new number is part of our monthly quota." He looked at Divko. "Attrition."

Attrition, whether articulated by that single word or not, had dominated Divko's life since the Selektion. As he marched off to his first day of work, he recalled Chernov's warning, that Munitions had one of the highest death rates in the camp. From that moment on, he had studied every component of the operation, looking for the easiest job, which often meant the one farthest from the harsh elements. As a result, he and every other member of his crew had lasted more than six months. That longevity, coupled with the respect he generated from the men, had resulted in his being named foreman.

As foreman, he had formed an uneasy alliance with Scharführer Müller, the overseer of his part of the plant. It was a partnership that was forged by their mutual goal of survival at any cost. With production goals escalating and working conditions and resources worsening, Müller was under constant pressure to maintain or exceed the prior month's numbers. His predecessor, who missed two months in a row, had been publicly rebuked and sent to the Russian Front, which, Müller remarked more than once to Divko, had the same mortality rate for Germans as Auschwitz had for Jews. For that reason, Müller met every morning with Divko to discuss the daily and weekly goals and how best to meet them.

As part of his own goal of self-preservation and his concern for his charges, Divko had managed to gain some major concessions about the conditions in which his crew lived and worked. Much of the munitions work took place in exposed conditions— a warehouse with a ceiling but limited walls. That was fine during the initial spring and summer months of Divko's Auschwitz imprisonment. But November brought with it a hardening of every element. The stinging cold gripped and hardened the hands, making the intricate work next to impossible some days. The wind found its way through and around the flimsy walls, clawing at the prisoners' garments, whipping their pants around their ankles until they chafed and sometimes bled.

Divko had met with Müller about the cold and its impact on production. And while he knew that the camp would never approve the purchase of portable heaters for Untermensch, he convinced Müller that it was in his own interests to move the one heater from his private office into a central location where the prisoners could drop by, albeit informally and just for a second, to bring their fingers back to life.

The other major change had to do with the daily three-kilometer march from the barracks to the factory. Even with a brisk pace, it took almost an hour to traverse the rutted and sometimes muddy route. And the march took its toll, with laggards or fallen prisoners given one chance to rejoin their peers before a trailing SS soldier put a bullet in their head and left the body for the trailing wagons.

Arguing again from a productivity standpoint, Divko convinced Müller to transport the prisoners to the warehouse, thus gaining two more hours of work and a higher—and better— yield on the finished munitions. The prisoners loved being out of the elements and Müller loved the increased productivity.

But all that had changed with this new addition to the camp lexicon. "Attrition" was now not just another term for the keepers of the books, like "typhus" or "dysentery," but a new, measurable metric that needed to be incorporated into camp activities and measurement.

"So let me get this straight," Divko said to him. "We're not dying fast enough to suit you? Despite the production numbers that are making you a hero?"

"Come on, Divko. You know better than anyone that you and your crew weren't intended to survive as long as you have. I've gone along with your proposals because the resulting production numbers made me look good and kept me away from the Russian Front. But now we're standing out. And for the wrong reasons."

"What's changed all of a sudden?"

"They're liquidating more ghettos, which means more incoming. And it's too expensive to build more barracks."

Divko looked out at the shop floor. Despite the cautions from his mentor—the wizened prisoner who was now, unbelievably, in his third year in the camp and still counseling Divko on all things Auschwitz—he had become close with some of these men. And now he and those same men were impediments to Müller's survival.

"So who do you want me to kill, Müller? And in what order? And how soon do you want them dead?"

"Don't be like that, Shimon. It stinks. I know that. But we've got a job to do."

Divko stood up. "This is where we part company. I'm sorry, Herr Scharführer, but there is no 'we' on this one." He looked down at him. "I'm not noble enough to volunteer myself as one of your casualties, but I won't be part of the Selektion process." He walked back to the table and the open missile it held.

As he moved around the table and inspected each station, he talked to the men. "Jacek, where's your brother? I haven't seen him all week."

"Kanada. Lucky bastard. The promised land. He empties the arriving suitcases and sorts them. A few items manage to stick to his fingers. And on top of that, he gets rations-and-a-half."

"No offense to your brother, but Kanada turns human beings into jackals."

"Well-fed jackals. With real shoes, not these wooden blister machines."

Divko grimaced at his own wooden clogs and eased one off, showing the new blisters and old wounds from the ill fit. "Maybe. But I'll take a year in these wooden torture traps over a day in a corpse's leather shoes doing a vulture's work."

"Nicely said, Shimon, but Ivan's new bunkmate has been there two years. Two years. No one here can say that."

# Nine

BARRACK 214 was preparing for lights-out. As one of the older camp structures, 214 showed its heritage. The floor was uneven and cement in places, tamped dirt in others, with the remains of a brick floor at the edges. The brick continued up the first meter of the walls, giving way to a construction of flimsy wood. The ceiling was peaked. Darkness grew up its sides, swallowing the sounds from below, and three weak overhead light bulbs tried but failed to light the entire building.

Over eight hundred women were settled in for the night, having clambered up into their bunks. This barrack had a veteran core of women who, early on, had established the rules about who claimed which positions and arbitrated any disputes about how much space and how much food each woman was allowed. This was a nice contrast to the barracks populated by newcomers, where fights persisted for the first month until a hierarchy and set of rules were established.

Due to her longevity and competence, Perla was now regarded as one of the veterans, someone newcomers sought out for advice. Like the other mentors, she charged for her services. Bread was always currency, as were cigarettes and any items that had made their way out of Kanada: buttons for uniforms, padding for shoes, or an extra blanket.

Three new prisoners, directed to Perla by one of the Kapos, were seated around her. It was the hour before lights-out and all the chores had been done. Perla let the last girl settle in and then began. "This is going to sound like I'm being philosophical. Trust me, I'm not. I just want to give you a clear picture of how things are here." She looked around the group, her eyes assessing each face and its owner's potential usefulness. "There are two types of prisoners here: the valuable and the dead. Your job is to get into the first group and stay there. If you either start out or slip into the second group, the only question is not if you're going to die, but how: gas, disease, beatings, or starvation."

She leaned forward. "It's a lot easier to go from the valuable to the dead than it is the other way around. If you wind up as the dead type, you're almost sure to stay there, and if you find yourself in that group, my advice to you is to take the initiative and run into the electric fence. It's a lot better than the alternative." She took a drag off a cigarette, not offering any of it to her listeners. "If you're one of the fortunate who wind up in the valuable group, remember this: The definition of 'valuable' changes day-to-day, job-to-job, Kapo-to-Kapo. So don't ever get too comfortable. Just keep your eyes open. Become as valuable as you can on that given day and you'll live until the next day. It's the best any of us can do."

She raised a cautionary finger, which had lost everything of substance except her bone. "Remember this: Even though the Kapos and the SS control your fate, don't kiss up to them. Your barrack mates will be watching you, and if there's any hint of collusion, you'll be smothered in your sleep. So do what they tell you, but no more."

She let the advice sink in and took one last drag off the cigarette, the ash burning down to her skin, before tossing it away and gesturing at their clothing. "Also, get your hands on a needle and thread, whatever the cost. The going rate here is a half portion of bread. Pay it. Right away. The Nazis, which means the Kapos as well, are fanatics about appearance. Missing buttons or torn garments mean beatings or no food until you fix the flaw."

She tapped her wooden shoes with her broken fingernails. "There's a saying here that we die from the ground up. It's true. Shoes that are too loose or too tight translate into open sores, which translate into disease. And if the disease doesn't kill you, your designation as 'unproductive' because you can't keep up will. So find shoes that fit. Trade with someone. Steal them if you have to. Then stuff them with cloth or newspaper to keep down the number and severity of sores."

She took off her clog and showed it toward the girls, letting them see but not hold it. "One final piece of advice. Learn as much German as you can, starting now. I've seen too many new prisoners shot or beaten simply because they couldn't understand what they were ordered to do."

She kept one piece of advice to herself. During the day, if you were working away from a permanent latrine, the Nazis used large buckets with a partially closed top as a substitute. And when that bucket became full, the last prisoner to use it, by the Kapo's estimation, was required to carry it over to the refuse tank and empty it. It was a duty that was not only physically taxing, but the spillage, coupled with the open sores generated by the shoes, could result in disease leading to death. So early in the shift, Perla would walk by the portable latrine while it was being used and gauge by the sound how full the bucket was, which told her when it was safe to use.

After she mentored the newcomers, Perla lay on her side in her outside position—another sign of her longevity—on a second-level bunk, her body shielding her motions from the watching

Kapos. She gnawed on a bread crust as she scrawled her daily report. "4 December, 1943: Day 194." She began to summarize the day's events, including the number of incoming, when a prisoner dropped a fresh pencil and paper on her pillow. Perla reached under the pillow and handed her supplier two cigarettes in return.

As she returned to her journal, a whistle blew, followed by the arrival of two Kapos. "Roll call. Everybody up!"

Perla jammed her pencil and journal under her thin mattress and joined the group of women scrambling to take their places on the open floor in front of their bunks. No one spoke a word. This was not a morning roll call, conducted outside in the large yard. This one required the women to jam tightly together, their chins almost resting on their neighbor's shoulder. They stood in this position, their faces impassive and patient.

The lead Kapo, Greta, called out, "Count off!" and then stood at parade-rest attention.

The women began counting down the line, then back up the next one, until the final woman called out, "Eight hundred fifty-three."

The women stayed at attention, though some of them were starting to sway, held up only by the proximity of their neighbors.

The Kapo knocked once on the door, which opened quickly. In walked Gisela Brandt, her uniform buttoned and flawless, followed by her secretary, also in black. "Total registered?" Brandt demanded.

"Eight hundred fifty-four."

"Accounted for?"

"Eight hundred fifty-three."

"And how do you expect to remedy your error, Kapo Greta?"

"I'm sorry, Fraülein Oberaufseherin. There must be—"

Brandt made a soothing motion, and then she held her hand out for Greta's whip. Holding it for a minute in front of her face, she began, in an almost casual motion, to strike the Kapo around the neck and face. "I don't need apologies. I need my prisoners." She changed her striking pattern to match each word. "Eight . . . hundred . . . fifty . . . four . . . to . . . be . . . precise." She handed the whip back as the welts on the Kapo's face and neck pushed their way to the surface. "You have ten minutes to find your missing prisoner or you can rejoin your charges as a member of their ranks. I'm sure they'd welcome you back with open arms."

Kapo Greta whirled away from Brandt and looked for the closest veterans. "You," she said, pointing at a nearby prisoner. "And you," she said, pointing at Perla. "Find her. The rest of you remain in your place."

The two women hustled to their task, concentrating first on the massive sleeping area. They looked under the beds at the head of each row and made their way down each aisle. Then they climbed up to each tier, throwing back bedding, until all the sleeping areas had been accounted for. Perla motioned that she would take the latrine and that her counterpart should take the showers.

The latrine held three long concrete benches, one with holes in it, the other two just boards suspended over the pools of waste. The smell was almost fog-like in its density over the pit. In the final row, in a small inset where the bench joined the wall, she found a young girl huddled and shaking. "You must come out, little one," Perla said softly.

The girl jammed herself more tightly against the wall. "I can't take anymore. I can't."

"I know. But this isn't just about you. You've put everyone at risk. Starting with me." When the girl still didn't move, Perla squatted next to her and stroked her hair. Then she straightened. "Come with me. And don't say a word."

They emerged from the latrine, Perla maneuvering to stand between the Kapo and the girl. "She had passed out and fallen behind the shitter. No wonder she was missed."

Brandt strode over and stood in front of Perla. Her face skeptical, she looked evenly at Perla, looking for any hint of initiative or rebellion. Perla returned the gaze evenly, her face a neutral mask, her posture showing neither weakness nor rebellion. She knew that the next two minutes determined not only the fate of the little girl but of herself as well. It all depended on the mood and the objectives of the Oberaufseherin. All she could do was wait for the drama to play itself out.

Brandt placed her own riding crop to the side of Perla's neck and moved her to the side, exposing the girl, who tried to stand straight but whose body seemed to shrink under Brandt's gaze. The Oberaufseherin returned her attention to Perla. "Show me your arm." Perla turned her forearm up, showing "127503." Brandt looked at her clipboard and read aloud: Divko, Perla: Clerk." She patted Perla on the cheek. "Good work, Divko, Perla. You'd make a fine Kapo." She looked sharply at Kapo Greta. "Should a vacancy arise."

"Thank you, Fräulein Oberaufseherin."

Brandt turned back to the waiting Kapos. "And what should we do about this one?" she asked, motioning toward the cowering girl.

"She'll hang at first light," Greta said. "In front of everyone. A lesson for all."

Brandt shook her head. "Then the only motivation for my girls would be fear. When it should be camaraderie." She stayed silent as she walked among the women, now all at full attention. "This barrack—this group—can be a model to the rest of

Auschwitz. But not with episodes like tonight's. We are a community, and members of a community look out for each other."

The women kept their eyes down as she walked among them. "Who are this girl's bunk-mates?"

"Show yourselves," Kapo Greta said in a near-scream.

Two women stepped forward. More girls than women, their shrunken bodies receding like turtles into their uniforms, they came to attention, their eyes fixed on their feet. Gisela walked behind them, continuing to address the group. "Mutual accountability. That's what's going to make us a tighter community. We each need to look after our neighbor."

With a sigh, she produced a Luger pistol and shot each girl at the base of the neck. Stepping back from the collapsed bodies, she said. "I hope we all learned a lesson tonight." She patted the girl on the cheek. "Especially you, my dear."

She looked back down at the dead bodies. "I think I just executed my best typist."

Perla stepped forward, looking Brandt steadily in the face. "I can type. Ninety words a minute."

"Well, lucky me. And lucky you, Greta, that I need a typist more than another Kapo." She turned back to Perla. "Report to my office in Kanada in the morning."

# Ten

KOMMANDANT HÖSS was at his desk, head down, intently looking through the morning reports. Behind him and to the right, Fritzsch stood, feet together, leaning slightly forward, at the ready. Höss reviewed each page closely, scribbled comments on most of them, and then handed them back to Fritzsch without looking up. Fritzsch then read the comments and made his own notes, placing each page in one of two stacks on a small table to his side. Both men ignored the prisoner who stood before them at attention.

Höss was working on the first draft of his year-end report, to be delivered to Himmler and the Führer in three weeks. Of course, he thought to himself, there was a good chance it might never be delivered, given the upcoming audit. On the flip side, he thought, a strong 1943 report might be the only thing that kept him from the gallows—or a bullet—should Himmler discover the theft, as was likely. So while he monitored the search for his killer and thief, he needed to put 1943, and himself, in the best possible light.

His goal, as he saw it, was to make Auschwitz look as productive and himself as essential as possible, especially if what he was hearing about 1944 was accurate. His Berlin sources were telling him that Hitler was intending to invade Hungary, even though the country had been an ostensive ally, and that all Hungarian Jews were to be immediately routed to Auschwitz and to the gas. No Selektions; no exceptions. And that went for many of the ghettos and remaining Jewish and Slav enclaves in already-occupied territories. If 1943 had been a year of preparation, 1944 was going to be a year of execution, which put Auschwitz, and him, in the spotlight at the right time.

And unlike the gold ledger, this time he didn't need to juggle the figures. The past year had been a successful one, by any reasonable standard. His team had brought the new gas chambers and crematoria online earlier that year, doubling the camp's efficiency. And he had two more units scheduled to be completed in the next two months. If 1944 was going to be the year of the Jewish Final Solution, Höss and Auschwitz would be ready. By his calculations, he would be able to gas and burn forty-five hundred a day, providing an annual yield of over a million and a half. The key was to make Rudolf Höss, and not the gas chambers and ovens, the essential ingredient in this operation.

To ensure that his report was not purely self-aggrandizing, he wrote an evenhanded, perhaps even overly critical, assessment of the Buna operation. On the plus side, construction of the factory and its supporting camp, a complex set of barracks and service units capable of holding twelve hundred laborers, had been completed on schedule and under budget, thanks to the low cost of labor and the enthusiastic prodding by his guards and Kapos. In addition, the operation had also been an exemplar of the "death by work" practice that Höss was continuing to refine, with one-fifth the population dying every month due to malnutrition, gas, or beatings. The only negative was that none of the promised synthetic rubber had yet been produced. But the fault there, Höss could argue convincingly, lay with the Farben managers, not with his team.

The section of the report he was proudest of was the technology and original thinking that lay behind the extermination process, and specifically how he and Fritzsch had evolved and perfected the techniques the Reich would need to win its war-within-a-war against its parasitic enemies.

When Höss's partnership with Fritzsch had begun at Dachau, mass extermination hadn't been part of the camp practices. Still, death was a constant there. According to Fritzsch's records, thirty thousand prisoners out of the two hundred thousand prisoner population had died from disease and starvation. Execution, mostly by rifle and torture, had been a distant third. But whether it was because Dachau was the earliest concentration camp whose purpose was detainment and torture or because it was on German soil, there were limits there that didn't transfer with Höss and Fritzsch to Auschwitz. So as mass killing became part of their professional responsibilities, they had to look beyond the camps for guidance.

When they started planning the killing operations for Auschwitz, Höss and Fritzsch looked to the Nazi campaign against its "useless eaters" for guidance. Based on Hitler's writings from jail in 1923, the campaign targeted the retarded, the physically handicapped, and those with hereditary diseases that the Reich didn't want passed down to future generations. The program not only tested new killing technology but the stomach of the German population for such a program within its own society. On that latter point, the population disappointed, with Catholic and Protestant clergy denouncing it and the majority of physicians and psychiatrists refusing to participate.

Luckily for Höss and Fritzsch, the SS staff attached to the killing operation had kept extensive records about killing techniques and outcomes that became their starting point in planning for Auschwitz's transition to a killing center. The early techniques used in the program were of little use to the two men. As if in response to the term "useless eater," the program's first killing technique had been systematic starvation, which was already in place throughout the entire camp system. The physicians had then turned to lethal injection, which was far too expensive and time-consuming to address the numbers Himmler was talking about. But the final phases of the program, in which the administrators created fixed gas chambers within the facilities, showed promise. However, the gas used was pure carbon monoxide, which, while effective, was both expensive and difficult to transport. Still, Höss and Fritzsch had their starting point.

They turned their attention next to the mobile killing units that accompanied the Einsatzgruppen, the cadres of soldiers attached to the troops advancing through Poland and Russia. The normal execution technique of the Einsatzgruppen was the rifle, with the troops digging huge open grounds outside town and herding their prisoners to them, where either firing squads or a single shot to the base of the neck would topple the dead—or in many cases, wounded—into the grave. They were then covered by bulldozers, the earth sometimes shaking for hours afterward from the efforts of the buried wounded to extract themselves from their grave.

While execution by rifle or pistol was impractical at Auschwitz, the Einsatzgruppen had also experimented with other killing techniques. The one of greatest interest to Höss and Fritzsch was the van program. Prisoners were loaded into vans, as if they were being transported to another camp. But the vans were constructed with the engine exhaust redirected into the sealed passenger area. While these mobile vans would hardly work for the numbers Auschwitz was being asked to address, he gave thought to the possibility that huge stationary diesel or gas engines attached to fixed gas chambers would work. Unfortunately, the process took too long, which was both costly and ineffective, since the prisoners, in their lengthy death process, fouled themselves, causing lengthy cleanup times before re-use.

The killing camps that had preceded Auschwitz—Belzec, Sobibor and Treblinka—held lessons of their own. Unlike Auschwitz, which was a massive Uber-camp with multiple labor projects, these camps focused exclusively on extermination, using small chambers and carbon monoxide, again from engines. But their inability to scale ruled out their techniques as well.

As was so often the case in scientific advances, the actual eureka moment for Höss and Auschwitz happened almost by chance, and it involved Kanada. After the first raft of large transports, the Germans were in possession of warehouses of clothing taken from arriving prisoners. Before they returned the clothing to Germany for distribution, they fumigated it with a pesticide called Zyklon B. During one of the first fumigations, a worker had been trapped inside the warehouse. It took only ten minutes for his peers to notice his absence, but by the time they opened the door and pulled him out, he was dead. When Fritzsch received the report, he had read it through twice and hastened down to the Kommandant's office.

They tested Zyklon B at two small farmhouses away from the camp. When the lethality proved even better than expected, they quickly constructed large-scale gas chambers with accompanying crematoria. The resulting operation was relatively quick and more efficient than any of its predecessors.

—⁂—

This process of gather, transport, select, plunder, gas, and burn was the only one capable of attaining Hitler's and Himmler's goals for 1944, and Höss wanted to make sure they remembered who had created it and who was the ideal man to run it.

Höss read through the last page of his report a second time and nodded approvingly. He stacked the remaining papers together and moved them to the side. Looking up, he seemed to notice the prisoner for the first time. He looked at Fritzsch and shrugged.

"Kapo Chernov," Fritzsch said. "He says he has a candidate for our detective search." He turned to the prisoner. "Say your piece and get out."

Chernov swallowed hard and looked at Fritzsch, afraid to look directly at the Kommandant. "I, I heard the Kommandant is looking for a detective among the prisoners."

"All ghetto police have been interviewed," Fritzsch snarled. "Not a single intelligent mind in the lot."

"I know someone—a real detective. Not ghetto police. Blue police." At Fritzsch's frown, he continued. "The blue police were before the ghetto. Shimon Divko was a lead detective with a tremendous record for arrests and convictions. In the ghetto, he was more a mayor to many of us than the actual official."

The Kommandant looked from Chernov to Fritzsch. "Well, let's take a look at this wonder detective."

The two men went back to work. Chernov stood there awkwardly for a couple of minutes, as if awaiting a response, dismissal, or reward. When none was forthcoming, he bowed and left the room.

—\infty—

"Eighty-one! Eighty-two! Eighty-three!"

The yard was packed with men trying to keep up with the Kapo's accelerated pace for their jumping jacks. Over one hundred men, in varying stages of fatigue, kept moving their arms and legs, trying futilely to keep up. The Kapos moved slowly up and down the rows, goading the less productive with their truncheons. Two SS officers sat in chairs at the front of the group, looking on with studied boredom.

There was no reason for this exercise except for punishment and sport. The prisoners were in a deliberately weakened state on the best of days, but most days brought some additional difficulty that further sapped their strength and any energy they might have. It could be the weather, with summer's swelter and winter's frigidity equally draining. It could be the absence of even the slightest hint of protein in the noon soup, which, many days, was indistinguishable from the ersatz coffee they were served morning and night. It could be a new work detail, which required them to walk up to five kilometers just to get to the site of their twelve-hour shift. Or it could be the guards making them do physically taxing exercises, betting on which of the prisoners would collapse first. Which was the case now.

"Ninety-one! Ninety-two!"

The prisoner next to Divko, who had been struggling from the beginning, suddenly went to a knee. He retched, his stomach shivering but giving nothing up. One of the under-Kapos walked over and put a foot on the man's back. As the man struggled to rise, the Kapo kept his foot firmly planted. The prisoner struggled once more, then fell, his face and chest taking the brunt of the fall.

"No more," the man said weakly, his mouth grabbing dirt. "I can't."

"You have a choice here, Jew. Either you're back on your feet in ten seconds or *my* feet will finish the job."

The prisoner got to one knee and steadied himself. For a moment, his other foot seemed to gain traction, but then it collapsed, bringing him face-down into the dirt again. What strength he'd had in his arms and shoulders was gone.

The Kapo looked over at the senior Kapo, who nodded back and placed his foot on the fallen man's neck, causing the muscles of the neck to twitch. Then he raised his heavy-booted foot and brought it down, heel-first, with full force. There was a crunching sound and then a crack. The prisoner's body lost its tension.

Without looking back at the senior Kapo, the executioner motioned to the two men next to the corpse. "Clean this mess up. Now."

Divko, one of the two selected, reached under the man's arms and hoisted him slightly. His compatriot grabbed the man's ankles. They looked around for some place to deposit the body but received no guidance, either from the guards or the landscape. As the Kapo motioned for the men to resume their exercises, Divko motioned with his head toward the barracks. Leaning the corpse up against the inside doorframe, the two men returned quickly to the yard.

Ten minutes later, the men were allowed to quit the exercise. They picked up their tin cups, spoons, and bowls and started shuffling down the road back toward their barracks. The prisoner who had helped Divko move the corpse was now moving unsteadily, his feet splaying, not lifting enough for a full step. He stumbled once, but Divko grabbed him by the elbow and righted him. The second stumble brought him to one knee.

Divko grabbed the man by the collar with one hand and put his other hand in the man's armpit. He tried to raise him, but the man was having none of it.

"I'm done. Done. Leave me."

"You need to move, Klemko. Now."

"Leave me," the man said, his words barely audible.

"I can't. Where will I find a new lead mechanic?"

The man's lips moved, but the sound was so low that Divko had to place his ear next to Klemko's mouth. At that moment, a truncheon thundered down on the back of his neck. Divko's right knee collapsed and he mirrored Klemko's posture. He got to his feet unsteadily, wavered for a moment, then found his footing. Seeing a second Kapo approach, his truncheon raised, he tried to bring Klemko to his feet.

The second blow was to the back of his knee, which stiffened for a moment before collapsing. Divko tried to brace his fall, but the awkward motion only served to turn him onto his back. Shielding his eyes with one hand against the morning light, he watched his assailant approach, truncheon fully raised, his eyes fixed on Divko's temple for a killing blow.

At that moment, a Kübelwagen pulled up, its gravelly braking drawing everyone's eyes, including those of Divko's assailant. Hauptsturmführer Fritzsch stepped down from the car, a paper in his hand, which he handed to the SS officer on duty.

The man read the paper in a loud voice. "Prisoner 127485! Shimon Divko."

Divko tried to speak, but his voice caught in his throat. Raising himself on one arm, he tried to thrust the other one into the air but failed. But, with all the other prisoners frozen in place, the motion was enough to catch the eye of the man in the Kübelwagen. He walked over and turned Divko's arm roughly, looking at the tattoo. "Put him in the car," he ordered the guard with the truncheon.

# Eleven

His body still pulsing in pain from the beating, Divko tried to steady himself as he sat across the desk from the Kommandant, who was reading a single piece of paper. He looked from the paper to Divko, frowning slightly, as if the words on the paper and the pathetic figure in front of him were at odds. Then he put it down.

"State Police. Homicide, twelve years. Three times decorated."

Fritzsch, who had been reading over the Kommandant's shoulder, regarded Divko with suspicion. "Ninety percent conviction rate? Those are Gestapo numbers."

Divko's feet found purchase on the floor, and he steadied himself. He kept his eyes down as he answered. "But with slightly more humane interrogation techniques."

"Your German is good for a Pole," said Höss. He checked the paper. "1916. Conscripted by the Kaiser. You fought for the Fatherland."

"A water boy. Nothing more."

Höss motioned for Fritzsch to hand Divko a glass of water. Divko grabbed it eagerly and drained the glass in one solid ripple of his throat. Water at Auschwitz was a precious commodity. The water from the faucets, both in the barracks and at the job sites, was brackish and impossible to drink. The only answer to thirst was in the lunchtime watered-down soup and the ersatz coffee that was part of morning and evening meals. As the clean, cool water slid down his throat, Divko felt like crying, something he hadn't done since before the ghetto. He had wondered if he'd lost the emotional capacity to cry or if the mechanism, like so many of his bodily functions, had simply been corroded by hunger and desperation.

He held out the empty glass to Fritzsch, whose eyes widened at the temerity. Divko lowered his eyes but kept his arm out straight. Finally, at Höss's nod, Fritzsch poured again, glaring at Divko as he did so. This time, Divko sipped at the water, nodding his gratitude to Fritzsch as he did so. His eyes never rose above the lip of the glass.

"You're wondering why you're here," the Kommandant said.

"I gave up wondering a long time ago."

"There's been a murder." Both men waited for a response, but Divko remained silent, his eyes now fixed on his knees. "You'll investigate," Höss continued. "If you succeed, you'll be awarded a comfortable position here in Kanada with double rations."

"And if I don't succeed?"

"You go up the chimney," Fritzsch, now standing behind him, called out, almost joyfully.

"Who was the victim?"

"The lead accountant in Kanada. You will find his killer and the ledger he stole."

Divko looked up for the first time. "The lead accountant? A demanding job, since there's so much to account for here." He lowered his eyes before they could see the slight smile that had formed on its own.

At Höss's slight nod, Fritzsch crashed his balled fists into the base of Divko's neck, knocking him off the chair. Still recovering from the earlier beating, it took him a long time to gather himself and regain his seat. His look remained determinedly passive.

"What is or isn't in the ledger isn't your concern. Nor are the workings of this camp. Your job is to find the ledger and the man who took it. In seven days. Less, preferably."

Divko rubbed his neck. This time his eyes returned the Kommandant's gaze.

"Thank you for the offer, Herr Kommandant, and for the water. But I must decline your kind offer."

"It was an order, Jew, not an offer. You have no choice in the matter."

"On the contrary. A choice is all I have left." He motioned out the window. "Look around you, sir. No one leaves here alive. My only choice is where and when I die. And I choose here and now rather than assist my enemy."

Fritzsch put his gun to Divko's head and looked to Höss with raised eyebrows. Höss waved him off with a tired hand.

"Show him our other water. You can beat him, but don't kill him." He looked at Divko with cool eyes. "We'll talk tomorrow."

"My answer will be the same."

"We'll see."

# Twelve

LATER THAT NIGHT, in the private study off the Kommandant's office, Gisela sat at a small table applying a light, finishing touch to her makeup. Proud of her natural beauty, she wore only a touch of makeup and rouge. No lipstick. As she applied the makeup, she held the telephone in a crook in her neck. Her voice was calm and factual.

"The camp changes almost daily. Another sub-camp is created, and they want me over there to teach the new SS and Kapos how to train and maintain order with over eight hundred women in a building."

She listened, nodding slightly. "I honestly don't know when they'll get their first yield. But it's a production problem, not a labor problem. My girls are actually better laborers than Weiss's men. You know how we women are. We know we aren't going to make it with brute force, so we rely on technique."

She smiled, leaned back, and lit a cigarette. "Back in SS training, we were learning how to kayak. I was the only women in a group of eight men. There's something called the Eskimo roll, where you go upside down and have to right yourself. To do that, you must calm yourself, put your paddle in the right position, and snap your hips. Brute force won't get you upright."

Her smile broadened. "I was the only one to execute it right the first time. For most of that day, the guys kept trying to muscle their way through and almost drowned in the process. It's the same thing with digging and building. My girls measure, use their technique, and get it right the first time. Weiss and his men jump in with their shovels and dig like dogs. Then they have to get out, remeasure, and fix the work they do."

She listened for a moment, and her face lost its smile. "Sorry. I'll try to stick to the topic at hand. What I'm saying is that the new support buildings are going up on time. The problem is, they may be empty for a while. The Buna engineers still haven't produced a single usable product, which means they won't need all the laborers we're building these barracks for. And I know how the Reich is about useless eaters."

It had been a long day, starting with the discipline at reveille and then moving to overseeing the Farben construction. Normally, her responsibilities focused on the women who supported the Kanada operation, but two of her barracks had been requisitioned for help with digging the foundation of an extension of the Buna rubber factory, so she had rotated her oversight between the two locations.

Of all the German companies that had allied themselves with the Nazi regime and benefited from the camps—both extermination camps and labor camps—Farben was easily the most important. The most obvious operation, and the one potentially most lucrative for both sides, was the Buna factory. There, Auschwitz prisoners who were paid a fraction of what their German predecessors had been paid helped produce the oil and synthetic rubber critical to the war effort. In addition to Buna, a Farben subsidiary produced Zyklon B. And Bayer, another Farben subsidiary, was working with the medical staff at Auschwitz to conduct medical experiments. So when Farben officials raised a concern, everyone from the Kommandant to the most junior Kapo leapt to action.

But Gisela had a checklist of her own, cataloguing every area where her group could be held responsible. She monitored those areas with a protective eye and a jaded attitude, looking for anything the Farben bastards could blame, other than themselves, for its lack of output. Along with most everyone associated with the project, she knew that the production issues stemmed from the formula, not the facilities. It was up to her to ensure that Rudolf—and Berlin—were aware of that as well.

At the sound of a key in the door, she spoke softly into the phone and hung up. Putting away her makeup, she turned to face the door. Höss walked in, his shoulders slumped, his face drawn. There was a beaten quality about him that she'd never seen before. He smiled slightly and nodded at Gisela before turning and locking the door behind him.

Gisela stood up and walked over to him. Taking his face in her hands, she kissed him briefly on the lips. "I wondered what happened to you." She tried a pout. "I was afraid you'd forgotten about me." When he didn't respond, she dropped the pout and flirtatious voice. "That bad?"

"It's bad."

"No suspects?"

"It's Kanada. Everyone's a suspect." He poured her a drink and handed it to her. She nodded, put the Scotch on the table next to her makeup, and looked at him. "Anything of substance today? Anything at all that we can build on?" She patted the chaise. "Come sit beside me."

He walked over, a lumber to his step, and stopped for a moment, standing over her. Then he settled heavily on the chaise. She nodded and produced a small pad of paper. He was all business now. "Okay. Let's look at this with fresh eyes. There's a solution here. We just need to find it."

—·—

They had started out as a cliché. The Kommandant was known as a cocksman capable of attracting and bedding anything in sight. Or he at least fancied himself as such. Out of uniform he was a relatively ordinary looking man with a serious face that rarely smiled, hair brushed back from a forehead that was beginning to recede, and strong brown-black eyes that fixed and held his target. His uniform not only identified his rank but seemed to boost everything about him—vitality, authority, and certainty—if only slightly. And he was rarely out of uniform.

"You're a regal Nazi, Rudy," Gisela had told him one night. "And a good-looking man to boot. But don't kid yourself. Rank is a type of aphrodisiac, especially in a place like Auschwitz. Consider all the women you've bedded here—and may be still bedding for that matter, though I better not catch you—and ask yourself if your success ratio would be that high if you were an enlisted man working the front gate."

No woman had ever spoken to him like that, not even his wife. But from the moment they had first met, Gisela was determined to be as unlike the previous women in his life as possible. Early on, to catch his interest and get into the game, she had played the ingenue, letting him flirt with her but not playing along, accepting the flowers with a girlish blush, and finally agreeing to a private dinner in his study. She had allowed herself to be bedded after a few of these dinners, and she'd praised his prowess and staying power.

But once the initial bedding was complete, she changed the rules. When the Kommandant called her a week later for a reprise, she begged off, citing a family emergency and saying she hoped he'd understand. Keeping the charade of the emergency going, she applied for and received family leave, which took her away from the camp for ten days, a period she hoped would enhance his interest in her.

When she returned, an invitation to dinner was waiting in her mailbox. It had been a private affair, catered to them in his private study. But this time, when he tried to guide her toward the bed, she demurred, explaining to him that she saw herself as a Nazi first and a woman second and that part of her personal Nazism was based on the Führer's principle that honor began with loyalty. Just as she was loyal to the Führer, she would be loyal to the right man, but only if that loyalty were reciprocated. She was sure that, as a loyal Nazi, he would understand and respect these principles.

Höss was impressed, but not enough to forego his sexual prowling. Subsequent dalliances with other women had proven uninspiring, with their compliments on his abilities seeming suddenly rote and hollow. He invited Oberaufseherin Brandt to another private dinner, and this time, it was his turn to surprise her. He sought out her opinion on camp matters and thanked her at the end of the evening without pursuing a sexual agenda. Since that night, they had become as much of a couple as Höss's obligations to his wife and family permitted. He returned home at the end of the day and had dinner with Hedwig and the children. But once the children were off to bed and Hedwig was ensconced in her bedroom, he would return to his office, usually for a late-night rendezvous with Gisela.

---

Höss looked at Gisela's expectant face and raised pencil, then down at the empty pad of paper. She retrieved her drink and handed it him. Once he'd taken a long swallow, he looked at her with a face somewhere between aggrieved and beaten. "I had an interesting thing happen this afternoon. A Polish Jew—a prisoner, a former head detective in the Warsaw police—refused to help investigate the murder."

"Refused? No one refuses the Kommandant. Make an example of him. Bring him before the roll call and—"

"Make him a hero? Don't be foolish."

She slipped into a girlish pout, then caught herself. "This is Auschwitz. You don't just refuse a Kommandant's order."

"You haven't met this Pole. Like it or not, I need him. And he knows it." He smiled bitterly. "And unlike the rest of the camp, he doesn't seem to be afraid of me." The smile caught at the corner of his mouth and twisted slightly. "Imagine that."

Gisela took her drink back from the Kommandant and swirled it. "Men who won't think about themselves often think about others. Most of my prisoners have family here. Maybe one of them—"

"Is family to my Jew. Good idea, my love."

She reached for the telephone. "What's your prisoner's name?" He said it, then spelled it out. She dialed the operator and asked to be transferred to Records. "I'll have them work all night if they have to. If he's got family here, we'll find it."

Seeing that this news had done nothing to change the defeated look on Höss's face, she took his hand in hers and gave him a wolfish smile. "And while my staff is digging, let's you and I clear our minds. Then we will revisit our problem . . . reinvigorated."

# Thirteen

HALF A MILE AWAY, in a dimly lit courtyard, Divko was running in place with a broom held parallel to the ground over his head. Whenever the broom dropped below eye level or his quick-shuffling feet, a guard would hit him with a fierce stream of water from an industrial hose, rotating between his face and stomach. Clad only in his uniform pants, he was shivering and drenched, and over the course of the first hour, the guard had ratcheted up the strength until it was at full force.

As they entered the third hour of the water treatment, the guard looked over at Fritzsch, who was ensconced in a folding chair, its front legs off the ground as he leaned back against the garage wall, a freshly lit cigarette tucked in the corner of his mouth. He nodded at the guard, who then flicked his wrist, directing the rage of water at Divko, hitting him first in the face, then his chest. Divko groaned and staggered under the attack but remained standing.

With an aggrieved sigh, Fritzsch tipped the chair forward and hoisted himself to his feet. He gestured impatiently at the hose, then flicked his cigarette at Divko, hitting him in the chest and sending a slight shower of sparks into the night air. "If you want something done right . . ." he said, turning the hose to full force and holding it by his side.

As Divko continued to run in place, the water on his pants and chest, now a thin sheet of ice, cracked as his body shifted. Fritzsch aimed the hose at Divko's groin. With a small cry, he fell to one knee and stayed there, the broom above his head. As Divko struggled to his feet, Fritzsch motioned to the guard to turn off the hose and walked over to a table, his eyes roving over the six tools, looking for the one that could bring the evening to an end in time for Fritzsch to get a good night's sleep.

Fritzsch was a founding member of the Kommandant's Disciplinary Review Committee, so on the ride over to Block 11, a building which housed a number of tools useful to that night's task, he had gone over his options.

Discipline and torture, like every other component of Auschwitz, were documented and measured for efficiency. At the Kommandant's direction, the Disciplinary Review Committee, made up of a dozen disciplinary experts, met every three months to review the results of previous activities and any new techniques.

The first half of the meeting was devoted to discipline, which was any activity that ended in the prisoner surviving the process and returning to work. This included the use of the standing cell—a cage to which a prisoner returned after a day of work that allowed only enough room for them to stand. Its metal walls were within inches of the person contained within, and there was only an airhole at the top. They remained there all night. The group discussed how many days a prisoner could tolerate the standing cell, with and without sustenance.

The conversations on torture, on the other hand, were as random and varied as the techniques themselves. It seemed that each participant was determined to bring a new form of torture to the meeting, and their suggestions were met with either respect or ridicule.

When it came to torture, there were two philosophical camps, with the divisions between the two long-standing and fixed. There were those who favored predictability, set in the belief that knowing what was to come brought more terror and anguish than the actual event. This group was countered by the "randomists," who believed that by selecting both the victim and the form of punishment at random, they could inflict the maximum damage on the largest percent of the population.

The same arguments existed when it came to longevity. The older guards preferred the standing cell for its terror and efficiency, while the newer ones preferred flogging, both for its public nature and its involvement of a larger portion of the Auschwitz population. In a tip of the hat to the randomists, the prisoners administered the floggings themselves, with the flogger chosen at random from their ranks. And in a further twist, should it be deemed by either the Kapo or SS guard that the flogger was going light with the lash, he was required to take the place of his victim. It was one of the few suggestions that was met with applause on both sides.

One of the Kapos, a veteran of the Lodz ghetto whose savagery had been shown the ultimate SS respect by his invitation to be a guest speaker, had told Fritzsch afterward that the DRC reminded him of rabbinical gatherings during which the assembled rabbis would "drash" the day's text to exhaustion.

Most of the time, the meeting members were engaged in debate and discussion just to hear themselves talk. But every now and then, the meetings unearthed a nugget. It was this Kapo who had coordinated with Fritzsch to develop such a nugget, which became one of Auschwitz's favorite forms of both discipline and torture. Within the Disciplinary Review

Committee and among the prisoners, it was called "restraint," and its reputation was growing, both for its simplicity and its results.

Restraint had come about completely by accident when Fritzsch had administered a relatively minor punishment to one of his prisoners. He had the prisoner stand in the corner of a room, facing the corner, and told him to remain there for his entire work shift. After three hours, the prisoner asked if he could relieve himself, a request that Fritzsch had casually denied, though he couldn't remember why. When the prisoner asked again an hour later, the anguish in his voice was obvious, verging on panic. Fritzsch denied the request again, but this time, he kept an eye on the prisoner and saw a progression of his anguish: minor tremors, then the legs shaking uncontrollably, then the inevitable pool of urine down the leg, followed by the collapse.

Intrigued, Fritzsch started experimenting with restraint, called that because all it asked of its victim was that they show restraint in their toilet behaviors. He expanded the time that he required each victim to stand, and he allowed them double rations the morning of the procedure, including access to Nazi clean water.

The Kapo had told the Disciplinary Review Committee that prisoners who had been flogged and post-hung said they found restraint to be the worst of all, simply because it was seemingly within their control, which made it unique among all their activities at Auschwitz.

—⁂—

At midnight, Fritzsch sent the guard home. He motioned for Divko to lower the broom but kept him standing at attention. Divko was shivering uncontrollably, the cold keeping down the swelling from the systematic beating that Fritzsch had administered with his truncheon. His uniform was frozen in places, cracking when Divko shifted his posture.

"One more time, Jew. Are you ready to help with the investigation?"

Divko kept his mouth shut and simply shook his head.

Fritzsch grabbed his folding chair and placed it in front of the table that held his torture tools. "Sit," he commanded, and Divko quickly complied. Fritzsch then fastened Divko's legs to the chair legs with wire. Leaving Divko at the table, Fritzsch disappeared into the garage and came back with a glass pitcher filled with water. He put the pitcher and a tin cup in front of Divko. "Drink," he said. "We've got a long night ahead of us." Divko grabbed the cup, filled it, and drank quickly. Then another cup and another. He stopped after four and looked cautiously at Fritzsch, his thirst diminished, his suspicions growing.

Fritzsch bound Divko's hands behind his back with heavy rope. Then he came back into Divko's view and smiled almost gently. "I should have warned you to go carefully with the water. My mistake. Anyway, here's what's going to happen." Fritzsch pulled an industrial truck battery from beneath the table and set it in front of Fritzsch. Extracting cables from a heavy canvas bag, he attached the first set of electrodes to the battery posts. Then he knelt and pulled down Divko's pants. Attaching the other ends to Divko's scrotum, he talked as he straightened up. "This is a variation of the restraint treatment that I'm sure you've heard of. In this case, the electrodes are sensitive to water and movement. If you urinate or try to shake them off, the electrodes will discharge automatically." He grabbed a second chair, sat down, and tipped his cap forward over his eyes. "Now, if you'll excuse me, I'm going to sleep. I would suggest you not do the same."

Fritzsch woke up at six, gathered his wits, and then inspected his prisoner. Divko was still upright in his chair. A pool of urine had formed around the two chair legs where his legs were bound. Fritzsch looked at the electrodes and saw that the skin on the scrotum was slightly charred. Divko looked at him with blank eyes. Then he passed out.

# Fourteen

PERLA ENTERED THE TYPING POOL, a cramped room with seven other prisoners bent over the machines. One of the workers, a member of her barracks, looked up and motioned her with a nod to the lone empty desk in the room. Perla sat down and looked around. A moment later, a woman Kapo came into the room with a pile of papers. She divided them among the other typists, then walked over to Perla's desk.

"Where's Wolkowitz?"

"Dead. I'm her replacement." The woman shrugged and placed a large pile of handwritten notes on the table. "These are incoming records from yesterday's transport. Those marked with a "Z" are to be entered into the "inactive" ledger, along with the date of their termination. The others are active. You are to record their date of arrival, their work assignment, and their barrack. There will be a second tracking system for them that you'll also work on. When your ledger is complete, bring it to me. I'm in the next office. If there are no more transports, you'll work on the second tracking system. Any questions? If not, then get to work."

Perla looked at the two stacks and then around the room. She said to her neighbor, a woman from her barrack, "Z?"

"For Zyklon." When Perla shrugged, she added, "The name of the gas."

By the end of her first day, Perla had the first system down, tracking the gassings as well as those who had died "ER" (en route). The perished were entered in small, tight rows of numbers that quickly filled the page and then the ledger. Perla did a quick reckoning of her own activity, then compared notes over lunch with the other women. There were two other women tasked with the same assignment. Doing the math, Perla calculated that the previous day, Auschwitz had gassed and burned over forty-five hundred arrivals. And her compatriots assured her that it had been a slow day.

"I'm stunned that we're documenting all this activity," she said to her jaded mentor at day's end. "This is damning testimony, should they lose the war."

"You'd think so, wouldn't you? But I've learned two things in my year here. First, the Nazis record everything, including when they take a shit. And second, they're not at all concerned about the aftermath. They're either going to win this war or they're going to scorch the earth on their way out." She motioned toward the office behind them. "These records will either go into the victors' archives in Berlin or into the ovens, along with the last transport."

Over the course of her first week in Incoming, Perla had searched the desks—her own, then the others, as schedules and breaks permitted—for something to record her findings in. At the end of that week, she found a small notebook no bigger than her hand in the stockroom with the typing supplies. She slipped it into her uniform top, then secured it later at her waist. Two days later, as they were totaling the week's numbers, she memorized what she could and jotted down what she couldn't on a scrap of paper and entered the data in her notebook that evening at lights out. Her new Oneg Shabbat had begun.

Near the end of that first week, Perla walked into the neighboring office with a ledger and a spool of ribbon in her hand. She handed the completed ledger to the Kapo, who handed her an empty replacement. Perla nodded at the ribbon. "I need a new ribbon."

"That closet," the Kapo replied, nodding at a door. "Ingrid there has the key."

Perla went to the desk nearest the closet door and stood, her hands behind her back, as the woman talked on the phone. Her eyes wandered to the wall above the desk where a series of magazine pages, each showing a different location, was pinned on the wall.

The woman hung up and looked at Perla, who tried a smile. "Berchtesgaden. I hear its beautiful. Have you been there?" Perla asked.

"If you must know, I collect stories of Reich leaders and their families. An inspiration for us all. Berchtesgaden is where our Führer has his Eagle's Nest and where Reichsführer Himmler vacations. Now, what was it you wanted?"

"Typewriter ribbon."

The woman handed her the key and went back to work. Perla opened the closet and entered. It was more a room than closet, the left side dominated by shelves of office supplies and ledgers. The right side also had shelves, but those contained stacks of clothing. She unfolded one, revealing a female SS jacket, and looked at the lower shelf, where she found its male counterpart. She folded both uniforms and put them back, then turned to the office supply shelves.

# Fifteen

AT THAT SAME MOMENT, a kilometer away, Divko, hollow-eyed and exhausted, sat with extreme difficulty in the back seat of an open Mercedes as it negotiated the roads connecting the different camps within the Auschwitz complex. In the front passenger seat, silent and comfortable, Höss looked straight ahead, motioning now and again to the driver.

Earlier that morning, Fritzsch had dragged a barely mobile Divko from the Kübelwagen to the Kommandant's office, where he had him stand in the hall while he went in to consult with his boss. Standing for Divko had been difficult, but it was preferable to sitting on his burnt scrotum. He had squirmed and rearranged his crotch on the ride over, and just when he found a position he could tolerate, the car lurched to a halt, causing him to scream in pain. Clenched teeth had caught most of the pain, but Fritzsch had looked over and given him a smile that was part triumph and part sympathy.

Now, at a slight raise of Höss's hand, the car came to a stop in a small courtyard. A group of soldiers leaned against a wall, a set of guns on the ground in front of them. Across the courtyard, tied to posts and slumped but erect, were two prisoners, their uniforms more red than grey.

Höss waited until the car halted and the engine quieted before calling over his shoulder, "Some people say that imagination can be more vivid than reality." He nodded to the soldiers, one of whom stood, took aim, and shot at one of the prisoners, who grunted, a fresh stain of red opening on his shoulder. "Me? I find that reality has its own persuasive charm."

An SS doctor with a stethoscope around his neck walked over and inspected the prisoner, listening to his heartbeat, his ear next to the gasping mouth. He nodded back to the group, which cheered and patted the shooter on the back.

"As a rule," the Kommandant said, "we shoot escapees on sight. But the guards must have their sport. And their target practice. The game here is to bet on how many bullets they can put into a prisoner before he . . . quits the game. The record is seventeen." He motioned for the men to continue.

As the next shot hit the second posted prisoner, Divko kept a stoic face, and when the doctor walked out again to make his assessment, Divko turned his head to face Höss. He gestured toward the outhouse at the end of the yard. "I need to use the latrine, Kommandant." Motioning to his stomach, he added, "Last night's activity took its toll."

At Höss's nod, Divko hurried toward the structure. Once inside, his face collapsed, the rest of his body soon following. He sat on the toilet and broke down, his cries coming in gulping breaths that he muffled with the back of his fist. Feeling his throat grab and convulse, he spun onto his knees just in time to vomit into the toilet. When he was done, he regained his seat and sat there for a minute, steadying himself.

He was done, he admitted to himself. Last night had started as resistance to the Kommandant's request, which Divko had no intention of agreeing to under any condition. Then it had evolved into a war of wills with Fritzsch, his only goal being to keep the look of frustration on Fritzsch's face for as long as possible. Then, once Fritzsch had wired him up, Divko's only thought was how to survive the night so he could die after one last confrontation with the Kommandant.

When it came to his actual death, though, there was a gulf between desire and accomplishment. Most inmates at Auschwitz committed suicide by going "into the wire," waiting until final roll call before exiting the barracks silently and running into the electrified fence. But Divko could now barely walk, much less run. Besides, Fritzsch would be on alert for just that move.

His primary hope was to get Fritzsch's gun away from him and turn it on Fritzsch—and even the Kommandant, should the possibility present itself—before taking his own life. It could be done. As a detective, he'd heard stories of seemingly incapacitated suspects grabbing a policeman's gun and doing maximum damage. But Fritzsch would also be on his guard for something like that. Still, it was his only option. He just had to be convincing in his presentation of himself as weakened and immobile. And given his current condition, that wouldn't be difficult. His only regret was that he would never see Perla again. He was not a believer, and the thought of an afterlife, though he hoped for it now, was a long shot at best. As much as he hated to admit it, Auschwitz had beaten him.

Divko washed his face and hands from the bucket of water, dried them with his sleeve, tried to slap some life into his cheeks, and headed back. Höss was already in the front seat when Divko returned. He leaned forward slightly, giving Divko access to the back seat but keeping the passage narrow, causing Divko to twist and angle his body, sending shivers of pain throughout his lower legs. At the Kommandant's nod, they drove off, and as they neared the corner, another gunshot rang out, this one generating no audible response.

"Your decision yesterday was courageous," Höss called over his shoulder. "But it was also rash. It didn't consider all the facts. As a detective, facts are your stock in trade, no? So let me show you some new facts that will assist you in your decision."

They rode the rest of the way in silence. Five minutes later, they pulled up in front of a low-lying building with a sign that read "Hospital" over the door. The driver jumped out and held the door open for the two men.

"Our next stop," Höss said. "This will show a more intimate and structured operation, rather than the target practice you just witnessed."

They moved down the aisle until the Kommandant held up his hand and stopped in front of an open door. Höss motioned Divko to take a look. Inside was a large room populated by a group of children at play. No striped uniforms; no gaunt physiques. Divko wondered if it was a center for the children of the Nazi guards.

It took Divko more than a minute of watching before he realized that the children he was observing were all twins. Höss nodded. "When the war is over, I know that much of the focus will be on our elimination program, which I certainly understand. But there are other programs here—important programs that I hope history will appreciate." He motioned to the doctor on duty, who hurried over.

He was a handsome, well-groomed man with startling blue-grey eyes and an eager smile. "Herr Kommandant, an unexpected honor."

Höss nodded. "Doctor Mengele. Please explain your experiments to our Jewish friend here."

Mengele nodded. "These children were all going to be eliminated with the rest of their peers. I saved them from that fate." He held up a hand, though Divko hadn't said anything. "This was not an act of mercy but of science. As you know, these children are enemies of the Reich because of the blood that flows through their veins, regardless of their age. But before they join their parents in the gas chamber, I'm determined to extract as much scientific value from them as possible. They owe us that much."

He motioned toward the group. "I have here the perfect test group for my medical theories and for experimentation on diseases that may save thousands of lives in the future, if not more. Whether it has to do with disease, innovative surgical procedures, or new medicines, I have the perfect subjects." His eyes seemed to dance as he continued. "Normally, your 'before and after' are the same subject. But when that subject dies and you're determining cause and measuring results, you're never sure about these things." His eyes moved to the room and the children. "But here, if a subject dies during one of my experiments, I can immediately have an orderly fetch the surviving twin and inject him, killing him instantly. I can then conduct side-by-side autopsies. Medical science doesn't get any more exact than that."

He nodded at the Kommandant. "This man shares my vision and has generously given me free rein in my experimentation. I trust that history will show that the two of us were more than Reich loyalists carrying out the distasteful but necessary extermination process. We were medical pioneers who actually saved lives. How many, only history will tell."

"I have a question for the doctor, if I may," Divko said to the Kommandant. When Höss nodded, Divko looked at Mengele, careful to keep his face earnest and interested. "Do you subscribe to the Reich's theory that we Jews are vermin and nothing more than an infectious threat to the Reich and its people?"

"I do," Mengele said, his head cocked slightly as he looked at his questioner.

"Then how are any of your experiments of any medical worth, since the lessons learned from these vermin can't have any validity for the Aryan species, which is so clearly both different from and superior to us diseased rats?" As Mengele's frown deepened, Divko continued. "Wouldn't your resources be both more valuable and more accurate if you used German twins? I'm sure their parents would be willing to donate them to the Reich once you explained to them the value of your experiments."

Mengele stared at Divko for a long moment before shifting his gaze to the Kommandant, whose eyes held a slight smile. Höss raised a questioning eyebrow at Mengele indicating that an answer was in order.

Mengele thought for a long moment. Finally he nodded, as if to himself. "I take it you're not a man of science, prisoner . . ."

"Divko."

"Prisoner Divko. If you were, you would know that we try our theories and experiments first on rats, then on dogs, and finally on monkeys. Here at Auschwitz, by working with Jews, we're starting at an even more basic level, one species below rats." He smiled condescendingly at Divko, who said nothing.

The Kommandant smiled at both men. "Outstanding, Doctor. I feel like I'm watching two grand masters playing chess."

Höss thanked Mengele and moved down the hall, stopping at a closed door, behind which was an operating theatre. He rapped on the door until the operating surgeon, his mask still on, opened it.

At the sight of Höss, he clicked his heels—a soundless gesture since his feet wore cotton operating booties—lowered his mask, and stepped out into the hall. "An honor, sir."

Höss nodded absently and looked past the doctor through the half-open door. "Doctor, please describe the procedure you're about to perform."

"Certainly. We are looking to the future, to diagnosing diseases in their earliest stages. So I'm performing a colposcopy to identify possibly cancerous cervical cells. And then I will perform a complete cervicectomy."

"The Reich, and I, admire the diligence of your research, Doctor. You have our thanks."

With a nod, the doctor returned to the operating room. Höss gestured after him.

"I'm told he uses no anesthesia but donates it instead to our clinics at the Russian Front."

"Admirable," Divko said, watching as the doctor approached the restrained woman and lifted the sheet.

"Unfortunately, the survival rate is low," the Kommandant said.

"Death is death."

"To you, perhaps. But not to the woman on the table, I can assure you." A shriek filled the air, but Höss didn't seem to notice. "Let's head back."

# Sixteen

BACK IN HIS OFFICE, Höss excused himself and went into his study while Fritzsch remained at attention by the door. He returned with the bottle of scotch and two glasses. He poured one for himself and took an admiring sip.

"I hope our field trip brought clarity to your situation," he said as he pushed the other glass toward Divko, who made no move for it.

"Only that it seems I have more ways to 'quit the game,' as you put it. So let's get on with it. Do I choose or do you?"

Höss nodded. "So principled and yet so naïve. In the wake of last night, I counted on this response. Which is why I have one last exhibit." He nodded at Fritzsch, who opened the door to the study. There stood Gisela Brandt. As the door swung fully open, Perla came into view, her arm held tight by Brandt's black-clad arm. Initially too stunned to speak, Divko moved toward the door. Höss nodded at Fritzsch, who closed the door before Divko could reach it.

"Now this is how things are going to work, my Jew. I'm going to allow you five minutes with your . . ." He looked at a sheet of paper. "Perla. At which time you will tell me one of two things. Either that you will lead my investigation or one of the fates we just witnessed—bullets or scalpel—will be Perla's. And then yours, of course."

At Höss's nod, Fritzsch opened the door. Divko stood there, still stunned, moving forward only when Höss gave him a push through the door and closed the door behind him. At the same moment, Gisela released Perla's arm and exited the study through the far door.

The two faced each other for a long, awkward moment, neither making the first move. Finally, Divko stepped forward and wrapped Perla in a tight hug. "I don't know what just happened, but this is a miracle. I thought I'd never see you again."

Perla hugged him back, her hands so tight on his thin uniform that she tore it slightly. She pulled her head back and looked up at him. "What are we doing here? Or more specifically, what are *you* doing here?"

"They want me to help them solve a murder." He looked around the room, suddenly avoiding her gaze.

"Shimon." She waited until he was looking at her. "Do I need to remind you what we did with collaborators back in the ghetto?"

⸻෴⸻

Legally, there was no such thing as collaboration in the ghetto, since it meant aiding the occupiers, and neither the Germans nor the Judenrat saw that as a crime. Which left it to the Jewish Council to define and enforce what was and wasn't aiding and abetting the enemy.

During their almost four years in the ghetto, both Divkos had been called to serve on the three-person juries that heard the most serious collaboration cases. Defining the term "collaborator" was in some ways as complex and nuanced an exercise as the arguments the rabbis conducted over specific Biblical and

Talmudic texts. In some ways, just by staying alive, everyone was guilty of some form of collusion with their oppressors. As one council member put it, "The only true heroes are dead, which doesn't help the living that much." But blatant collaboration, especially that which led to punishment or death for ghetto residents, could not go unpunished, lest it spread like a disease.

The initial jury panels had been made up entirely of men. But when a young mother was accused of collaboration with the Nazis for having sex with two German soldiers, and when the men on the panel demanded death as the penalty, Shimon had demanded that they bring Perla into the discussion before carrying out the sentence. Perla heard the men out, assessed the logic of their arguments and judgment, and then met with the accused woman.

"What she did clearly falls under the definition of 'collaboration,'" she said to the panel. "But I sat in that crowded apartment and saw the bones peeking through her children's skin, and I realized that even as a woman, I couldn't judge her." When pressed for a decision, she had said, "Look, I have no children and can't begin to understand what must go through a mother's mind as she watches them die in front of her. So I can't say what I would do in her place"

"So what are you saying?" the presiding rabbi asked.

"What I'm saying is that if I can't judge her—and I have the advantage over the three of you in that I'm a woman—then you certainly aren't in a position to do so. What I'd suggest is that you create a mother-only, or better yet, a mother's only jury to decide this case and cases of its kind going forward. If they convict her and sentence her to death, I'll carry out the sentence myself."

The one inviolable rule had to do with children. Specifically, children caught in the act of smuggling. In the earliest ghetto days, when the Nazis were trying to starve the community to death with diets of eight hundred calories a day or less, the only way to survive was by smuggling food in from the outside. There were professional smugglers on both sides of the wall, but only the most well-off ghetto residents could afford their services. So after the wall went up in late 1940, a large number of families relied on their children to go through, under, or over the ten-foot wall, scrounge and barter with their Polish sources, and return to the ghetto that night with the day's yield hidden in their coats.

The Nazis took delight in catching the children, usually at day's end, and administering justice the next morning. The penalty for smuggling was hanging, and the hanging of a child was a particularly gruesome sight since most children didn't have the weight to snap their neck when the gallows floor disappeared. Instead, they danced in the air, their feet seeking a purchase that wasn't there, slowly strangling while the ghetto residents were forced to watch. Parents were forced to watch the hanging along with the residents of the apartment that would have benefited from the goods the child in question was smuggling. If they looked away or cried out, they were the next to ascend the gallows' steps.

The sentence for informing on child smugglers was death. And with members of the jury expected to carry out their share of the death sentences, Shimon had executed five collaborators. Perla three.

———〜〜〜———

"I know what this looks like, Perla. But it isn't collaboration. Not even close."

"Then tell me what it is."

"I can't, not in five minutes. Which is all we have to decide if we live or die. Today." He held Perla's gaze, trying to penetrate and assuage her doubt, but her eyes were stiff, withholding judgment. "The only thing you need to know is that I told them to go to hell—that I'd die before I helped the Reich. They've tried everything to get me to change my mind. You're their last card."

She nodded at the door. "Well, it's an easy call then. We open that door and tell them to go to hell. We walk into the gas chamber holding hands." She tried a smile. "What could be more romantic than that?"

"If you're sure that's what we want to do."

"Why wouldn't we? We're not collaborators."

He put his hands along her jawline, his thumbs tight on her cheeks, forcing her to hold his eyes. "'Whatever it takes to survive.' Do you remember extracting that promise from me on the platform? Do you?"

"That was the romantic in me—the part that disappeared at the first Selektion. Look, Shimon, I want to survive this place, but I won't help these bastards. And to find you in the company of that murderer . . ." She motioned toward the closed door.

He kept his hands tight on her face. She didn't resist. In fact, she seemed to lean in to them. "Listen to me. Yesterday I told the Kommandant I'd die before I'd help him. They spent all last night beating the hell out of me and burning me, trying to get me to change my mind. Five minutes ago, I told them for the final time to fuck off. And then I saw you."

Before she could object, he continued. "Perla, listen to me. I'm not speaking as your husband right now. This is not me gushing romantically. I'm speaking as a cop. We're witnesses to murder on a scale history has never seen and the world seems to know nothing about. So right now, in less than two minutes, we've got a decision to make. We can stick to our principles and go to the gas chamber together—if we're lucky enough to be given that option. Or we can stay alive and find a way to fight these bastards and bring these events to life."

"What are you proposing?"

"I honestly don't know. As I said, five minutes ago, I was ready to die. Then I saw you and something shifted in me." He looked at her almost fiercely. "Because not only was I looking at the love of my life—someone I never thought I'd see again—I was also looking at the best journalist and the best investigative partner I've ever known. And in that moment, I wondered what impact the two us could have if we applied our skills together."

—◊◊◊—

They had met in Warsaw in 1938. Divko was still the rising young detective with the impressive track record. Perla was an independent investigative journalist selling her pieces to the Polish, Jewish, and Socialist newspapers that competed for her services and gave her investigative and literary leeway. Her work alternated between crime and social justice.

For the social justice investigations, she was an avid and proud advocate for the common citizenry, gaining a reputation as "the voice of the people." She published her address and investigated every complaint brought to her, whether it was about government policies, usurers who were preying on the poor, or landlords who demanded exorbitant rents while keeping their tenants in deplorable conditions.

As a crime reporter, she had a unique standing, both within the press community and with the police. She was often on the scene of major crimes within minutes of the police and sometimes even before the police arrived. And while the police had resented her initially, eventually, they came to see her as an extension of their investigations rather than as a journalistic foe. Because she had a deserved reputation for protecting her sources, and because she sometimes held back information that would enhance her reputation but hinder the investigation, the police often shared information with her that other reporters would have killed for. They knew she would use that information judiciously with her own sources, most of whom viewed the police with distrust, and report back anything new that might move the investigation forward and bring the perpetrators to justice.

She'd met Shimon Divko when he was investigating the death of a young union leader. The man had been clubbed to death outside the factory he was trying to organize, but the circumstances felt staged to Divko. The factory owners were bothered by the threat of unionization, but they seemed to view the organizer more as a pest than as a significant threat. Unless they were better actors than Divko had encountered in the past, they weren't murderers or parties to murder.

Broadening his search, Divko went to the victim's apartment and began to go through his notes and records. As he started to pack up after a fruitless hour, there was a firm knock at the door. Before he could answer it, a woman in her late twenties opened it, strode into the room, and introduced herself with a firm handshake. "Perla Litvak."

Divko knew of her, as did every policeman, but he was not going to allow a civilian to sully his scene, whether or not anything there proved to be related to the crime. But as he started to escort her off the premises, she asked him a series of questions he didn't have answers for. That suggested she might know things about the case that he didn't. The two sparred for ten minutes. When it was clear that each was not going to reveal anything to the other without a quid pro quo, Perla suggested they retire to a nearby café and compare notes.

The difference in how each had become involved with the case increased the range of information that could be shared.

Divko had come to the case by a single event: the murder. Perla, on the other hand, had been in the neighborhood for the past week, working on a story about the building in which the victim lived. Residents had called her attention to this specific building, but there were many more like it, all owned and operated by the same man. She had reviewed the conditions, investigated the unanswered complaints, and researched the threats issued against those who withheld payment of rent until conditions improved. Then she went to the owner, who dismissed both her story and the complaints out of hand while at the same time suggesting what bad luck it might be to take the story any further.

It was in interviewing the residents that she chanced upon the young man who became Divko's murder victim. She learned that in addition to his labor activities, he was a resident of the building and was organizing the residents to conduct a rent strike until the living conditions were brought up to a habitable level. And that residents of the other buildings owned by the same landlord had asked him to help them organize.

Working both apart and separately, it took Shimon and Perla two months to tie the murder to the owner and his three rent collectors. Impressed with Perla's research skills and intuition, Divko brought her in on his next two thorny investigations. In both cases, her insights helped lead to a conviction. Perhaps he would have reached the same conclusions and gained the same convictions, he admitted when others asked him about the alliance, but not as quickly or cleanly.

Within the year, they were married.

---

"I like your idea of odds, Divko," she said. "The two of us against the Third Reich. You're the Jewish Don Quixote."

"That door is going to open any minute, taking the decision away from us. All I'm saying is that for now, we buy some time to see if there's anything we can do. Not to stop this thing. I'm not that naïve. But maybe expose it." He smiled. "How about it? We can always die tomorrow. Together, hopefully."

"Always the sweet talker." They both turned as they heard the doorknob turn. "Okay," she said. "I'll be your Sancho Panza. For now." She kissed his cheek and whispered in his ear, "Don't make me regret this, my love."

# Seventeen

DIVKO STOOD IN FRONT of the Kommandant and Fritzsch at
loose attention. Perla had departed with Gisela, who had been
standing guard just outside the study, and the two men were
awaiting his answer.

"Yesterday, on our tour," Divko began, "you talked of facts.
Here are mine: You sanitized a murder scene, you have no witnesses, and virtually everyone in Kanada is a suspect. Am I
missing anything?"

"Only that you have six days to solve this murder and recover my ledger. On the seventh day, you can either rest, as your
God did, or you will die."

Divko looked down at the floor, as if considering his decision. Höss and Fritzsch traded looks of surprise. Fritzsch started
to move forward but Höss raised a restraining hand.

Finally, Divko looked up. "I'll do it. But with conditions."

"You're trying my patience, detective."

"I must be able to move freely through the camp."

"An investigator must investigate. Done."

"I must object, sir," Fritzsch said, taking a step forward.
"Some sectors must remain off-limits due to their sensitivity."

"Very well, Fritzsch. You select the sectors where you're certain the killer will definitely not be found and I'll put them on the list."

Höss looked back at Divko. "You have total access to the camp. What else?"

"I must be able to question anyone in the camp." He gave a pointed look at Höss. "Anyone."

Fritzsch moved toward Divko. "You Jewish piece of shit! You dare to—"

Höss waved him back. "You've got balls, Jew. I'll give you that. But you raise a problem. The questioning. You have the mistaken impression that you are a person. But here at Auschwitz, you are vermin. Lice. Nazis don't answer questions asked by lice. I'll see about getting you some help in this matter. But yes, you can interview everyone in the camp. Myself included. Any more requests while you're at it?"

"One more. That my wife be transferred here to help with the investigation."

Höss smiled condescendingly. "If you haven't noticed, detective, this isn't a honeymoon lodge."

"You've given me a week and hundreds of suspects, sir. Without help, I've got no chance." His eyes tightened on Höss. The Kommandant returned the gaze, his eyes flat, snake-like, and apprising. "I'm good at what I do, Kommandant," Divko continued, "but a major part of my success has been due to Perla. We're a team. This is not false humility at work here. I'm the best bulldog you'll ever meet. I get my teeth into a case and shake it until it gives up its secrets. But in certain areas of an investigation, Perla is simply better than me. She sees things and connects them in a way no one else can."

"Give me an example. And make it convincing. I want to know that you're not just saying this to get one last whiff of your wife before you both go up the chimney."

"I could give you any number of examples, but I'll give you a recent one, since it involves the ghetto that your Reich created."

"Save the political statements, Jew. Just give me your report."

"Fine. There was a rash of infant deaths at the main hospital, all from different causes. They went unrecognized for a few months, given the impact of the ghetto on staffing and reporting. But finally, the numbers caught the attention of a night nurse who went back into the files, noticed the pattern, and called us in."

Divko shifted. The pain in his groin was causing him to adjust his posture, which made Fritzsch grin. "The numbers and schedules directed our attention to two doctors. But the evidence was minimal, to the point that I wasn't certain if I had the right suspects."

"I'm tiring of this story already, Jew. War is hell. Ghettos are tough. I get it. Get to the part about your wife."

"It was Perla who cracked the case. She volunteered at the hospital, stripping beds and emptying bedpans, which enabled her to observe without drawing attention to herself. And she saw how minimal the post-ghetto record-keeping was. So she started keeping her own records for the infant ward. Things like doctors, type of procedure, and attending staff. And after two weeks, she had her suspect: a volunteer nurse whose two children had died of starvation three months earlier."

He paused and looked squarely at the Kommandant. "Maybe I would have found the woman on my own once I eliminated the doctors as suspects. But she was the one who broke the case."

Höss waved his hand. "Fine. You can have her on your team. But don't disappoint me, my detective. You've seen the fate of those who have disappointed me. And for far less."

As Divko moved to leave, Höss leaned forward. "And what happened to the nurse? Did you execute her?"

"Perla and I confronted her and she confessed immediately. She said that she was saving them from the drawn-out pain and helplessness of starvation. We listened and let her go. She had suffered enough." Divko gestured out the window. "Given what I saw in the ghetto and what I've seen here, she probably had the right idea."

# Eighteen

PERLA STOOD IN FRONT of Gisela Brandt, who was at her desk attending to the day's list of assignments. It was an hour after the meeting in the Kommandant's study, and Perla was now clad in a red headscarf and a fresh prison uniform with leather shoes instead of clogs.

Finally, Gisela looked up. As if noticing Perla for the first time, she motioned for her to sit. "You're leading a charmed life, Divko, Perla. From prisoner to chief typist to—a first for Auschwitz—a prisoner detective. And a woman at that. At this rate, you'll be running the camp by week's end."

"I'm indebted to you for the promotion, Fraülein Oberaufseherin. As for the rest, I can only—"

"Please. Lose the humble act. I didn't ask you in here for thanks. I did it to remind you that you're still a prisoner. *My* prisoner. And that this is not *your* investigation. It's *our* investigation. Starting this moment."

"Again, Fraülein Oberaufseherin, I'm aware of both my status and my debt to you. And I'm grateful for the opportunities you've—"

"Gratitude means nothing here, my dear. It goes up in smoke with every transport. What I want, what I *expect* from you, are results. And loyalty. Am I clear?"

"Very. I will be sure to copy you on anything we provide the—"

"Stop." The word wasn't said loudly or with any malice, but it cut the air. Perla stopped and tilted her head slightly, waiting for Brandt to continue. "Anything you and your husband learn, anything you even suspect, I hear about before anyone else. And that includes the Kommandant."

Gisela rose and moved behind Perla. She placed her hands gently on Perla's shoulders and began a slow massage that was almost sexual in nature. Perla flinched slightly under the working hands. "Life at Auschwitz exists on so many planes," Gisela said softly in her ear as she increased the massage's soothing touch. "You can go from this . . ." She quit the massage and placed her forearms on either side of Perla's neck. Then she locked her elbows, trapping the neck in a vise. Leaning forward, she used her shoulder to twist Perla's neck to the point of peril. "To this . . . in an instant. The choice is yours. And, as you can see," she said, squeezing slightly, "Mine. Again, do I make myself clear?"

Perla nodded with difficulty, a small choking sound escaping her tightly shut mouth.

Gisela released her grip and moved back to her chair. "Then let's get started," she said in a cheery voice.

Perla took out the pad of paper and pencil that Brandt had given her earlier and began to speak, but her overseer held up her hand.

"Before we go any further, let's get a few things straight. First, our working relationship. We're enemies, and I'm sure you've got strong opinions about the war and our program here at Auschwitz. But we don't have time for that crap right now, either of us. For the next week, we're allies. Get used to it." When Perla didn't respond, Gisela continued. "Second, as your ally, my job is to get you whatever you need to further this investigation. As absurd as it sounds, I work for you. If you encounter any obstacles or resistance in the coming week, you come to me, not to Fritzsch, and I'll take care of it if it's within my power. Are we clear?"

"We are. And thank you, Fraülein," Perla said, taking advantage of this change in dynamics to drop the formal "Oberaufseherin" from Brandt's title.

Gisela looked up at the familiarity and started to respond but closed her mouth into a small smile. "Third, let's clear something up right now. I'm a Nazi, not an idiot. I don't believe this Untermensch crap that Goebbels has been spouting for the past decade. I don't believe you're a large cockroach trying to take over the world." She raised both hands from the table slightly. "I hope I didn't need to state that, but there we are." She motioned to Perla's notebook. "Now that we've got all that out of the way, what do you need to know?"

"Every investigation begins with the scene of the crime," Perla began. "I need to get as big and accurate a picture of Auschwitz as possible. Even with my position in Records, I have only the vaguest feel for this place. I need to know its history, its current size, who the soldiers are, and how the soldiers wind up here—things like that. Is Auschwitz unique, or are there other camps as large and with the same purpose. Whatever you can tell me." She motioned with her pen for Gisela to pick up the narrative.

Gisela nodded and placed both hands, palms-down, on her desktop. "Let's start by being clear about one fact. Auschwitz is a Vernichtungslager." She looked up to see Perla frowning as she wrote. "An extermination camp," she clarified. "It started out as something completely different, but for the past two years, its primary purpose has been the elimination of as many people as quickly and efficiently as possible. The soldiers who have been here the longest did not start their duty at a death camp. And when our charter changed, many of them transferred out. Those of the old guard who stayed, such as myself, were promoted. We made sure that the new soldiers had the stomach for what was ahead before we transferred them here. So depending on how you look at it, the new guard is either the best of the best or the worst of the worst."

"I appreciate your honesty, Fraülein. What do I need to know about Auschwitz's history to start this investigation?"

Gisela lit a cigarette and then pushed the pack and matches over to Perla, who nodded her gratitude and lit up. "Auschwitz was a small camp at first, one of hundreds just like it, constructed only to house those Poles who had resisted the invasion or those who struck us as strong laborers for the camp's ultimate purpose."

"Which was?"

"Believe it or not, the opposite of our current function. Auschwitz was to serve as a model and recruiting tool for our Lebensraum program. You're familiar with term?"

"Room to live. Your justification for invading your neighbors. Acquiring the land Germany needs to reach its full potential."

Brandt nodded. "As the invasion progressed quickly and it looked like it would be a quick war, the question was how best to settle this newly conquered area. The idea was to establish a town—a rather substantial town at that—in the center of the land. It would be significant and cosmopolitan enough to attract German city dwellers, but its primary purpose was to be as a resource center for those farmers who came to settle around it and develop the countryside.

"And Auschwitz was to be that center?"

Brandt leaned back and blew her smoke toward the ceiling. "Rudolf, the Kommandant, showed me a model of the main town. It was to be an Aryan showcase, a jewel of a town showcasing the might and glory of the Reich. Proof to the Poles and Germans we wanted to settle here that we Germans were clearly the superior race. The camps surrounding Auschwitz would be filled with Untermensch whose main role in life was to support the Reich with their labor."

"What changed?"

"Rudolf gave me a brief history lesson, but—and this is my interpretation of events, not his—I believe Auschwitz's evolution was due more to chance than design. First off, the Blitzkrieg and subsequent invasion happened faster than anyone had predicted. Which left us with more prisoners—or potential laborers—than we needed. Or could feed. Or shoot, even."

She stubbed out the cigarette and picked up her pack, checking to see if Perla was finished with hers. Then she lit two cigarettes and passed one over. "The second thing that happened came in the summer of forty-one when the Russian invasion stalled. Forget any talk of a model city. Every resource was directed to achieving our war objectives. Finally, both Himmler and Hitler woke up to the knowledge that the world didn't give a damn about the Jews. They could do whatever he liked to you people and the world would just shrug. Which, by the way, has turned out to be the case. And so Auschwitz became a Vernichtungslager."

"And what of Kanada, since it's our crime scene?"

"You won't find Kanada on any early camp blueprints. It evolved out of necessity. Initially, we just gathered and burned the possessions that came our way."

"A nice euphemism, 'came our way.'"

"Don't try to anger me, Frau Divko. I may have to be your ally, but I can still make your life difficult beyond words." She wrapped the tabletop with her knuckles to make her point. "Anyway, burning was both time-consuming and wasteful. And at some point, some genius either supposed or realized that your people were hiding valuables in the linings of your clothing and your suitcases. At that point, we started gathering everything. Which led to Kanada. And as you've witnessed for yourself, while we've gotten better at harvesting the valuables, we have no idea what to do with the rest."

"And the gold operation? Was that there from the start?"

"Hardly. Someone—I can't remember who—noticed that some of the prisoners were extracting their gold teeth and using them as barter, either among themselves or with the guards. It was only then that we realized how stupid we had been not to check the mouths of the dead. Or the incoming, for that matter. After that, it was an easy and logical step to realize that these bodies might hold more than gold. New prisoners, looking to curry favor with their SS overseers, informed them that, as news of the camps reached the ghettoes, the inhabitants who had diamonds put them in the one place they wouldn't be found—their colons."

Without looking up, Perla said, "And so now we have both a 'public Kanada,' with its vast warehouses of clothes, glasses, and hair, and a 'private Kanada,' which traffics only in gold and diamonds. Correct?"

"Correct. The Kommandant may have been late in his recognition of this hidden source of riches, but once he did, he developed an efficient and secret operation in record time. And he brought the Reichsführer into the picture from the beginning." As Perla raised her eyebrows, Brandt nodded. "Genius, no? The only problem was that Himmler, being the efficient bureaucrat he is, didn't just receive these new riches, he set up an audit to ensure he was getting his fair share. So here we are."

"What is the relationship between the Kommandant and the Reichsführer?"

"They are cautious allies. Himmler admires Rudolf's initiative, but I don't think he trusts him. Rudolf, for his part, knows that shit rolls downhill and if the war goes bad, he'll be on his own. The gold is how he hopes to leave this war, regardless of its outcome: a wealthy man with a new identity."

"Forgive this next question, Fraülein, but are you part of that post-war future?" She held up a hand. "This is not a matter of gossip but of knowing who is who in this equation."

Brandt's patient smile disappeared. "You're overstepping, Jew. The answer to that question has nothing to do with this investigation" She calmed herself. "Any more questions before we both get to work?"

"Just one. I work in Incoming, where we have thick ledgers of clean numbers tracking all types of items. And yet I'm told we're looking for a child's notebook with hand-drawn figures. Is that the norm for all of Kanada or just the gold operation?"

Gisela almost laughed. "Hardly. For what you call the 'public Kanada,' we use a machine. It's the only way we can keep up."

"What kind of machine?"

"A numbers machine. I can never remember the name." She looked through the papers on her desk and then walked over to a file cabinet. "Here it is. A Hollerith. From an American company." She looked at the bottom of the page. "International Business Machines or whatever that translates to in German. It uses cards with holes in them. We couldn't run the camp without it. Same with the trains. The machine runs both the train schedule and a listing of every traveler. The company has its office in Krakow, but it also maintains an operations center here in the Farben complex."

"We heard some allusion to a machine like that in the ghetto. I remember a few times when I went to the offices of the occupiers…" She saw Brandt look up sharply. "Sorry, but that's what we called them. At any rate, I went there with questions about how resources were being allocated and how the thousands of new residents were being housed and there was always some vague mention of 'the machine.'"

"That was the Hollerith. We couldn't have done the census—in particular, the determination of what percent Jewish a certain person was—without it. A man I was dating at the time—and remember, this was in the early days of the Nazi regime—was in charge of finding and registering all the Jews in Heidelberg and its environs. He told me about the research his office needed to undertake to track an individual's heritage, from birth records to synagogue registries to marriage records and burials. And I know I'm forgetting some things here. If that was for one individual, you can appreciate the volume of work his office was tasked with. And that was just for Heidelberg. Then along came the Hollerith."

"But how would the machine deal with someone like me?" Perla asked. "I have no religious affiliation and was never bat mitzvahed. The only time I've been in a synagogue was to attend weddings."

"The Hollerith didn't care. According to Herr Goebbels and Nazi law, you were still a Jew. And if you'd married a Christian rather than your Shimon, you were still a Jew. As my boyfriend explained one night, after one too many beers, Doctor Goebbels had distilled anti-Semitism down to its essence. Anti-Semitism used to be religious, and the message to the Jews was convert or die. Then it became cultural and economic, and we put them in ghettos. But now, we define Jews biologically, which means that the moment a Jew is born, he has broken the law by being a threat to our society. Genius, no?"

Perla started to respond, then checked herself. "But this machine was never used for the gold operation? Because perhaps we can go back and rebuild—"

"No. It would have involved too many people knowing about it. And it would have been difficult to manipulate. Unlike Elster and his notebooks."

"Based on what you just told me, a thought occurs. We know that the Kommandant has placed his life at risk because he has not sent all the gold yield to Herr Himmler. Correct?" Gisela nodded. "Then who's to say that Herr Himmler isn't doing the same?"

"I'm not sure where you are going with this."

"If the Kommandant can't produce an accounting and explanation of his own—for sake of a better term, 'larceny'— that will satisfy Herr Himmler, perhaps he should just threaten to send his totals directly to Berlin before he and Herr Himmler remove their take."

"A scorched-earth threat? A scenario where someone draws Hitler's attention to the discrepancy?" She thought for a long moment. "Considering how calculated Himmler is, I have to believe he has anticipated such a move and put his own numbers in place. But to be honest, I'm not at all sure, and I doubt that the Kommandant has considered it." She looked at Perla, her admiration showing. "I like the way you think, Frau Divko."

# Nineteen

THREE HOURS LATER, Divko and Perla stood before Höss, with Fritzsch at the Kommandant's side. A third uniformed Nazi stood along the back wall, just behind Divko and Perla.

"Okay, let's start with the victim." Divko looked at Fritzsch. "May we have something with which to take notes?"

Fritzsch glared at Divko and refused to move. It was only after Höss looked at him with some annoyance that he left to get pen and paper.

"Obersturmführer Georg Elster," Höss said. "Chief Accountant. A numbers man whose only focus was Kanada. He knew little of the rest of the camp's business and cared even less."

"And his role in your operation?"

"Six days a week, he recorded what was reported from the standard operation."

"And I'm assuming that on the seventh day he didn't rest?"

"On the seventh day, he and I would meet and . . . make adjustments."

Perla spoke up. "Which were recorded in the second ledger, the one we seek?"

"German as good as your husband's, I see." Höss raised his hand as she started to reply. "That was an observation, not a question. But yes. You are correct."

The door opened and Fritzsch appeared, pens and notebooks in hand. Grudgingly, he handed them to Perla, who kept a set and handed the other to her husband. "Danke, Herr Hauptsturmführer," she said.

Höss opened his desk drawer, extracted a ledger, and handed it to Divko. "Your job is complete when I have both the killer and this book's twin in hand."

"These are hardly standard ledgers," Perla observed. "These are more like children's school notebooks. Was the choice deliberate?"

"Yes. We didn't want to use standard ledgers in case they wound up in the normal bureaucratic shuffle. No one would mistake this for an official document."

Divko opened his notebook. "What is the population of Kanada? Put another way, what is our starting suspect pool?"

Höss looked to Fritzsch, who said, "Almost three thousand. Prisoners and staff combined."

"Ruling out the prisoners for now—a question of access—how many staff?"

"Including SS, Gestapo, and Wehrmacht, two hundred fifty."

"Those with legitimate access to this area?"

"Thirty by day, twenty by night. Though that number is fluid, depending on the transport schedule."

"We'll need to begin by speaking with—"

"You're forgetting our earlier conversation. This is Auschwitz. When was the last time you heard a Jew ask a question here?"

"But if they know I'm acting on your behalf—"

"Which is exactly what they are *not* to know. The Kommandant looking into his own malfeasance? And a Jew leading an investigation? You might as well be a talking dog.

Which is why you'll be teamed with Unterscharführer Graf here. As far as the camp is concerned, it is his investigation. Not mine, and certainly not yours. You are his translator and Frau Divko your recorder."

The man who had been standing behind the Divkos stepped around them and stood to the side of the Kommandant's desk. Earnest and fresh-faced, his hair parted sharply and close-cut, he brought his heels together softly, as if unsure of the protocol. His Adam's apple protruded and bobbed once as he gathered himself. "It is an honor, Kommandant."

Höss waved an acknowledging hand and turned back to Divko. "This, as far as Auschwitz is concerned, is our lead investigator."

"We don't work like this."

This time it was Fritzsch who spoke up. "Then change how you work. No one in Auschwitz will submit to questions from an Untermensch."

Divko faced Graf. "What is your prior experience in law enforcement?"

"I was a postal inspector, investigating thefts in our—"

"*This* is your lead investigator?" Divko interrupted, turning to Höss. "It will never work."

Perla stepped forward slightly, and everyone turned to her. "We'll make it work." Then she turned to Divko. "We will."

"You'll discuss strategy with Unterscharführer Graf before each interview. Provide him with a list of questions in advance."

"And should something come up during your questioning that needs follow-up?"

"The prisoner may suggest additional questions on a notepad," Graf said.

Before Divko could say anything, Perla spoke up again. "Not ideal, but workable." She turned to Graf. "We look forward to working with you, sir."

When Graf refused to acknowledge her, she turned back to Höss. "How many people had the combination to the safe, sir?"

"The answer, Frau Divko, is discouraging." He held up two fingers. "One of them sits before you. The other lies on a morgue slab."

Divko nodded. "So we're assuming that the thief got the combination."

"Look at the man's guts, idiot," said Fritzsch. "He was sliced to ribbons. Tortured."

"Perhaps. But we'll wait to see the body before making a final determination. Torture is not as persuasive as the torturer would like, as I'm sure your Gestapo has found out over the years. The tortured person will sing, to be sure, but what song?" He shrugged. "Some things are more compelling. Such as fear."

He turned to Höss. "The Kommandant recently gave me a persuasive tour of the tools of intimidation at his disposal. I'm assuming you gave the same tour to Herr Elster?"

"I did. And I explained what would happen to his family as well should the operation be compromised. As a newlywed, he was doubly incented."

"Then if our victim went to his death silently, let's go see what he has to tell us now." He gestured at Graf. "After you, Detective."

As they started to leave, Höss coughed once, harshly, stopping the three in their tracks. "One last thing. I expect nightly updates." His eyes fixed on Divko. "From you, my Jew." His gaze broadened to take in the entire group. "To be clear. I expect daily progress. And success. Don't disappoint me. Herr Divko can tell you what happens to those who disappoint me."

Divko, Perla, and Graf left the Kommandant's office and immediately made their way to the morgue. But when they arrived, they found an SS doctor with a clipboard blocking the morgue door. Refusing to acknowledge Perla and Divko, he focused his glare on Graf. "I won't have my work questioned by anyone. Especially the likes of these."

"I appreciate your principled stance, Doctor. And I'm sure the Kommandant will as well when I inform him."

The morgue doctor paused dramatically before stepping aside.

"If you please," Divko said, motioning at the clipboard. The doctor hesitated for a moment, then looked at Graf, who nodded. Clearly annoyed, he sailed the clipboard at Divko, hitting him in the chest. It dropped to the floor with a loud clatter. Divko picked it up and smiled slightly at Perla as he straightened. She rolled her eyes but grinned back at him.

Once inside, Divko circled the bright bluish-silver table, making observations about the corpse that Perla, sitting on a stool, noted in her book. Graf stood against a wall, observing. Perla glanced over at him to check his pallor and see if he looked away from the body, but he was stoically focused on the task at hand.

Divko stopped and focused his attention on the stomach. "Two centimeters, give or take. None of them immediately fatal, but certainly attention-getting if torture is your goal."

Perla stood up and joined him. She leaned forward and nodded up at Divko. "Shallow. There seems to be no desire to make any of them fatal." She motioned to Graf with her head, asking if he wanted to come closer. But he remained where he was.

"No defensive wounds or signs of a struggle," Divko added. "Four long significant stab wounds to the gut. And yet no scratches or signs of restraint."

Perla started to sit back down but stopped midway and looked around the room. She walked over to a pile of bloody clothing, picked up Elster's shirt, and held it up.

"He was found in his office that morning," Graf said, consulting his notes. "Whether he had come in early or never made it home—"

"Excuse me, Herr Unterscharführer," Perla said, holding up the shirt. "Look at this shirt, gentlemen. Four long wounds to the abdomen and this is all he bled?"

"Meaning what?" Graf asked.

"Remember the Perlman case?" she said to Divko, who nodded.

She turned to Graf. "Help me turn him over, if you would, Herr Graf." He did so, and when Elster was face down, Perla asked Graf to hold up Elster's hair at the bottom. When Graf followed the instructions, a small red hole appeared at the base of the neck.

"There it is," Divko said. "Good work, Perla."

"The wounds to the abdomen are postmortem," Perla explained to Graf. "They were administered after he died to make us think he was tortured. The actual cause of death was an ice pick or similar medical implement to the base of the brain. Death was instantaneous."

"Which tells us what?"

"That we're dealing with a smarter murderer than we thought. Or hoped, at any rate."

Divko lifted Elster's left arm. On the underside, up near the armpit, was the tattoo "AB." He looked inquiringly at Graf.

"All SS are blood typed," Graf said. He tapped his arm. "Type O."

"As am I," Divko replied. Graf's frown to that went unnoticed by Divko, who was focused on the corpse. Fingers moving like a pianist's over Elster's body, he stopped at the elbow, peered more closely, and pointed at three small pricks at the crease of the elbow. "And these marks? Are they also something that every SS man shares with the deceased?"

Graf frowned again and leaned in for a closer look. "Clinic records will show if he was recently seen by a doctor. And recently received any injections."

"But since we are here, and in the interest of time, we speculate. These marks look sloppy, as if they were self-administered. Which suggests . . ." He nodded at Graf to continue.

"Drug addict?"

"Or user, at least. It's hard to believe an addict would have been capable of documenting two major operations. But a user? Definitely."

Perla moved to the base of the table and lifted his foot by the ankle. She spread his toes and leaned forward. Then she motioned to the two men to join her.

"We can check the clinic to be sure, but I believe we'll come up empty. Doctors don't seek to hide their work." She nodded to Graf to peer closer. "Between the toes is how serious drug users inject themselves to hide their habit."

"Then why the injections on his arm?"

"It's a good question, Herr Graf," she replied. "Perhaps— and I'm only speculating here—the ones on his arm were administered in the comfort and safety of his room while the one between the toes might have happened in the workplace, in a quick run to the restroom. Or the ones on the arms are recent vaccinations and the toes are self-administered. As you said, we'll see what the clinic records have to say."

Divko took a seat and glanced up at Graf. "Herr Graf, we do not have the knowledge of the soldier population at Auschwitz that you do. Or a sense of it. To the best of your knowledge, is drug use a problem among the ranks?"

Graf took a step forward and grasped the side of the morgue table, leaning across it to confront Divko. His knuckles tightened to the point of white, as did his voice. "You do not question the integrity or behavior of your superiors, Jew. These are soldiers of the Third Reich you're talking about. They—"

"Are human beings," Perla gently interrupted, "a long way from home and in an environment unlike anything they've ever experienced. Drug use in these circumstances would be more than understandable. For some individuals, it might be necessary."

Graf's face softened slightly as he turned to Perla. "I've heard nothing about drugs, but in the postal exchange, I have little interaction with the SS guards, especially those working the chambers. Those men face different challenges and stresses than the rest of us, so you might be right." He paused. "What kind of drugs are we talking about?"

"It could be anything from morphine to amphetamines, depending on whether he was looking to deaden or heighten the experience." She looked back at the corpse. "What was it, Herr Elster?"

⸺⁕⸺

As they drove away from the morgue, a figure stepped out from behind a neighboring building. He followed the departing vehicle until it was out of sight, then looked at his watch. After making a series of notations in a small book, he closed it and stepped back into the shadows. A moment later, there was the sound of an engine starting up and slipping into gear.

# Twenty

"YOU TWO FINISH UP HERE," Perla said. "I'm going to check the intake book." She returned a moment later. "I'm forgetting my place here. The nurses looked at me like I was from another planet, requesting their records." She smiled, though with little warmth. "Herr Graf, if you would be so kind as to request the intake books for the past two weeks."

Graf frowned and left the room. Perla turned to Divko. "Honey, I know Graf was thrust upon us, but we need him. You've got to bury your animosity. Or at least hide it better than you've done so far."

He nodded. "You're right. It's just that I've never worked with a Nazi before. Certainly not like this. In the ghetto, at least we had the Judenrat to shield us from direct contact with the Germans." He looked toward the door through which Graf had exited. "I know I was the one who advocated doing this investigation, but the more we help these bastards, the sleazier I feel."

Perla nodded. "But I also see the wisdom behind our decision. And it's *our* decision, honey. I could have said no. Look at how much we've been able to gather about the killing operation already. And I can get my hands on a lot more in the next few days. And whether we do an Oneg Shabbat and have to bury the evidence for others to find or we find a way to smuggle it out . . ." She tried a small smile. "Or even—and I know the odds are incredibly long—we're the ones who smuggle it out, I'm glad we're doing this. It's the first time since we've been here that I've felt useful."

The door opened and Graf walked in with two binders. Perla took one and handed the other to Divko, and the two sat down and started scanning the pages.

Graf looked over Perla's shoulder. "What are we looking for?"

Perla looked at Divko. "Honey, why don't you explain to Herr Graf the romance of detective life—especially the elimination process."

Divko motioned Graf over with a nod of his head. When Graf joined him, he pointed at the page. "The true answer about what we're looking for is this: We don't know. And I mean it. We're looking everywhere right now, hoping that something pops up and slaps us in the face. But getting to that point is a lot of drudgery and false starts. Take the morgue for example. We're looking for anything out of the ordinary."

"But how are we to know what is ordinary?"

"Congratulations, Herr Graf. That's the first question a detective has to ask. And quite often we forget to do it as we get caught up in the chase."

"Shimon uses the term 'ordinary,' Perla said. "I like 'normal.' And the only way to determine what is abnormal and suspicious is to establish what the norm is. Which means a lot of observation and research, neither of which we have much time for in this case. But we call the process of establishing the norm 'baselining.'"

"Here," Divko said, pointing to the page he was on, which drew Graf's eyes back to it. "Here's an aberration. It might be something. Probably nothing. But since we're grasping at straws, we will follow up on it." He tapped his pencil on an entry. "The process here seems to be to incinerate the corpse three days after the time of death. I'm assuming that's to give Dr. Mengele and his team the option of autopsying the body, should it be of interest."

Graf leaned in to look at where Divko was pointing. "Okay, I can see the dates. But what are they telling us?" He leaned in closer, as if that would help reveal the answer.

"So the night Elster died, there were two other SS deaths: one from a heart attack and the other from typhus. Both went to the ovens the same day, not three days later. Normally we wouldn't even see that fact, much less think anything of it. But since it involves our friend Herr Elster, we need to follow up." He stopped and smiled at Graf. "Correction. That's what *you* need to find out."

Graf didn't return the smile, but he straightened up with an enthusiasm and resolve that had been previously absent. "I'll be right back," he said, and he headed down the hall. He was back within five minutes. "You're right. Same-day cremation is not standard practice. Except in the case of typhus, which has everyone here in a panic, including the medical personnel. So anyone dying of typhus is immediately cremated. And as long as they were incinerating the first corpse, they included the heart attack as well."

"So a dead end," Perla said. "Welcome to the glamorous world of detecting, Herr Graf." This time, Graf smiled back.

"If we had the time," Divko added, "we'd spend some time here looking for drug-related deaths and see if we found any patterns or behaviors that traced back to Kanada. But we don't have time for anything that isn't directly related to the murder and theft."

"Besides," Perla added, "even if there were a spate of drug-related deaths, no one here would want his name associated with that kind of activity. Which means that those deaths would be recorded with some other cause of death. So back to work."

Graf shared his pack of cigarettes with the couple, and they took a cigarette break before heading back to Kanada. Sheltered in the doorway of the morgue, they stared out at the camp as they smoked.

"This baselining," Graf said. "Can you give me a real-world example of how it works and how you two used it in your work? As you can see, I've got a bit to learn and not much time."

Perla looked over at Divko. "What would be a good example of baselining?"

He thought for a moment. "Probably the Landsmen."

"Landsmen?" Graf asked.

"Erecting the ghetto walls was just the start of the Nazi plan for Poland," Perla replied. "That just locked us city dwellers in place. But the ultimate goal was Lebensraum, which meant taking ownership of whatever land they seized and bringing Germans there to farm the land once the war was over. For the normal Polish peasant, that just meant eviction from their land. But the Jewish peasants not only lost their land, they were immediately transported to one of the major ghettoes: Warsaw, Lodz, Bialystok. That was phase two." She stopped to see if any of this was news to her listener.

He motioned for her to continue. "I'm aware of what you're talking about. So your baselining was comparing phase one to phase two."

"Not really, though you're on the right track. Think of what phase two meant to the phase one residents of the ghetto. As bad as things had been, they were suddenly much worse. It wasn't just the yellow star and the meager diet. Now they were told that they had to make room in their two-bedroom apartment for ten refugees. Strangers. Peasants. And they may have already taken in family members who had lived outside the walls."

"Perla doesn't use the term 'peasants' as an insult," Divko clarified. "But these people were not as knowledgeable in the ways of the ghetto as their Warsaw hosts. And actually, the term that everyone used for them wasn't 'peasant.' It was 'landsman.'"

"Someone from your hometown or country," Graf said.

"The Nazis were using it sarcastically, telling us to take care of our landsmen, as if we were related just because we were all Jews," Divko replied.

"So how did baselining come into play?"

Divko picked up the story. "We all knew that people were taking advantage of the landsmen. We just didn't know how bad it was. What we did know was that the new arrivals, the landsmen, were dying at a much greater rate than the city dwellers. How much greater and why, we didn't know, because our record-keeping was so spotty. Was it due to something criminal or just bad luck? Perla investigated it first, so it's better if she continues the story."

Perla accepted a second cigarette from Graf, nodding her thanks. "When the landsmen were jammed into the ghetto, it was part of the initial Nazi plan for Warsaw, what they called 'attrition.'" She looked up at Graf as he was lighting his own cigarette. "You know the term?"

"Not in this context."

"Systematic starvation," Perla said in a steely voice. "So the first baseline was to work with the death centers before disease could take hold and decimate the ghetto. The death centers weren't morgues, really. They were just places that collected and disposed of corpses as quickly as they could. But I got them to at least track whether the corpse was a recent arrival to Warsaw or an established resident."

"Which was what you needed to build your baseline," Graf said.

She nodded. "My initial baseline. The second came after I invited Shimon in. We looked at any number of contributing factors: living conditions; what jobs they'd been assigned to; separation from family. But we came up with nothing. And the number of deaths kept mounting."

Divko continued the story. "So as you often have to do when an investigation is stalled, we went back to square one. And the answer was so obvious that we'd missed it the first time around. Not to offend you, Herr Graf, but I'll pose the same question to you that we asked ourselves. When someone dies of starvation, what's the actual cause of death?"

Graf cocked his head, looking to see if he was being mocked. But the question and the curiosity behind it seemed real. "Not getting enough food."

"Correct. But here's the key: We were focusing on the wrong part of your answer. We were focused on the word 'food' when we should have focused on the word 'getting.'"

"It all came down to ration cards," Perla said. "Every resident of the ghetto was issued a ration card by the Nazis. Any Warsaw Jew worth his salt knew that you kept your own ration card and trusted no one with it. But many of the building administrators who had been assigned by the Judenrat to each building convinced the landmen that they were to entrust their ration cards to the administrators, who could use the power of bulk buying to get everyone a little extra."

"And the landsmen wound up receiving even less than the normal resident."

"Exactly. And the building administrators got fat and wealthy, by ghetto standards at least."

"What wound up happening?"

"Shimon arrested and charged the administrators with theft and extortion. The Jewish Council tried them, and when they found them guilty, they stripped them of their jobs and replaced them—informally, of course—with honest brokers."

"And why didn't the administrators just go to the army and report this?"

"Because we took a page out of the Nazi handbook and told them what would happen to their families should they do so. It wasn't a major victory. It just made the starvation more democratic." She paused. "But sometimes little victories are all you get."

They got in the car and headed back toward Kanada. "So where are you from originally?" Divko asked Graf.

"Kelsterbach," Graf replied. "A village near Frankfurt."

"Were you with the postal service before the war?"

"Two years."

"Have you family?" Perla asked. "A wife? Children?"

After a few minutes of silence, Graf pulled over and cut off the engine. "Let's get one thing straight. We're not friends. Remember that." He gestured at the crematorium smokestack up ahead. "The only thing keeping you from being ash is this investigation. Keep that in mind." Then he started up the Kübelwagen and drove on.

# Twenty-one

"HIS HEAD WAS SLUMPED a bit more to the side, like he was sleeping," Sturmmann Feurer said.

Divko, playing the role of the deceased Elster, shifted his head to the side and adjusted his neck slightly to be more a curve than a straight line. Feuer nodded to Graf. "Like that."

Perla, who was standing against the wall, made a note in her book.

"Which is what you thought he was doing," Graf said, motioning for Feuer to take up the story. "Sleeping?"

"Until I saw the blood."

"The blood," Divko said, raising his head. "Liquid or tacky?"

Graf and Feuer both stared at Divko. Feuer looked at Graf, who nodded. "Liquid, I suppose."

"The safe," Graf said. "Open or closed?"

"Open, but only slightly so. To be honest, I didn't even notice it until later, when he—the Kommandant—drew my attention to it."

Perla handed her notebook to Graf, who read it and then turned to Feuer. "Was Elster close to anyone here? Anyone close enough to share the safe combination with?"

Instead of answering, Feuer stared pointedly at Divko. "What is he doing here?"

Graf refused to follow Feuer's eyes. He kept his gaze firmly fixed on the Sturmmann, who seemed to feel the eyes and shift his gaze back to Graf. "Elster and Frankel were partners," Feuer replied. "Frankel sold typhus medicine to the prisoners and guards. It's an epidemic here. Frankel ran the operation, and in return for a cut, Elster didn't record the theft."

"The Kommandant is under the belief that Elster was a timid numbers man with no initiative of his own. You're painting a different picture," Graf said.

"The Kommandant's assessment was accurate, at the start. But after two years of watching Frankel get rich and the Kommandant caring only about his own operation, Elster grew some balls and branched out."

Divko pushed a piece of paper across the desk to Graf, who read it before resuming his questioning. "You saw no one else in the building that morning?"

"This is Kanada. There's always someone in the building. But it was early morning, so the traffic was lighter."

This time Perla spoke up. "After you sounded the alert, Sturmbannführer Frankel was the first to arrive?"

He looked at her for a moment, then back at Graf. "Correct."

"How quickly?" Graf asked.

"Within a minute, now that you mention it."

Divko joined in. His tone now had the backbone of authority to it. "There's something you're not telling us about the relationship between Frankel and Elster. It would be better if you volunteered it now, rather than—"

Graf started to speak, but Perla motioned for him to hang back. The three of them waited Feuer out.

"Recently they started trafficking in a new medicine. I heard them arguing about who was taking the risks and who was entitled to what size cut."

"This other medicine," Graf said. "Did it have a name?"

"I never heard them mention it by name. All I heard was Frankel telling Elster to shut up, that they were both going to exit the war rich men."

As they left the barracks, walking down the gravel path outside Feuer's barracks, Divko spoke up. "You've got a lot to learn about being a detective."

"And you've got a lot to learn about knowing your place. You speak up like you did in there with a senior officer and you'll be shot for insubordination. On the spot. No questions and no recriminations. So where to, 'Detective'?"

"Kanada. Receiving. It's time to see Herr Frankel in his lair."

"You two take care of Frankel," Perla said, turning back to the barracks. "I've got to check in with Fraulein Brandt."

Ten minutes later, Graf and Divko strode into the major warehouse area at Kanada. Off to the side of the receiving area was a mid-size office, where they found Sturmbannführer Frankel sitting at a long table eating his lunch. He was peeling an apple with a dagger, spearing the pieces and delicately placing them on his tongue.

He looked up. "Ah, the detectives approach. Or should I say the detective and his mascot?"

The two men stopped in front of his desk. "What was your relationship with Obersturmführer Elster?" Graf asked.

"Getting right to the point, huh?" He looked at Divko. "You're training him well." He took a bite of his apple and chewed it slowly. For a moment it looked like he had no intention of answering them, but the investigators waited him out. Finally, he said, "Elster came here every morning, gathered our sheets, took a random audit at times, and then retreated to his cave. I wouldn't see him until the next morning."

"Where were you at the time of the murder?"

"I believe that is what Prisoner Divko here—excuse me, '*Inspector* Divko'—would call a 'trap question.'" He smiled condescendingly at Graf. "Since I don't know when the murder took place, I can't answer that. I can tell you where I was when the body was discovered."

"And that was . . .?"

"In the bathroom. Alone." He aimed another smile at Divko. "Let me correct myself. With a magazine." He raised his eyebrows, widening his smile at the same time.

"Did you notice anything unusual—"

"Prior to Feuer's girlish screams? Only his mincing footsteps in the hallway a few moments before." Again, he looked to Divko and smiled, but Divko maintained a blank expression and dead eyes.

"You say Herr Elster never showed any curiosity in your operation," Divko said finally. "Not even to certain . . . pharmaceuticals?"

"Don't speak in riddles, Jew. If you have something to say, say it."

"Herr Sturmbannführer, let me be clear. I care nothing about the workings, legal and otherwise, of this camp. Or who profits from them. I've seen enough of Kanada to know that you and a few select lieutenants—and I believe Elster was one of them—will exit this war rich men. That is your business, not mine. My only goal is to solve a crime. You can help us in this effort, for which we would be most grateful. Or you can resist and attract not only our interest, but the Kommandant's interest as well."

Frankel listened to Divko without interruption or change of expression. He idly picked up his dagger from the table, turning it into a position that transformed it from utensil into weapon. His eyes held Divko's and tightened into a twitching, menacing glare. Each man seemed comfortable in the moment, playing it out to see where it led. Frankel's fingers clenched the dagger's hilt so tightly that the vein in his wrist pulsed visibly. Then he barked a sound that was somewhere between a laugh and a snarl. "By God, Jew. Circumcised or not, you've got a set of balls on you. No one, German or Jew, talks to me like that."

"Well, as we both know, I've got very little to lose at this point."

"I don't want you tattling on me to the Kommandant," Frankel said gruffly. Then his voice took on a syrupy tone. "So how can I be of the greatest assistance to you and the investigation?"

Ignoring the mockery, Divko stepped back and deferred to Graf, who stepped in. "To start, you can give us a tour of your section of Kanada, starting with Incoming and Processing."

For the next hour, Frankel escorted Divko and Graf through the various parts of Kanada, starting with the offices where they processed the lists of each transport, then to the mountain of confiscated baggage, and finally to the warehouses devoted to specific items. He swung back large doors and showed them, in sequence, warehouses filled with suitcases, clothing, eyeglasses, shoes, hair, and finally, a room stacked to the ceiling with bones.

He paused in front of a separate door with a complicated lock and a feel of strength to it that they hadn't encountered up to that point. "Beyond that door lies Hauptsturmführer Fritzsch's operation, which is another level up from mine in terms of complexity and finances. And beyond that is the Kommandant's operation, which is another level altogether. And before you ask me, no, I've not been behind either of those doors. I believe in self-preservation through ignorance."

They returned to Frankel's office, where he pointed them to chairs. He leaned back in his own chair, his hands behind his head in a gesture that felt less like arrogance than openness. "Yes, Elster was my partner. For the past two years we've sold typhus medication. To prisoners and guards alike. Typhus doesn't discriminate. It's in the blood."

"And we'll want to know more about this operation," Graf said. "But we're also hearing of another drug, one that——"

Divko suddenly stood up and put a hand on Graf's arm. "I think we have enough for now. Thank you for your cooperation, Sturmbannführer."

Frankel and Graf both looked at Divko, surprised at his abrupt change in tone and direction. Frankel recovered first, picking up his dagger and returning to his meal. Graf shook off Divko's hand and stared across the table at Frankel for a long moment while Frankel continued to eat his meal without taking notice. Divko returned his hand to Graf's arm and kept it there until he looked up, and without saying a word, simply raised his eyebrows and nodded toward the car.

Shaking off Divko's hand again, Graf stood up and strode quickly toward the waiting vehicle. It wasn't until he started the car that he realized Divko wasn't with him, and he finally spotted him at the single window in the receiving area. He waited for a moment, then he honked the horn. When there was still no response, he turned off the engine and walked angrily toward Divko, whose back was to him.

Graf halted next to Divko and made an impatient noise. When Divko gave no notice, Graf joined him at the window and followed his gaze to see a line of Jews shuffling toward the low-lying building. From their vantage point, Divko and Graf could see the vents in the ceilings and the men placing the canisters next to each vent. Graf put his hand on Divko's arm, but it was with a gentle touch that he turned him toward the car.

# Twenty-two

"YOU'RE GOING TO have to be more specific, Frau Divko," Brandt said. "Kanada is like one of those Russian nested dolls. I need to know which doll you're inquiring about."

"I know you hate flattery, Oberaufseherin, but you know Kanada better than anyone. So my question to you, before we go further in our investigation, is a political and pragmatic one, designed to save us time and frustration. Who, in your opinion, has the nerve to attempt something like this, much less pull it off."

Brandt smiled broadly. "Nerve? You mean balls, don't you? Come on, it's just us two women here." She mimicked Perla's neutral tone. "Well, I'm sure you considered Fritzsch and dismissed him as too obvious."

"And then put him back on the list in case he's counting on our dismissing him for just that reason."

Brandt nodded. "You're a clever woman, Frau Divko. I'm glad I didn't underestimate you, starting with that night in the latrine. In answer to your question, the nerve you're describing springs from one of two sources, great intelligence or great stupidity."

"You can take stupid off the table," Perla said. "The crime scene was staged to make us believe that Elster was tortured to extract the combination. But the wounds were inflicted post-mortem as a distraction."

"There!" Brandt said, the word erupting almost as an explosion. "That right there is the type of information I'm looking for. Anything that can help the Kommandant—and our cause." She reached into her desk drawer, extracted two cigarettes, and handed them to Perla. "One for you; one for your husband." She reached into the drawer again and pulled out two more cigarettes. She lit them both and handed one to Perla, who nodded her gratitude.

"What else?"

"It's early yet, but you told me to give you anything we're working on. It seems that Herr Elster had a drug problem. Whether that factored into his death, we don't know yet. But he and Frankel were involved in at least one drug ring, and possibly more than one. I'll know more tomorrow." She took a drag on the cigarette, exhaled, and watched the smoke drift up to the ceiling for a few seconds. "To that end, it would be extremely helpful if you could get me access to the clinic's records about disease outbreaks here. The sooner, the better. It may be nothing, but we're chasing all leads at this point."

Brandt stood up. "Consider it done. See my secretary Helena about accessing the clinic records." She reached over the desk and patted Perla's cheek. "You're off to an excellent start, Divko, Perla. But it's just a start. I'll see you tomorrow. Bring me more of the same."

—⁓—

That night the three investigators sat around a table in an upstairs room in one of the barracks. By order of the Kommandant, this was now Graf's quarters. The Divkos were allowed to be there at any time, though a guard was stationed outside the door and was tasked with escorting them back to their barracks when they left. And in an attempt to ensure alertness instead of the fatigue that usually accompanied the Auschwitz prisoner diet, the Divkos had been provided dinner from the SS evening menu. Dinner finished, the dishes were now stacked by the door.

Graf was sitting on his bed, reading through the day's notes, and the Divkos sat at one end of the rectangular table that served both for dinner and as the gathering place for the investigation.

"You had to see it," Divko said to Perla in Polish. "I thought the ghetto was as low as humans could go, but that operation today—"

"You know the rules," Graf interrupted. "German only in this room."

Divko switched back to German. "I was telling Perla about what we saw today. And I appreciate, Herr Graf, that you didn't try to defend it."

"That's because there is nothing to defend. This is war, and in war . . ." His voice hardened. "You know the term 'Organisierung'?"

"We don't have a term for it in Polish, but everyone here, regardless of their native language, knows the term," Perla answered. "It's how this camp runs. You turn what you've got into what you want to get. Or need. I give you two cigarettes for an extra piece of bread."

"Exactly. What we saw today is just another form of Organisierung. Another weapon in this war. We take from those who no longer need it and send it back to the homeland. Nothing more."

"Hardly," Divko said. "Hardly, Herr Graf. If it didn't register with you today, let me clarify. Every article we saw today belonged to a person. A person not that different from me . . . or you, sir, regardless of what your Herr Goebbels says about us and our vermin-like status." He stood up. "You've seen us at work, sir. You've learned from us. You've broken bread with us. Do we strike you as vermin?"

Graf stood up and started toward Divko, but Perla leapt to her feet and placed herself between the two men. "Gentlemen. We have an investigation to conduct. One that our lives depend on solving—Shimon's and mine, definitely, and perhaps yours to, Herr Graf." She looked from one man to the other. "So put your manhood back in your pants and let's get back to work."

Neither man quit staring at the other at first, but finally, they took their seats and directed their attention to her.

"First off, let me review what I discovered in the clinic. Typhus has been rampant in the camp since its founding. All the conditions are there for a major outbreak: no sanitation, overcrowding, lice in abundance, and no treatment for those afflicted. My understanding is that before the gassing operations were instituted, it was the number three source of death here, behind dysentery and starvation. But the Germans don't track those first two causes. They just categorize them as 'Durchfall,' their general medical phrase for diarrhea, intestinal disorder—all the medical conditions that this camp creates."

"So why do they track typhus separately?" Graf asked.

"Because according to one of the prisoners here, Mengele and his troops are investigating whether they can use it as a weapon in the war. They're looking for a strain they can duplicate and use to infect the enemy."

Divko glared over at Graf, who kept his head down, scratching something into his notebook. Perla broke the tension by moving to the blackboard and picking up a piece of chalk. "I'm sure you have your own style of investigating, Herr Graf, but may I show you ours?"

"Go on. As your husband likes to point out, my investigative background is no match for yours."

She wrote in a scratchy script, creating three columns: Opportunity; Means; Motive. Then she turned back to Graf. "Let's start with means. We know that two weapons were involved. The first, an icepick or its equivalent, was the murder weapon. But the postmortem wounds were inflicted by something very different."

Divko looked up from his notebook. "The depth and type of wounds from the post-mortem. That's it. When we were with Frankel today, something was itching my mind, but I couldn't quite scratch it. But I get it now."

Without thinking, he reached for Graf's dagger. The German reared back, his face showing his shock at Divko's brazen behavior. He stood up, dagger in hand, and glared at Divko, who only nodded absently. "My apologies. I should have asked." He held out his hand. "May I?"

Graf cocked his head and searched Divko's face with his eyes. When Divko's expression didn't change, Graf turned the dagger around and extended it, handle first.

Divko leaned forward and examined it without touching it, his face close to the blade, with Graf's fingers just beyond the handle. "Two centimeters, give or take. Am I correct that every SS officer here has a knife like this one?"

"That's correct."

Perla looked at the board. "Looks like means just got a bit more crowded. Which brings us to opportunity. Elster was killed from behind. Unless he was surprised—unlikely given the room's dimensions—his killer was someone he knew."

"And trusted," Divko continued. "Which both limits the field and brings us to motive. And what we saw today . . . well, let's just say that motive moved to the top of the list."

Graf straightened. "What are you implying, Jew?"

"I'm *implying* nothing, German. I'm *stating* that from what we saw today, all you need to emerge from Kanada a rich man is a uniform with pockets. That makes for a large suspect pool."

Perla slowly stepped forward so both men could see her. "I know we're just getting started, Herr Graf, but what was your initial take on Feuer and Frankel?"

Graf looked surprised by the question and was silent for a time. "Feuer, no. Too junior. He seemed genuine in his reactions and statements. Frankel, on the other hand . . ." He gestured at the board. "If he and Elster were partners and that partnership went sour, he could fit all three of your categories."

"But how did he get access to the ledger, and why would he take it?"

"Again, if he and Elster were partners, perhaps Elster was less conscientious about what he said around Frankel." Again he pointed at the board. "And that might have allowed Frankel to see an unexpected opportunity. Or perhaps he surprised Elster while the safe was open, saw the opportunity, and killed him, taking the contents of the safe to make it look like a robbery."

Divko nodded. "You're thinking like a detective now."

Graf almost smiled but caught himself and faced Divko. "Earlier today, with Frankel, I had more questions. Why did you cut the interview short?"

"Because when he mentioned typhus being in the blood, it reminded me that we were out of sequence with our investigation. There's a phrase we teach all our investigators: 'Follow the blood.' In this case, the murder scene was bloody enough that some of the victim's blood could have transferred to the murderer's clothing. Which means we have some closets to check tomorrow. Starting with Frankel and Feuer."

# Twenty-three

WITH GRAF'S SENTRY BEHIND HIM, Divko knocked on the Kommandant's door that evening and waited silently. When he heard Fritzsch's voice, he entered and took a passive stance of attention just inside the door. Both men ignored him for over two minutes, attending to paperwork on the Kommandant's desk, and looked up together once they had completed their task.

"Given your empty hands and expression, I'm assuming you're not here to present me with my murderer and ledger," Höss said.

"It's far too early for that. If this could have been solved in a day, you wouldn't have needed us. I'm here with an update, a question, and a request."

"We'll deal with the request last. Start with the update," Höss replied.

Divko looked at Fritzsch, and the silence in the room grew past the point of comfort. "This meeting might be more productive were it conducted in private," Divko said finally.

"You don't call the shots here, Jew," Fritzsch snarled.

"With all due respect, Hauptsturmführer, neither do you. Begging your pardon, my questions for the Kommandant are of a delicate nature."

Höss stared at Divko without animosity and cocked his head, his forehead creasing. Then he turned to his lieutenant. "Leave us, Fritzsch."

"Then I must insist on searching the prisoner before leaving."

"I would have it no other way."

Fritzsch started with Divko's upper body, then his ankles and knees. Finally, he brought his hands up hard into Divko's groin, eliciting a groan and a wince before ending his search and leaving the room.

"Your update," the Kommandant prompted, motioning for Divko to sit.

Divko eased himself into the chair, his face tightening for a moment. Then he was at ease. "First off, and this may not matter at all, Elster was not who you thought him to be. Loyal to you, or at least intimidated by you, yes. But he had enough spine and smarts to have his own operation in addition to yours. Which opens up a new set of suspects and the possibility that your ledger was stolen unintentionally rather than as the primary target. I would prefer that our investigation be shrinking in focus at this point, not expanding. But that's the reality we're dealing with."

Höss frowned. "That's unfortunate. If what you're saying is true, then I misjudged the man. Something I rarely do."

"I'm not trying to curry your favor here, Kommandant, but you've got an entire camp to run. Some things are, by necessity, going to escape your attention. That's just the way it is. Put yourself in Elster's place. He sees the scope of the camp activities and sees the limited time you can spend managing them all.

"If I were Elster, I would have bided my time, surveyed the entire operation, and found my niche. Remember, I'm the one keeping track of everything. I would have kept my take small but constant and enriched myself with virtually no chance of being discovered. And once I'd perfected my formula, I would have expanded it, seeking a partner such as Herr Frankel. I'd keep the same formula, just expand it to a larger and more lucrative operation. The yield would grow, but the risk, minimal as it was, would remain the same."

Höss, who had been listening stoically, finally spoke. "You put it that way and I have to respect the man, don't I?"

"Well, at least acknowledge his initiative."

When Höss simply stared back at him, Divko continued. "The Kanada operation I witnessed is impressive in its scope. It's also both the scene of the crime and the possible motive, which complicates the issue and requires us to look at it from all angles. Our initial observation is that Kanada has enough holes in it to make an army of industrious managers rich. It appears that Elster was one of them. My guess is that he kept your particular ledgers scrupulously honest, even to the point of pointing out the occasional irregularity or theft in another area to create an even greater trust between the two of you." He peered at Höss. "Does any of that scenario sound familiar?"

"Enough of it to make me feel like a fool. In retrospect, I could have been more aware of—and perhaps suspicious of—Elster. But you're right. He maintained the books immaculately and always projected a timid air when we were together. He never gave off even the slightest whiff of initiative or leadership."

Höss looked down at his desktop and straightened some papers that were already in place. "Perhaps I would have noticed something, but just when our operation hit its stride, along comes that damn Eichmann and his 'Final Solution.' And suddenly my job—and this entire camp—changed direction."

Divko let Höss stew for a few moments before coughing softly. "Let's turn our attention now to how Elster's activities impact our investigation." He waited until Höss looked up and focused on him. "He maintained your gold operation impeccably while seeking an unexploited niche that he could call his own. The answer was drugs. Specifically, typhus. But we're fairly sure that he had expanded into a new operation. And perhaps that, rather than his role in your gold operation, is what led to his murder." He raised his eyebrows at Höss. "This is where I need your insights."

Höss gave him a hint of a smile. "Do I look like a drug addict to you?"

"Not an addict, sir. An authority. Since I have no experience with today's Germany and today's Germans, I need your help in this area. We know that Elster selected drugs as his area and typhus as his initial focus. But the major target for any typhus operation is the prisoners, and that is a market that is both poor and . . . shall we say, 'transient.' If I'm Elster, now that I'm ready to expand my operation dramatically, I'm looking for a drug that is both popular and poorly supervised in the camp. And a market outside the prisoner base."

He stopped talking and let silence settle into the room. Neither man seemed willing to break it for a time, leading to a brittle atmosphere between them. Höss cracked first. "You're talking about my personnel. The SS and regular army that work the camp."

"Which I believe number more than five thousand."

"More like seven thousand, give or take." He looked out the window, his hands interlaced in front of his lips. Then he lowered them. "All right, you've got my interest. What do you need from me?"

"Your insight, to start. When it comes to identifying this new drug, I'm at a distinct disadvantage on two fronts. First, I'm a Pole, not a German. I haven't been in Germany since before

Herr Hitler assumed power. And I have to believe that the country and the people I knew don't exist today."

Höss nodded. "If your memories are from the Weimar days, we're not that people anymore. Not by a long shot."

"I believe you." The Germans I remember were . . ." He paused and shifted gears. "Back to the drug angle. Do you—"

"No, no," Höss interrupted. "Continue. We were what? Noble? Honorable?"

Divko eyed the Kommandant but didn't see any mockery in the face or question. "Yes to both."

"That may be true, but you forgot 'destitute' and 'betrayed.' What year were you last in Germany?"

"Nineteen twenty-eight."

"And did you see how many men were missing limbs? Proud men who were reduced to sitting on the street with a cup, relying on the kindness of people who needed every Pfennig?"

"I did."

"And the women with wheelbarrows full of marks heading to the store and coming back with only some eggs and bread?"

"I saw something like that, yes."

"Tell me, my Jew. Where is the honor and nobility in that?"

"I take your point, Kommandant. But where is the honor and nobility in murdering thousands—perhaps millions—of innocent people?"

"Point taken. But if you're trying to understand this New Germany, you need to go back a decade earlier than your last memory. Do you know how many enemy soldiers there were on German soil on November 11, 1918?"

"Very few, I believe."

"The answer is none. Up until the armistice, the normal German, myself included, believed we were actually winning the war. Which is where our sense of betrayal began." He paused for a moment before continuing. "We could have a long discussion about all this, my Jew. Perhaps over some excellent liquor. But I don't know how it will help your investigation."

"My experience with drugs is limited, Kommandant. It wasn't my area of criminal specialty. But what I know is that people take drugs for one of two reasons: to heighten an experience or to deaden one. And given the horrors of war, my money is on the second option. So I'm wondering, sir, is there a recent drug that I'm ignorant of, one that may have been popular in Germany before the war and has made its way into your camp? One that would make life here more tolerable?"

Höss cocked his head and surveyed Divko, a look of genuine puzzlement on his face. "You've never heard of Pervitin?" Divko stared back blankly. "The troops called it 'The Nazi Jolt.'" Again, the blank response. "It's a type of methamphetamine that became popular in the years leading up to the war, not just in the military but within the general population. And when the war began, our doctors took over its manufacturing and upped its power."

Höss motioned out the window. "Remember the Blitzkrieg?"

"How could I not? Warsaw was its initial target."

"That was Pervitin at work. Our soldiers went five days without sleep. Five days."

"Impressive. But the Blitzkrieg was a short-term mission. How does this Pervitin work in a sustained operation such as Auschwitz?"

Again, Höss took his time answering. "Killing is hard work, my Jew. You've heard of the Einsatzgruppen?"

"Your mobile killing squads. Instead of bringing the Jews to camps like this one, your soldiers seek them out and kill them where they live."

"Correct. It's a messy and very psychologically demanding job, much different from our operation here. It's one-to-one killing. Over and over. That kind of activity takes a toll, physically and otherwise. But they work only once or twice a week, so the officers in charge let them fortify themselves for the task ahead by drinking heavily the night before and the morning of the operation. You don't need to be sober, just upright, to shoot a passive figure in the neck. And afterwards, the men feel little remorse. They just sleep it off. So that's one way to motivate and support our executioners. But here at Auschwitz we can't use alcohol because we run a twenty-four-hour operation that requires efficiency and precision. We can't afford the drunkenness and sloppiness that the Einsatzgruppen allow."

"But, like the Einsatzgruppen commanders, you need something to both motivate and dull your executioners."

"Which is where Pervitin comes in." As he saw Divko reach for his notebook, Höss grabbed a pen and wrote out the word for him. "It lets them work harder and longer. And as important, it reduces any inhibition they have about their work."

Divko nodded as he wrote. "This is helpful, Kommandant." He paused for a moment before continuing. "But if you've been using this Pervitin since the start of the war, why are we only now seeing a black market? What changed in the last few months?"

Höss put his chin in his hand and closed his eyes. The skin around his eyes wrinkled as he concentrated. Then, suddenly, he pushed back his chair, stood up, and went to a bookcase on the far wall, where he took down a large ledger and brought it back to his desk. He thumbed through it for a few moments and then stopped. "There. We used to store and administer Pervitin at the clinic, but as all the gas chambers came online and increased their capacity, the demand exceeded our doctors' ability to perform their other duties. So we——"

"Moved it to Kanada."

"Yes. Looking at it through fresh eyes, Pervitin and Kanada are a volatile combination. I can see how what you're suggesting could happen." He looked across the desk. "I have to admit, my Jew, I'm impressed."

He took a pack of cigarettes from his desk drawer and pushed them across the desk. "Take these. They're Auschwitz's universal currency. Buy something for yourself. And your wife. You earned them."

# Twenty-four

THE KOMMANDANT lay back on the chaise, still panting slightly. His face was florid, the sweat still visible at his temples and forehead. His pants were next to the chaise, as was most of his uniform, save his shirt, which was damp with sweat and down to its last button. Beside him, half-sitting, half-lying down, was Gisela Brandt, completely naked, her face composed and looking at Höss as he gathered himself.

"I'm impressed with you Rudolf, I must say."

He grinned and straightened his spine. "Well, you bring out the best in me, my dear."

"Not many men would be able to get it up with the gallows—or worse—staring at them."

He flinched. "I told you. It's under control. You don't need to worry."

"Oh, but I do, darling. I'm a pragmatist. And this pragmatist has two large concerns."

"And they are?"

"The first, as you mentioned earlier in one of our less romantic moments, is that if you go down, I'm going with you."

"I wasn't trying to be callous, honey, but the reality is—"

"I *know* what the reality is, darling. Which is why I'm not offended by what you said. Just concerned. For myself and for us."

"So what can I do to allay that concern?"

She sat up. "You can take me into your confidence. Your full confidence. If I'm at risk, then I need to be a full partner in this investigation."

"Noted. And your second concern?"

"That I'm just a camp fling, as temporary as those Jews out there." She nodded toward the crematorium.

"How many times do I have to tell you? You're my future."

"And your wife and family?"

"My past. And Hedwig would concur. This war, and my role in it, has sapped whatever love we once had for each other. The only reason she is still here is that she and the children are safer here than in Berlin. We've agreed that once the war is over, I'll give her a share of the gold, enough to set her and the children up for life. And then it's just you and me." He reached over and held her chin in his palm. "Gisela. Believe me. You're my future."

Her eyes lost their hard edge, and she reached out and touched his cheek. "Then let me help you. With this investigation to start. And planning for whatever's beyond that." She brought her other hand up and cradled his face. "I'm serious, Rudi. You're wasting a valuable asset here. No one, not even Fritzsch, knows Kanada the way I do. So let me help."

He thought for a moment. "It looks like I don't know as much about Kanada as I thought I did. It turns out that Elster and his counterpart, Frankel, had a sideline business. Quite a lucrative one if my Jew detective is to be believed. And I don't see any reason not to believe him."

"A sideline doing what?"

"Selling Pervitin. Once we moved it from the clinic to Kanada, we lost oversight of it. And Elster and Frankel took advantage of it and turned it into a cottage industry."

"Even if that's true, how does it figure into the investigation?"

"It may be why Elster was killed and my ledger was taken—along with the Pervitin ledgers. If so, we've been looking at this completely wrong. It might prove to be nothing, but until we rule it out, we have to investigate it. Which takes up resources we don't have."

Gisela thought for a moment. "I've heard some loose talk about a drug operation, but I thought it was just some of the guards making some extra money with the typhus medicine. I'll look into this Pervitin angle." She stopped his objection before he could voice it. "Discreetly. It's easily enough done."

Höss walked over to the window and looked out into the yard. Without looking back at her he said, "If we're going to be full partners going forward, there's something else I need to share with you."

Gisela stared at his back and started to respond but kept her mouth closed. Höss kept his gaze locked on the yard. "As I'm sure you've gathered from the recent reports from Berlin—all the talk about new sacrifices—the war is not going well."

"I gathered as much. How bad is it?"

"One of the first things you learn in military training is that it's never a good idea to engage in a two-front war. It's an even worse idea to be losing on both fronts."

"Is it a temporary setback or a permanent one?"

"It's temporary. For now. Which I guess is the definition of 'temporary.' But if we keep fighting this war the way we govern, it will be permanent."

"You're speaking in riddles, Rudi."

He moved over to his desk and sat down. Reaching into his drawer, he pulled out a pack of cigarettes and lit one for himself, not offering her one. Gisela helped herself to a cigarette, lit it, and waited.

"I forget sometimes how young you are, Gisela." When she started to speak, he held up a hand. "I'm not objecting, darling. Far from it. It's just that I forget that the Nazi system is all you've known in your adult life."

"And what's wrong with that?"

"Nothing. It's just that the leaders you've known all your life who have brought us to such power may not be the right ones to fight this war. They're losing it, in fact."

He took up a pen and drew a hard line down the middle of the paper, his pen point digging into the paper. "When Hitler came to power, he knew that all the institutions in place—government, schools, media, you name it—saw us as just another government they would weather until a new form of democracy took root. He was smart enough to realize he couldn't fire all the administrators or make over each institution, at least not in the timeframe he envisioned. He also recognized that the Party had no experience in governing. So he came up with an ingenious solution. He kept the institutions in place and created a Nazi version of each one—a shadow government, so to speak. And he let them coexist. Side by side in most cases. Any government decision had to be approved by its Nazi counterpart. And any Nazi decision had to be instituted by the government."

"I remember how confusing it was at the start," said Gisela. "We were always unclear who we should see about what."

"It was only for the first five years or so. Eventually, the institutions all either came on board with the party or were replaced. And the parallel operations and redundancy ended."

"But waging a war is different than governing," Gisela said.

"Exactly. The military is the one institution that didn't give way to Nazification. When Hitler saw that, he just established shadow armies—"

"Such as the Gestapo and SS."

He nodded. "And there's the problem. Now Hitler has two sets of military advisors: the generals he doesn't trust but who are experts in war and the Nazis he trusts who know nothing of war." His face hardened. "He needs to choose one and eliminate the other, but he can't bring himself to do it. And the paralysis is killing us."

Gisela had sat, wide-eyed and open-faced, letting the Kommandant educate her. He was telling her nothing that she hadn't figured out already for herself, but it was important to let him play the teacher. As a woman guided more by pragmatism than idealism, she had watched the war carefully from its onset and had reached the same conclusions a year ago. She knew that Hitler, with Goebbels and Himmler whispering in his ear, saw himself as a twentieth century Alexander the Great. And down that road, she knew, lay disaster.

"I'd heard rumors, of course, but you're making me see it all in a new light," she said when Rudolph wrapped up his tutorial. "I'm hearing you, Rudi." She caught herself, as if afraid of his reaction for what she was about to say. He leaned forward, an encouraging look on his face. "I'm listening with both my brain and my heart, Rudi. My brain, the Nazi side of me, wants to hear more about the war. But my heart, the woman side of me, wonders what this all means for you. And for us."

Höss issued a harsh laugh. "For me? What it means for me?" He stood up, buttoned his shirt, and reached for his pants. "If Germany loses the war, Auschwitz will become a swear word and I'll be the poster child for mass murder."

Gisela walked over to him, locked her hands around the back of his neck, and looked into his eyes. "I know that wasn't easy to say, but it just makes me love you even more. You're a good man, Rudi, a decent man put in an awful situation." She straightened his tie, though it didn't need it. "So tell me. What can I do beyond acting as your Kanada eyes and ears?"

"If the war continues the way it's going, Auschwitz will fall within the year. To protect both the Reich and myself, I have no intention of giving the Russians or Americans—whoever gets here first—the evidence to convict me. To that end, I'm developing plans to destroy as many records and facilities as possible."

"While you're doing that, what can I do?"

Höss went back to the window and looked out. He was quiet for over three minutes, his eyes seemingly taking in the entire camp. Then he turned to face her, leaning back against the windowsill. "I was going to wait for the right moment to bring this up, but this seems to be that moment. When the camp is captured, I plan to disappear in the commotion." His eyes tightened on her. "Hopefully, with you."

She lowered her head and then looked up at him, her eyes glistening. "Rudi, we really *are* partners, aren't we?"

He nodded. "I was going to surprise you with all of this, including my plans for after the war. But now that you know, we can split up the duties. While I'm working on destroying the evidence, I need you to coordinate our escape."

"I can do that. How many people are we talking about?"

"Just the two of us. Plus our Jews."

"Why them? And why would they want to help us?"

"Because they speak the language and know the area. We don't. We'd be picked up and executed before we got a hundred kilometers from here. And they want to survive this war as much as you and I do. You can see it in their eyes. It's a devil's bargain. We use them and they use us."

"Understood, but can we trust them? They don't strike me as the type that can be bribed. And as you discovered with the husband, threats don't seem to work."

"All true. For the moment, though, let's see what they come up with. If we feel we can't trust them, we use their ideas but find more willing—or pliable—prisoners to help us pull it off."

She nodded. "I'll start cultivating the wife immediately. You do the same with the husband. But keep two things in mind, Rudolf. First, as you said, they're smart. And second, they hate our guts."

# Twenty-five



"AS I SAID, the laundry is on Friday, so . . ."

Frankel's prisoner houseboy stood by helplessly as Graf opened the closet door, widening it so the Divkos could see in as well. They were in Frankel's private quarters, a room built on to one of the main barracks but radically different from the building it was attached to. There was a double bed with a beautiful bedspread and satin throw pillows. A variety of oil paintings adorned the wall, complemented by a set of antique chairs and a delicate desk.

Divko looked at the houseboy and waved his arm to take in the room. "All this. Where from?"

"When they liquidated the Lodz ghetto, he had one of his lieutenants there with a truck."

Graf reached into the closet and pulled an overcoat off a hanger. He handed it to the houseboy and nodded to the bed. The houseboy smoothed the garment and laid it out, moving one of the pillows. The same procedure followed for two uniform jackets, trousers, and a velvet smoking jacket, the latter garment causing Shimon to look up at his wife with a slight smile.

Divko held up one of the uniform jackets. "Blood against Nazi black is hard to spot. But this looks clean." He checked the second jacket, also clean.

He looked at the houseboy. "Did Frankel ever do his own laundry? Especially recently."

The prisoner scoffed. "He wouldn't know soap from soup."

Divko held up each garment in turn, passing it to Perla, who in turn handed it back to the houseboy. Meanwhile, Graf stayed with the closet. As he turned the six pair of shoes over, looking at the soles for traces of blood, he noticed a loose board in the closet floor. He pried it with his free hand, and the board came up easily. The box he pulled out was filled with vials of medicine. He held one up for review. The label read "Pervitin."

The three of them went back to Graf's room to process the morning's activities. The idea of a valet in a concentration camp produced surprise coupled with mild amusement in Graf and Perla, while Divko remained silent. Perla was also impressed by the quality of the furniture and rugs in Frankel's quarters.

"There's definitely a black market for confiscated goods," Graf said. "If you're SS and friends in the military alert you to a campaign to take a key city or region, you simply place your order with your friends, and for a fee or percentage, they'll deliver whatever was on your list. And that's just the Polish cities. Think what it's going to be like if we take St. Petersburg or Moscow."

Divko started to respond, but Graf held up a hand. "I'm going to agree with your outrage before you even voice it. I understand that to the victor go the spoils. That's been a part of every war in history. But too much of that activity can create moral rot as well as morale problems. Regular troops will begin to wonder if certain actions were taken for their strategic value or because of the booty they would yield."

Perla nodded. "We mean no disrespect with this next question, Herr Graf, and we appreciate how loyal you are to your compatriots. But for the purpose of determining the size of our suspect pool, we need to ask if Sturmbannführer Frankel—with his valet and stolen goods—is the norm or the exception here."

Graf was silent for a few moments before answering. "I was stationed at two different camps before this one, and I can assure you that there were no Frankels there. But here . . . there are more Frankels than I'd like to admit."

"And why do you think that is?" Perla asked.

"As Auschwitz's charter has shifted toward death in volume, the type of soldier stationed here has changed as well."

"How so?" Perla asked.

"As the charter changed, the original soldiers who had problems with this new mission were allowed to transfer out without it reflecting poorly on them. And they were replaced with troops who were selected either for their anti-Semitism or a particularly violent nature."

"People like Frankel."

Graf nodded. "People like Frankel."

"Again, I ask this with all due respect," Perla said cautiously. "Why are you here? You don't appear to have either of those traits."

"I'm removed from the killing operation here. We don't function under the same rules as those brought in after the chambers and crematoria were put in place." His mouth took on a sour look. "But I will transfer out of here the first chance I get, even if it's to the Russian Front. I didn't bargain for this."

—⚜—

Their first stop that afternoon was Feuer's room. It was the opposite of Frankel's: sparsely furnished and spartan in feel. This time it was Divko who went to the closet and handed out the two remaining uniforms to Graf, who held them up for Perla to review.

"Herr Feuer doesn't have the luxury of a valet like our friend Frankel. He seems to be behind in his laundry."

Perla held up a uniform coat and motioned to the cuff. A ring of blood halfway encircled it. "Let's go visit Herr Feuer," she said.

Once Feuer was in front of them, they encountered the shifting stance that only a nervous man would adopt. In the space of two minutes, he went from innocent to puzzled and finally to adamant as they began their questioning.

When he insisted he'd already told them everything about the morning of the murder, Graf said, "We're more concerned about the evening before."

"There was no evening before, at least in my dealings with Herr Elster," Feur replied as he looked from Graf to the Divkos and back to Graf. "Other than being the one who found him, I've got nothing to do with your investigation. And before you ask, I didn't know the combination of the safe. Elster was the only one."

"And he didn't give up the combination, even at the point of your knife?" Graf gestured at Feuer's dagger and shifted to a lower voice. "Sturmmann Feuer, you've seen how the SS exacts revenge. Not just on the party involved but his entire family. We are not the standard SS. You have my word that, if you come clean, you will be the only one to suffer the consequences. So tell us, at what time did you kill Elster?"

"*Kill* him? I *found* him. Why would I choose to be the one to 'find' him if I killed him?"

"Because if you hadn't been in his office first thing in the morning, as is your habit, it would have drawn all our attention to you," Graf said. "You hoped that someone else would find him, but when no one did, it fell to you to make the discovery."

"You also swore you never touched him," Divko said in an aggressive voice.

Feuer's head swiveled to his new accuser. "Which is the truth."

"And yet your uniform cuff was literally drenched in his blood."

Feuer considered for a moment while his questioners waited patiently. Then he issued a small grunt and smiled. "That's what this is about? The blood? That was *my* blood." He pushed up his sleeve to expose a bandaged wrist. "Last week, that cold snap? Elster's office is next to the boiler. He complained about the noise and ordered me to fix it. The boiler door was partially open. When it wouldn't close properly, I tried to force it. My hand slipped and I cut my wrist on the corner."

He pushed his arm aggressively at Graf, who motioned Perla forward. Perla unwound the bandage, exposing a nasty and deep two-inch cut.

—⁓—

Perla and Graf watched as Divko ran his finger along the boiler's frame. "It's sharp. And there's dried blood." He looked at Graf. "I hate it when suspects are telling the truth."

"He could have inflicted the wound after the attack as a way to explain the blood."

"Possible but unlikely. But again, you're thinking like a detective now."

They were about to leave when Perla walked around to the back of the boiler and came upon a large, square metallic door. "And this is what?"

"A coal chute," Graf answered.

Perla looked up at the chute and then back to the two men. "Well, the opportunity column just got a lot larger."

Divko tried the handle, which turned easily. He swung the door open, showing the same kind of handle on the inside. He peered in and then looked back at Graf. "Do you have a torch?" Graf reached into his briefcase and produced a small flashlight. Divko turned it on and nodded at the strong beam. Then he hoisted himself up and crawled into the tunnel.

Graf and Perla were standing beneath a grate at shoulder-height on the outside wall when it opened noisily and Divko's head emerged. He extracted half his body before asking Graf for help. Graf stepped forward, grabbed Divko by the shoulders, and walked backwards until Divko's feet came out of the shoot and he dropped to the ground. He nodded his thanks and straightened up, dusting himself off.

Divko nodded up at the grate. "I'll come back tomorrow and see if I can get in and out of there on my own. If it's a two-person job, that changes things."

"And how do we know our killer employed that chute at all?" Graf asked.

"We don't," Perla replied. "It's just another loose string we have to pull."

As Perla talked to Graf, Divko surveyed the yard. His eyes came to rest on a prisoner he estimated to be in his sixties raking the yard in front of the adjacent building. At Divko's approach, the man looked up, squinting.

"You, Father," Divko said in Polish. "Is this your regular job?"

"Dawn to dusk, except Sundays."

"Do you remember where you were working five days ago?"

The man thought back, at one point counting backwards on his fingers, folding them down in sequence. Then he nodded and pointed to the administration building. "There. Building K."

"Was there any traffic near that building over there where my friends are standing?"

"There's always some form of traffic. It's a shortcut."

"Did you see anybody enter or leave the coal chute on that day? Take your time and think back."

"No need to take my time. It was the end of the day. The man stood by the side of the building for a while, then beneath the chute, as if expecting a delivery. Then he hoisted himself up and pulled himself into the chute. I remember thinking it was an odd time of day to be cleaning the chute. That's usually a first-thing-in-the-morning task, before the delivery. And besides, where were his cleaning tools?"

"Would you recognize this person if you saw him again?"

"I wouldn't recognize you, again, sir. Bastards took my glasses on day one. All I can tell you is that he was SS." As Divko started to respond, he said, "From the outline of his hat. That much I could see."

# Twenty-six

THAT EVENING, during the hour before dinner, Perla sat in Gisela Brandt's office, a cup of hot tea in front of each woman. Brandt pushed a cigarette across the desk to Perla, who put it in her pocket.

"So what have you found?"

"Found? Not much yet. Seen? Quite a bit."

Brandt looked up from her tea. "Mind your tone, Prisoner Divko. We're at war, if you haven't noticed."

"With all due respect, Fräulein Oberaufseherin, this is not war. This is murder. Organized, institutional murder. On a scale the world has never seen. And we both know it."

"Don't presume to tell me . . ." Brandt caught herself and turned her attention to her tea. She sipped at it, calming herself as she blew across the surface. "We'll leave this conversation for another time. Perhaps after the war. For now, your observations."

"The drug angle is showing promise. We discovered Pervitin in Frankel's quarters. His houseboy has been cautioned not to tell him about our discovery, so we'll see whether he's more afraid of Herr Frankel or the Kommandant. Either way, my husband is briefing the Kommandant later tonight, and we'll figure out at that time how and when to come at Frankel."

"Is he your prime suspect?"

"Suspect? Not at this point. Person of interest? Definitely. But there may be more persons of interest—private operators within Kanada—that we simply don't know about. We'll definitely pursue the Pervitin angle, but that's all we have time for, given our deadline."

They discussed the investigation for the next ten minutes as Perla walked through the day in detail. Finally, she closed her notebook and stood up. Brandt stayed where she was. As Perla reached the door, Brandt called to her back. "Actually, there is one more thing." She motioned for Perla to sit back down, and as Perla returned to her seat, Brandt opened her desk drawer and took out a map. She unfolded it and turned it around so Perla could read it.

"You know us Nazis and our thoroughness." She smiled disarmingly, but Perla stared at her with flat eyes. "The Kommandant has been instructed to prepare for all contingencies. My assignment? If we had to evacuate a small group of senior personnel with key records and personal effects, how could we best negotiate Poland to a safe destination?"

Perla didn't even glance at the map. "Fraülein Oberaufseherin, I'm a city girl. I'm not only ignorant about this subject, but as you just pointed out, the clock is ticking on our investigation." She motioned toward the map. "And this is simply not my job."

Brandt, who had been bent over the map in a spirit of complicity, jerked her head back, as if slapped. "Your *job*, Prisoner Divko, is whatever I say it is." Again, she seemed to catch herself. "But I take your point. So let's regard this as an additional task that may bring with it additional rewards." She folded the map carefully and handed it to Perla.

"Take this back and pose the challenge to your husband. I'll reward any idea with double rations. For the right plan, I'll bring a cot into your processing room and give the two of you one night of privacy—without any SS oversight."

—m—

The dinner dishes had been gathered and placed outside the door. Divko, Perla, and Graf were standing at the blackboard, chalked notes now covering more than half of it.

"How far back does the discovery of the coal chute set us?"

"The chute is a knife that cuts both ways," Divko said. "On the negative side, the suspect pool has expanded greatly. But in another way, it helps."

"Helps how?"

"Earlier we thought this was purely an inside job, which meant we were looking for a single suspect. And as we're finding out, a very smart suspect. That insider, who remains our primary suspect, realized he couldn't do the job on his own. He needed outside help."

"Help for what?" Graf asked. "A stranger would have alarmed Elster. He couldn't have gotten close enough to . . ." He looked back at the blackboard. "The safe. He was needed for the safe. Elster was already dead."

Both the Divkos looked at Graf with a new appreciation. His chin came up slightly in recognition and he looked at the blackboard anew. Divko joined him and drew two lines, connecting different parts of the board. "Tomorrow is going to be a long day. Let's get some sleep and come at it fresh tomorrow." He turned toward the door and the sentry behind it.

Perla stopped the men with a raised hand. "Before we do, there's something I have to tell you two about. It's a request from Fraülein Brandt, though it feels like it has the Kommandant's fingerprints on it." She looked at Graf. "I used the word 'request' just now, but it was more a command, an assignment with potential negative ramifications." She looked at Graf. "The assignment is only required of Shimon and myself. I would suggest that you stay away from this one, Herr Graf."

Graf appeared surprised by the consideration. "I appreciate that, Frau Divko, but you two are my charges. I can't leave you alone, by order of the Kommandant. So it looks like I'm part of the assignment, whether I want to be or not. So what's this assignment?"

The three of them sat down at the table. Perla reached behind her back and pulled the map from her underwear. As she opened and smoothed it, she looked up at Graf. "Before we begin, Herr Graf, may I ask what rumors you hear about how the war is going?"

Graf shifted uncomfortably. "Officially, we are winning on both fronts. Unofficially, there are questions. And rumors. Why?"

"I've been asked to develop an escape plan for the Kommandant and a select few, one of whom, I assume, would be Fraülein Brandt. The unofficial nature of the request makes me think the request is informal and perhaps illegal, originating not in Berlin but in the Kommandant's office. Which is why I'm again asking if you'd rather not be a part of this."

"I understand. But my responsibilities are to oversee and assist your activities, and this task falls within that charter."

Perla nodded in sympathy. "We recognize that we, and this investigation, were forced on you, sir. But you've treated us better than anyone else in this godforsaken place. If this request is of an informal nature, then what we're doing places us, and now you, in a bind. Should the Germans prevail, our actions would be regarded as treasonous. And should the Allies win, we're enabling a war criminal to go free." She knocked her knuckles lightly on the table. "We have no choice in the matter, but you do. So I'd think of myself and my family before I go any further down this road."

Graf smiled sadly. "Again, I appreciate your concern, but my wife was killed in an air raid. Along with our baby."

Helmut Graf was ten years old when World War I came to its sudden and unexpected end. His father, who had lost a leg at the Battle of Arras, was a vocal opponent of the surrender, as well as the subsequent attempts at German democracy, which he felt were jammed down Germany's throat by the conquerors. Germany was an international pariah: not invited into the new League of Nations, blamed for the millions of deaths and shattered cities, and saddled with onerous terms that placed a huge burden on the average German. Helmut remembered his mother leaving the house every morning with a satchel stuffed with Deutsche Marks, returning with only enough for that evening's meager supper.

In 1923, his father finally found a reason to leave the house. His frustration and unfocused hatred had found a voice in Adolf Hitler. He began attending Nazi meetings and bringing home the pamphlets. When Hitler was imprisoned for his failed putsch, it only inflamed his father's ardor.

As Hitler and the Nazis rose from street thugs to an organized political party, Helmut's father tried to interest his son in the cause. But Helmut had no interest in politics, only sports and his friends. And while his mother had joined his father in his Nazi activities, Helmut continued his politics-free lifestyle. Never a strong student, he secured a job at the post office after Gymnasium and married a postal clerk, Anna Berger. Four years later, Karl-Heinz was born.

When Hitler came to power in 1933, all government institutions were immediately Nazified, and the postal service was no exception. Helmut joined the party, as did all his compatriots, but his participation in Nazi events was limited to doing the minimum his bosses required. For the postal service, the change in regimes was initially reflected only in the photos on the walls of the buildings. The Nazis then turned their attention to the outside world, monitoring outgoing communications, noting anything that ran contrary to the Nazi goal of creating the concept of a "new Germany"—one that should be welcomed, not feared—a campaign that crested with the 1936 Olympics.

Once the Olympics were concluded, the façade of the humane Germany was abandoned. Germany ratcheted up its military might, along with its campaign against the Jews. The laws, the Brown Shirt activities in the street, the boycotts, and the culmination of those activities in Kristallnacht, the organized pogrom that left synagogues burned and Jews battered and imprisoned, finally alerted the world to the Nazi agenda. And the Nazis were unrepentant.

The ramifications for the postal service were dramatic and immediate. The initial focus on outgoing communications was expanded to include anything between or in support of Germany's Jews. Designated postal employees, Helmut among them, could open, reject, or censor any piece of mail, international or domestic. And if they found anything of interest or concern, they turned it over to the Gestapo official attached to each post office. Helmut wasn't excited about the new job, but it came with a 20 percent bump in salary. And as his supervisor pointed out, "no" was a dangerous word to utter in this new Reich.

Then came the war and the expanded concentration camp infrastructure. The outside world was bent on communicating with the prisoners, a delicate dance that the postal service was tasked with conducting, made harder by the fact that most of the recipients were no longer alive. And of course, there was the monitoring and censoring of the communications of the soldiers to their families back home. Not only were the postal monitors told to edit anything mentioning camp protocols or activities, especially those related to the Jews, they were also told to alert commanding officers if they read anything that indicated that a soldier was developing a queasy stomach or guilty conscience regarding this new campaign against the Jews.

All of which brought Helmut to Auschwitz, which was where he was stationed when he received the news about Anna and Karl-Heinz.

# Twenty-seven

PERLA'S FACE FELL at Graf's news of his family, and Divko looked down at the tabletop. "I'm very sorry to hear that, Herr Graf," Perla said after a long moment. "Very sorry."

Graf's eyes moistened. He swallowed hard. "And you two? Any children?"

"Maybe later," Perla said. "If there is a later. But for now, thank God, no." She motioned toward the map. "Okay, let me tell you about this new assignment."

She was interrupted by a knock on the door. Graf crossed the room and opened it, and the guard motioned him into the hall. A moment later, he returned, his face long and troubled.

"Our investigation just took another turn. Frankel is dead."

As Graf had ordered, the body had been left exactly as they found him. Frankel was on the floor, faceup. He was clad in his uniform blouse and trousers, shoes, and socks. His shirt showed the same blood pattern as Elster. There was the same puncture wound where his hair met his neck. With Graf looking on, the Divkos bent to their tasks. Shimon pried the mouth open, smelt the breath, and moved his finger around inside. Then he looked at Frankel's hands, focusing on the fingernails.

Meanwhile, Perla removed Frankel's shoes and socks and looked between the toes. "Fresh injections," she noted.

Divko cocked his head. He moved his gaze from Frankel's hand up to his elbow crook.

"No signs of injection here. How fresh?"

"Fresh. The blood is still smeared." She looked up at Graf. "Herr Graf, how often would you estimate that the guards here bathe?"

"There's a fear of lice and other diseases that can be picked up from the arrivals, so it's drummed into us to bathe regularly. Daily, ideally, every other day at the least."

"What are you thinking?" Perla asked Divko.

"That the stab wounds may not be the only things conducted postmortem."

"My thinking as well. I think we're being played."

"I'm sorry," Graf said. "I'm not following."

"We know we're up against a clever thief and killer," Divko explained. "That was clear from the initial stab wounds on the chest when the actual cause of death was on the other side of the body. In short, they were distractions meant to throw any investigator off the track. It's possible that these needle marks are the same thing. Something administered postmortem to send us in the wrong direction."

Graf looked at the feet and nodded. Then he went to the closet, pulled back the board, and looked up at Divko and Perla. "The drugs are gone."

"Okay," Perla said. "Let's take stock here. We know the torture was an attempt at misdirect. It's possible the drugs are too. But 'possible' means we still need to investigate."

Perla noticed Graf's confusion. "We're now looking at two possible paths to the murder and missing ledger. And unfortunately, we have to pursue them both." She held up an index finger. "The first path is the initial basis of this investigation, that the gold is the primary target and the drugs are a distraction. And if they *are* a distraction, is it intentional, meaning plotted and carried out by our murderer, or coincidental?"

She added a raised middle finger to the index finger. "The second path is that the drugs are the primary focus and the gold is a coincidental component."

Divko picked up the thread. "Under that logic, the gold may not be missing at all but simply misplaced." At Graf's frown, he continued. "It's possible that he had placed the Kommandant's gold in a safe location, one he would reveal to the Kommandant as they finalized the ledger in anticipation of Himmler's visit."

"But he never got the opportunity," Graf said.

Divko nodded. "Exactly." He looked around the room, his exasperation just below the surface. "These distractions, whether intentional or coincidental, are just what the murderer ordered. They're forcing us to divide our resources at a time when we need everything and everyone focused on a single line of inquiry."

Perla placed a calming hand on his arm. "It's not the first time we've had to divide and conquer, honey. Which one do you want?"

"I'll take the drug angle and see how much I can learn in one day, two tops. You two stay focused on the gold."

"Then we need to see the operation in action," Perla said, "not just hear about it second-hand."

Divko winced. "Which means having another conversation with the Kommandant that he doesn't want to have."

# Twenty-eight

"DETECTIVE DIVKO," the Kommandant said, the beginnings of a sardonic smile touching his lips. "Here for my nightly update. And empty-handed once again. This is becoming a dangerous habit of yours, my Jew."

"Trust me, Herr Kommandant, no one wishes more than Perla and me that we were coming to you with both the ledger and thief in hand." He paused, waiting to see if Höss wanted to express further disappointment. But the Kommandant just motioned for him to continue. "Sir, at the risk of antagonizing you, I'm going to articulate our situation just this once. No complaints, just facts." Again, Divko paused, but the Kommandant simply motioned for him to continue again. "Sir, even with my full detective corps back in Warsaw, this would be a difficult investigation in the time allotted. With the circumstances we are facing here, it's almost impossible. That's not a complaint, just a statement of fact."

"And in less than a week you and your bride are ash. That's not a threat, just a statement of fact." He regarded Divko with flat eyes. "Now, your update."

"We're pursuing dual fronts, sir. The second line of inquiry, in addition to your gold operation, is the Pervitin angle that you and I discussed yesterday. It took a turn—which direction I can't say yet—when the ringleader was found dead yesterday."

"Does the ringleader have a name?"

"Frankel." Divko kept his eyes tight on Hoss as he issued the name. He saw the corners of the Kommandant's eyes tighten. It was a slight movement, but telling. "Is the Kommandant acquainted with Sturmbannführer Frankel?"

"By reputation only."

Divko sat down, though the Kommandant hadn't given him leave to do so, and leaned forward. "Sir, you assigned me to this investigation because of my expertise. And that expertise is telling me that you have more to say about Sturmbannführer Frankel than the answer you just gave me."

Divko quit speaking and let the silence in the room grow. Höss tried to stare him down briefly, but Divko simply stared back with flat, nonjudgmental eyes. Höss then shifted his eyes to the office window and its dark contents. Finally, he sighed and returned his eyes to Divko. "This death may be my doing. I ordered Frankel to monitor your team's activities and report back to me if at any point you were going places you shouldn't go or asking questions you shouldn't be asking."

"And were you sharing with him any of our preliminary thoughts and suspicions? This is important, Kommandant."

"No. He was to be your shadow only, not a second investigator." He looked at Divko. "So what are your thoughts about his death? Are they related to your investigation?"

"We're acting on the suspicion that he was getting too close to the truth or was too much a threat. But whether that was because of his drug-dealing activities or his actions on your behalf, I can't say. But I'm hoping that the Kommandant can see the problems raised by this subterfuge."

Höss looked away. "You're doing something that no one in this camp has ever done, Detective. You're reprimanding the Kommandant of this camp. Which on any other day, for any other reason, would be a death sentence. But in this case, you are correct. I complicated your job by my actions. It won't happen again."

"I appreciate that, Kommandant. Is there anything else, any other activities that you are engaged in that I need to be aware of?" He held up a hand. "It's a question, not a second reprimand."

Höss gestured at the two ledgers on his desktop. "I have engaged an accountant—someone not related to Kanada or known to the personnel there—and am working with him to create the impression that together we are recreating the ledger."

"Thus rendering the one in our murderer's hands irrelevant." Divko nodded his appreciation. "It's a longshot but definitely worth a try. How visible are you with this charade?"

"I've dropped by a couple of times to check in with him, but we're just getting started."

"May I suggest that you set up shop with him tomorrow from two until four. That way both shifts will see your activities."

"Good idea, my Jew. Now back to your report. What further do you have to tell me?"

"As I mentioned, we have divided our efforts to reflect the two paths of this inquiry. You're now up to speed on the drug component. Now we need to turn our attention to your gold operation. And to properly understand it, we need a tour of Kanada. Not the public Kanada. We're familiar with that. We need to see *your* Kanada at work."

"I believe you received a thorough tour yesterday, including a glimpse of Fritzsch's operation. That's more than anyone else can claim. What more do you want?"

"The Kanada we saw yesterday was the public Kanada, Herr Kommandant. Impressive for both its scope and, as we discussed yesterday, for the number and size of holes in the operation. We will continue to investigate that Kanada, to be sure, because it is the site of the drug operation. But we also need to see your gold operation. In action."

Höss shook his head. "I can assure you that the killer didn't come from that operation. Fritzsch is the only person, other than the inmates and the unfortunate Elster, to see that operation in action."

"May I remind the Kommandant that you assured me that Elster was a frightened lamb of a man who would never do anything to cross you." As Höss started to rise, his face flushed with anger, Divko put both hands up, palms facing the Kommandant. "Sir, that is not a criticism but an observation. Please take it as such."

Höss settled back into his chair and forced calmness into his posture and voice. "Fine. I'll have Fritzsch give you a tour."

"Begging your pardon, sir, but this is not Fritzsch's operation. It's yours. We need to see it through your eyes, to get your perspective of what we're looking at and how it was developed, including any changes or improvements in the operation."

Höss was silent for over a minute. When he looked back at Divko, he said, "I try to have as little to do with the actual operation as possible. I find the whole operation distasteful." He noticed Divko's reaction and responded with a wry smile. "You find it hard to believe that I might be a bit . . . squeamish about our little operation?"

"Honestly, sir? Yes, I do."

"The irony is not lost on me, either, Prisoner Divko. But we all have our idiosyncrasies. For example, my children have an odd menagerie of pets. Come playtime, I can handle their frogs, their tortoises, and even their rats. But I would cut off a finger before I would handle their snake."

"And the gold operation is your snake?"

"Not something I want to admit, especially to a prisoner, but yes." He smiled at Divko's amazement. "I can watch our gas chambers in full operation without batting an eye or losing a wink of sleep. But there's something about the gold operation, the invasive nature of it, that makes those corpses more . . ."

"Human?"

"I wouldn't go that far, but more real, certainly. It's the individual nature of it that is bothersome." Höss stood up, walked over to the window, and stayed there long enough without saying a word that Divko thought he was being dismissed. But then Höss turned. "Tomorrow afternoon at two. We'll start in Elster's office."

—⁓—

Perla took her lunch that day in the barracks. Magda, her partner in her Oneg Shabbat campaign to preserve evidence of the camp and its gas chambers, had caught her eye earlier that morning as she and her group were heading out and indicated that they needed to talk. Mornings were too rushed for any conversation with Magda, who was taking care of herself as well as marshalling the construction group she headed up. And Perla spent most evenings in the warehouse investigation room. So she headed over to the gathering ground in front of the barracks and waited for Magda and her group to come trudging back.

"I got your signal," Perla said, joining Magda in line. "What are you doing back here in the middle of the day?"

"We start on a new foundation tomorrow, so we're spending the afternoon shift back here sharpening our shovels and picks. The winter ground has blunted most of them."

"Have you found a site yet?"

Magda reached the soup station. A new inmate was working it, her ladle moving quickly, slopping some of the thin, watery substance onto the table. As she started to deposit the contents of her large spoon onto Magda's plate, Magda grabbed her wrist and held it until the woman met her eyes. "Dig deeper," she said in a calm voice that had a harsh underbelly. "Twice," she said, nodding at Perla as well.

The server, alarm suddenly replacing the bored look on her face, looked to the Kapo, who nodded. She did as asked. The next station gave both women a larger slice of bread than normal. Perla nodded her thanks; Magda accepted it as her due.

"How are you doing with the evidence?" Magda asked as they sat down on the ground.

"I've got evidence of three complete transports as well as the output from Crematorium Zwei for an entire month."

"One of the Kapos told me that Zwei runs twenty-four hours a day now and is processing more than a thousand a day."

"More like fourteen hundred," Perla said. "And there are already two others like it, with a fourth one due to come into operation by end of summer. You do the math."

"I can't. I never got past second level. Had to go work the farm. You do it for me."

"Even allowing for downtime and other factors, if the trains, gas chambers, and ovens run like they're running now, you're talking a million and a half up the chimney."

"Fucking Nazis. I can't even get my head around that number." Magda looked around, her eyes hard. "Good work, Perla. Get me what you've got and I'll make sure it's safe and buried."

"What do you have in mind?"

"You said you used metal milk containers in the ghetto. I can't steal anything like that. It would be noticed. And also, where would I hide it? But this afternoon, when we're sharpening the tools, I'll make sure I keep one of the toolboxes empty. And tomorrow, if all goes right, I can stay behind and tell the Kapos that I want to check the group's work, that they're getting sloppy, that I'll catch the later transport back. And while the foundation cement is still settling, I'll bury the toolbox with whatever you can fill it with"

She stood up and walked over to the corner of the barracks, where she bent over, as if she were adjusting her wooden clogs and reached behind the steps and came out with a small woolen coat. When she returned to Perla, she put the coat down on the ground and sat on it. "The one from Vilna, she died last night. This is her coat. Wrap up whatever papers you've got in this and bring it to the morning meal. I'll get the papers into the toolbox."

⸻❦⸻

Perla sat in Gisela Brandt's office, staring at the wall festooned with postcards from around Germany and photos of the Nazi hierarchy: Hitler, Himmler, Goebbels, and Göring. Brandt leafed through a volume of reports, handing them to her lieutenant as she finished each. Finally, she handed over the last report, dismissed the orderly, and turned to Perla.

"I believe you have two reports for me. Let's start with the investigation."

"There's been limited progress. One of our key suspects, Frankel, is dead, which narrows our suspect pool while expanding the confusion. He died under the same circumstances as Elster: ice pick to the neck and an attempt to cover it up with slashes to the stomach. Which indicates that the killer isn't aware that his mode of execution has been discovered."

"And how is that relevant?"

"As we discussed yesterday, this is an inside-out job. Our insider had to employ the services of an outsider—a safecracker, to be precise. At this point, we're trying to assess how much of the operation our murderer would have to know to pull this off. The deeper the information needed, the narrower the pool."

"You're talking about Fritzsch, aren't you?"

"Among others, yes. Herr Fritzsch qualifies as an excellent candidate, as we've discussed. But if he is in fact the murderer, he's hiding his tracks well. And he's a convincing actor."

"If he is the murderer, how will you catch him?"

"My husband has a plan for that, one he is discussing with the Kommandant even as we speak."

Brandt nodded. "Not the progress I had hoped for, but I realize you're operating under difficult circumstances. Now what of your second assignment?"

Perla unrolled the map and secured its four corners with objects on the desk. She let Brandt look at it and waited for her to raise her eyes. "For this plan to have any chance of success, I need clarification on two points." She stared at Brandt, her face studiously neutral, the look of a peer.

"And those are?" Brandt finally asked.

"First off, I'm assuming this escape plan is not for a large group but only for yourself and the Kommandant."

Brandt returned the stare, neither woman blinking, letting the moment grow. Finally, her face relaxed into a smile. "Very good, Frau Divko. To be honest, it's good to be able to talk to someone about this. Especially another woman."

"My second assumption—and your look just now confirmed it—is that this is an unauthorized operation."

"Again, correct."

"I'd assumed as much, so I'm glad I didn't waste time on the wrong scenarios." She nodded at the map. "We're still working on the route, but when the critical moment arrives, either you or the Kommandant will need to put your hands on a small transport vehicle."

"That shouldn't be a problem. What else?"

"Clothing will be critical. Anyone wearing SS black, from the junior clerk to the Kommandant, will be shot on sight. And it won't work to try and pass yourself off as a prisoner. You don't speak the language and you're far too healthy. You need to secure the uniforms of some of the Latvian guards. And when the moment comes, you are heading to the north, to the mother country, to be tried for collaboration."

"And if we're stopped? We obviously don't speak Latvian."

"That's where Shimon and I come in. He is a detective escorting you to the Allies for trial. Since there's nothing to identify you as SS, they won't shoot you on the spot. And they'll respect him and his badge."

Brandt looked at her admiringly, an expression she had never worn in the presence of a Jew. "You are a brilliant woman, Perla. And I don't use that term lightly. Let me discuss this with Rud . . . with the Kommandant." She looked down at the map. "In the meantime, how did you come up with this? It's brilliant."

"The ghetto. You learned to innovate there or you died."

As the second year of the Nazi occupation began and the war continued to go Germany's way, the leaders of the Warsaw ghetto had realized they needed to shift their focus from simply enduring the Nazi campaign of attrition through starvation to one of resistance and survival. A small group, including both Divkos, was convened to determine the right strategy. After a week of constant discussion and consideration of different approaches, they determined that they should pursue two goals simultaneously: helping as many inhabitants escape as possible while infiltrating the Nazis to gain as much insight as possible into their plans for the ghetto.

Because of his facility in German and his military training, Shimon was put in charge of the infiltration program. The plan was simple in concept but complicated in execution: Find a certain number of ghetto inhabitants who were fluent, or at least capable, in German, extract them from the ghetto with the right Polish documents, and present them to the Germans as much-needed interpreters. These interpreters, some of whom were housed beyond the walls of the ghetto, were able to overhear or discern plans in their earliest stages and report back to Divko, who would in turn bring the news to the Jewish Council. Forewarned, the council could then move its most damning material—presses, libraries, documentation—in advance of any incursion.

While Shimon ran the infiltration operation, Perla took charge of the exfiltration program. Her job was to manage the departure of as many Warsaw residents as possible, not just getting them outside the wall but to a safe destination beyond the city.

Once she had mapped out and developed the escape routes, Perla shifted her focus to building a support network. Due to her ability to pass as a Polish Catholic, she spent more time outside the ghetto than any other resident. She worked from a list of "good Poles"—Polish nationals sympathetic to their plight—that new arrivals provided. But as she explained to Shimon, it was a small list to begin with, and there was a huge difference between sympathy and willingness to actively oppose a regime that delighted in retribution. She determined that only one in five was a candidate for the program.

Shimon was impressed that it was as high as one in five. As for his own program, it had started out strong, but a month into the program, two of his people were discovered and executed on the spot. Once word got out about those executions, another three of his people disappeared into the general population.

---

It was her network, Perla told Gisela, with resources ranging from food to transportation to news of possible roadblocks, that she would tap into if they made it out of Auschwitz and could stay ahead of the advancing troops, whether Russian or American. Though, she had to admit, she had serious doubts how much of her network was still intact. Which meant, she told Divko with a slight smile, that Gisela Brandt was now in the awkward position of rooting against the efforts of the SS troops tasked with rooting out the resistance.

# Twenty-nine

"BEFORE WE BEGIN THIS TOUR, let's get a few things straight," Höss said, his eyes settling on each of the investigators in turn. He sat at his desk, Fritzsch standing off to one side and slightly behind him. There was one empty chair, but none of the investigators made a move for it.

"First, this is a presentation, not a conversation." Höss pointed at Divko. "You. Spare me the outrage about what is happening to your people. 'People' isn't a word that applies to Jews at Auschwitz. Here you are vermin. What you're about to see is just an extension of the extermination process. Am I clear?"

As both Divkos nodded, he turned to Graf. "And you. Spare me your outrage that some of us are benefiting from our time at Auschwitz. If you'd ever had the opportunity to visit any of our superiors' offices or homes, especially those in Berlin, you'd find that not every piece of Jewish art or wealth is reaching the Reich's vaults. Am I clear?"

At Graf's nod, Höss wordlessly exited the office and moved down the hall. At the end of the hall, he stopped in front of the main warehouse door and turned to Perla. "Before we begin, why don't you explain to Herr Graf what happens when you're informed that you are being transported to one of our camps?"

Perla turned to Graf. "You're given twenty-four hours to report to the train station. You're told you're being resettled to a work camp and can bring only one piece of luggage. So you pack your most valuable possessions or hide them somewhere on your person and bring them to the train platform at the pre-scribed hour."

Höss motioned to Fritzsch, who opened the door. The Kommandant walked in authoritatively and stopped next to a huge pile of luggage of all sizes, shapes, and colors. The only element in common was that they had all been opened, and in most cases, ripped apart.

Höss motioned for Fritzsch to take up the narrative. "When you disembark at the camp, that luggage is immediately taken from you and brought here, where it is disassembled and sepa-rated by category." He looked at Höss, who motioned for him to continue. "Since you were here yesterday for a brief tour, I'll just summarize. We go through every suitcase and every coat. Watches, jewelry, currency, diamonds—all are separated out, recorded, and transported to Berlin."

"And before you cast doubt on my most loyal adjutant here," Höss added, "since the beginning of our time together at Auschwitz, I have compensated Fritzsch with 2 percent of the valuables recovered for his efforts in the Reich's behalf."

Fritzsch opened a large barn-type door, sliding it back on its rollers to reveal a mountain of clothing. "These clothes, espe-cially the coats and shoes, go back to the German population—especially now, during this particularly harsh winter."

He repeated the process at the next door, revealing pile upon pile of hair. He motioned to the Divkos' heads. "As you know, all prisoners who survive the Selektion are shaved. The hair behind me will go to Mannheim, where it will be used to stuff the mat-tresses for the U-boats."

"We saw two warehouses filled with eyeglasses," Divko said.

Höss nodded. "We're still figuring out what to do with those, as you saw. The current option under discussion is to grind them up for use in manufacturing. It would be wonderful if we could determine the prescription of each pair and match it with someone who needs it in our general population, but we don't have the resources at this time."

The next warehouse was packed to the ceiling with bones. "After incineration, the remaining bones are ground up and used for fertilizer and for road construction. And the fats—"

"Are used for soap," Perla said. "Or so we've heard."

"Actually, that's a myth. One we allow to propagate. Actually, what little fat we do garner from these corpses—and there is precious little of it—is recycled as an accelerant to help the bodies burn faster."

Höss stopped before a heavy steel door. "What you just saw is what my Jew detective calls 'the public Kanada.' Now let's see 'the private Kanada,' since it seems to be the source of not only the gold but the confusion surrounding the theft." He motioned to Fritzsch, who unlocked and swung back the heavy steel door, which opened silently.

Höss stepped forward into a large open area, the far wall of which was dominated by a stack of corpses. Already skeletal in appearance, the majority of the faces were contorted from their last strained breaths. Legs and arms were intertwined, making the first task of the two attending prisoners the separation of the selected corpse from his brethren. Hoisting them by the wrists and ankles, they brought each corpse over to a metal table, where another prisoner waited. All three prisoners seemed to find the presence of an audience disconcerting. Höss stopped by the table where a body was about to be processed. The prisoner opened the corpse's mouth, peered inside, took a chisel and hammer, and went to work.

Divko kept his eyes on Höss as the prisoner did his work. The Kommandant tried to adopt a look of cavalier indifference, but Divko saw him waver slightly on his feet and finally look away from the grisly task. He continued his narrative but with his back to the corpse and the task at hand. "Once Kanada opened, it was clear that each corpse contained its own possibilities." He motioned again to Fritzsch.

"Originally, we only harvested the teeth. But as news of the camps reached the ghettos, we found that the incoming prisoners were hiding their gold and valuables in other cavities. Hence we were forced to introduce this phase of this operation."

He motioned to the prisoner, who had extracted two gold-filled teeth and put them in a metal dish, making a small clanging noise with each tooth. The prisoner put down the chisel and took up a scalpel. With his free hand, covered with a thin glove, he inserted a finger into the corpse's anal cavity. He rooted around for ten seconds, removed his finger, and shook his head at the two carriers, who removed the body and placed it on a pile next to a large door. They then returned to the pile of corpses for their next body.

"Anything that isn't gold in these corpses—and that usually is diamonds—is taken over by Fritzsch's unit and brought back out to the area we just visited. Everything that remains is strictly gold-based."

He gestured around the room. "Harvesting is here, smelting through that curtain, and the pouring and cooling operation beyond. As I believe you'll see, unlike the operations in what my Jew calls 'the public Kanada,' there are few holes, if any, in this operation. The prisoners are searched every night as they exit, as are the guards." He looked at Divko. "And before you ask—because I know you will—yes, the personnel here are rotated every two months."

"And by 'rotated,' can we interpret that to mean 'eliminated'?"

"You can."

The Kommandant stopped at the final station, the tableful of gold ingots, and turned to the investigators. In a flat, hurried tone that didn't invite questions, he talked them through each step of his process. As he finished, he nodded to Fritzsch, who moved to open the door for him.

"Herr Kommandant," Perla called, causing him to turn back. "While we appreciate your taking the time from your busy schedule, we need more time here. This is too critical a part of the investigation to rush through. Ideally, we'd like you to walk us through the process in greater detail, but if we have used up all the time on your schedule, perhaps Herr Fritzsch can remain behind to answer whatever questions may arise."

Höss's face adopted a peevish look and he glanced as his watch. "Thirty minutes. Ask your questions."

"That should be enough," Perla said. She picked up one of the unstamped gold ingots. "Let's trace this gorgeous river back to its source and see what we learn along the way."

—⁂—

Back in the warehouse, the three investigators stared at the blackboard, dejection gripping all three. Graf took out three cigarettes from the pack on the table, and Perla lit them. All three squinted through the smoke at the board.

"That first tour of Kanada," Graf said, his voice low, prompting the Divkos to lean forward, "the shoes, hair, glasses, clothes. I said it was Organisierung at work. And I meant it. There are always spoils of war." He grimaced. "But what we saw today, all those corpses violated like that. A part of me knew they were already dead, but the larger part of me wanted to scream. He looked down at his hands, which were joined awkwardly together.

"I've never been an eager Nazi, but I've been a loyal one. But I can't defend what I saw today. That is not my Reich."

A dead air settled over the room. The three sat together in silence, each one seemingly hesitant to break it. Finally, Perla clapped her hands once, then rested them, palms down, on the table. "May I make a suggestion? I think we're in shock right now. Let's take the rest of the afternoon off to get ourselves right, then reconvene here for dinner and a working session." She started for the door.

"Before you go," Divko said, "we need to get something out in the open." He looked from one to the other. "You realize we're all dead in three days, right?"

"If we don't find the ledger and murderer, definitely," Graf admitted. "The Kommandant made that very clear."

"*Especially* if we find the ledger and murderer, Herr Graf. At that point, we become witnesses, ones the Kommandant can't afford to have around."

"But he gave us his word that—"

"The man called Perla and me vermin. And while you *may* escape our fate, I wouldn't be expecting a commendation or promotion, if I were you. Ultimately, you're a reminder of his failure. And worse, a witness to his criminality. Neither of which is convenient for the Kommandant."

When Graf didn't answer, Divko went over to the table and pointed at Perla's map. "Which makes our other assignment in some ways as important as the investigation. If we're going to survive beyond this week, we need to be of value beyond the gold. We have to be essential to their escape."

"I've told Fraülein Brandt the core of our plan," Perla said. "That you and I will be Polish police bringing them to justice."

"Then we just need a role for Herr Graf."

Graf looked up, surprised to be included in the plan.

"Not a problem. If we're escorting two prisoners, it can just as easily be three."

"I don't see the Kommandant and his girlfriend being interested in company," Graf muttered.

"Well, we'll just have to find a way to make you an essential part of the plan, won't we?" Perla said, smiling at him. "Maybe you're the one who carries all the gold. In the meantime, how the hell are we going to find our safecracker?"

"I've got an idea on that front," Divko said, "but it will depend on yet another visit to the Kommandant. And this time, he needs to meet with all of us."

# Thirty

THEY RECONVENED that evening over dinner, dividing the board in half: the left side for the gold operation; the right for the drugs. New items were recorded in the upper corner and then discussed before being assigned to the appropriate investigation. Underlined items were known facts. The rest were suppositions and questions. The board contained few underlined items.

"I know we have to investigate the drug angle," Divko said to Graf, "but my gut says it's either an intended misdirection or is coincidental to the gold investigation. Still, we need to run it to ground." He looked at the German. "What's your take?"

Graf seemed surprised to be asked, but he gave the question due consideration. "I agree that ultimately, it will come down to the gold. But I have to admit that I have a problem envisioning someone courageous—or stupid—enough to take on the Auschwitz Kommandant."

Perla weighed in. "One question we haven't considered and may not be able to get to is what happened to the gold. Is it still here in Auschwitz, and if so, how does our thief plan to extract it?"

"Storing it at Auschwitz would be easy for anyone who knows the warehouse system here," Graf said. "And that's a lot of people."

"But they'll have to extract it at some point," Divko said, "and I can't believe they'd wait until the Russians are at the gate."

"Again, if they know anything about storage, transporting it would be easy with everything that comes in and goes out of the camp on a daily basis."

"But wouldn't that require someone on the receiving end?" Divko asked. "Yet another player?"

"Not necessarily. If it were me, I'd box the bars up and mark them as containing 'dangerous chemicals'—perhaps even 'Zyklon B'—to guarantee that the box would be tucked in a corner and remain untouched until I claimed it."

They continued working until nine o'clock, when there was a knock at the door. Graf answered it and was called out into the hall. When he returned, he had a half-grin on his face and a bottle of beer in each hand. "I've been summoned back to my barracks."

Both Divkos stood up, awaiting the guard's entrance to escort them back to their own barracks. But Graf shook his head. "You two are to stay here. For the entire night. There is a message from Fraülein Brandt. 'I keep my word. Enjoy.'" He smiled at them. "I'm not sure what that means, but let me add my wishes to hers." He put the beers on the table and left the room.

—✺—

Their beers half-empty, Shimon and Perla stood next to the bed. She looked over at him, her face luminous. "I've never seen anything so beautiful in my life. Sheets."

Divko looked back down at the bed and smiled crookedly. "I'll say this for Auschwitz: It's certainly lowered the bar on what can make you happy."

He sat on the bed and felt the mattress. Then he put the beer down and fell backwards, swinging his feet and pushing his toes until his shoes fell to the floor. "Are you going to join me?" he asked, raising his eyebrows.

Perla smiled and eased herself onto the bed, settling into the crook of his outstretched arm. "I never thought I'd see you again. Much less touch you," she whispered into his neck.

"This was Gisela Brandt's doing?"

"Our reward for the escape plan. She'd mentioned something like this, but I'm so used to Nazis breaking their word that I never even mentioned it to you."

He reached over with his free arm, lifted her chin, and kissed her deeply. "I never thought I'd get to do that again, either."

Perla got up and turned off the light. When she slipped back into bed, she curled up against him. "Shimon," she said, raising her head in the dark, even though she couldn't see his face, "don't take this the wrong way, but . . ."

He reached over in the dark and put a finger on her chin, then slid it up to her lips. "You don't have to say anything. I feel the same way."

"As much as I'd love to make love to you, to feel you inside me one last time, it would feel—"

"Shameful," he said. "I know it sounds ridiculous, but I'd feel like the dead were watching us. That's no way to make love."

She burrowed deeper against him and settled in for the night. "I love it when you talk dirty."

After thirty minutes of comfortable silence, Perla spoke into his chest. "I'm glad you talked me into this Romeo and Juliet adventure. It's been so good to work together again and maybe even do something to hurt these bastards."

They brought each other up to date on their activities since the Selektion. She told him about her Oneg Shabbat activities with Magda. He told her about sabotaging the missiles. They downplayed the horrors they'd seen and the toll the past seven months had taken on them, physically and mentally. But inevitably, the talk came back to the investigation.

"What odds do you give us?" Perla asked.

"That we solve it before Himmler's visit? Less than fifty-fifty. Too many options; too little time."

"So to use our friend Rudy's phrase, we're ash by this time next week?"

"Maybe. There are two ifs on that front. If he survives the audit, which I think is doubtful. And if he wants to eliminate us more than he wants to keep us alive. Whether we find the ledger and murderer or don't, we're dead before the week's end without your escape plan. But with your plan, it comes down to whether he wants to eliminate us as witnesses or preserve us as accomplices."

Just before they drifted off, Divko spoke into the top of Perla's head. "Speaking of escape, if all hell breaks loose when Himmler arrives, we need to consider whether there's an opportunity for us to escape. I know the odds are dramatically against us, but it may be our only shot." He raised his head up slightly. "You're the escape expert. Any thoughts?"

Perla nodded. "I've given it some thought. Every option I come up with requires me to pass as a German. Which is difficult with this gorgeous hairdo. Plus the fact that I look like a walking skeleton."

"You're being too hard on yourself. Our recent diet has put some color in your cheeks and skin on your bones. With an SS cap and some makeup, you could definitely pass. And I could be a prisoner you're conducting to another camp."

Perla sat up. "Better yet, I know where I can get my hands on some SS uniforms. Male and female. We bandage you up as a wounded soldier, and I'm escorting you back to Berlin."

He nodded. "It might work. What the hell, it's a lot better than our odds five days ago." He pulled her back down gently and wrapped one arm around her shoulder and the other around her waist. "One last thing, Perla, and I don't want to argue about this. Not on this night. I love the idea of planning an escape with you. Even better, I love planning an escape where we both survive. But if our escape gets compromised in any way—and I'm dead serious about this—you've got to be the one to survive."

When Perla started to speak, he put a finger to her lips. "I've got no intention of letting you out of here without me. But if it comes to that, you're the one who can pass as German. You're the one with the evidence of the transports and gassing. And when this is all over, you're the one who knows where the remaining evidence is buried. So if it comes down to which of us survives, we need to be clear that it's you." He took his finger away. "So let's hear your argument to the contrary."

They lay there in silence for the next five minutes. Finally, Perla said into his chest, but loud enough for him to hear. "No argument. You're right."

They awoke when Graf tapped lightly on the door. He waited a few discreet moments, then opened the door, carrying a full breakfast, including steaming cups of real coffee.

# Thirty-one

"AS WE STATED BEFORE, Herr Kommandant," Perla began, "my husband is pursuing the drug angle while Herr Graf and I are pursuing the gold operation. Also, as I stated once before, we are not in the habit of asking the same question twice. But in moving forward, we have to be sure that no one else besides you and Herr Elster knew the combination to the safe."

"That's correct. No one else, not even Fritzsch."

"Then everything points to an inside job. But it also means that our thief and murderer had to rely on a third party, specifically, a safecracker."

Höss snorted. "A safecracker? On my staff? You're showing very little knowledge or respect for the SS vetting process."

"On the contrary, sir. Because of that vetting process, we don't believe the safecracker came from within your ranks or the SS population in general. We believe that this person was discovered and recruited from the general soldier population, where they would have been beyond your more strenuous vetting process."

"If that's the case, then how do you propose to find this . . . safecracker?"

"We have great respect for the Reich's recording and record keeping capabilities. We saw them at work first-hand in the ghetto.

To that end, sir, we would like to speak to you about your numbers machine. Specifically, we need access to it."

"Careful, Jewess," Fritzsch snarled. "You're stepping into dangerous territory."

"With all respect, Herr Fritzsch, there is no more dangerous territory than where we are standing right now."

"Let her continue, Fritzsch," the Kommandant said. -

Perla resumed speaking. "In Warsaw, we heard of a high-speed counting and sorting machine that was the backbone of the German census. One supplied by the Americans. It used cards with holes."

"Even if you are correct, why this stroll down memory lane?" the Kommandant asked.

"Because if this machine was used to maintain the vast numbers associated with the ghetto, it only makes sense that it would be used here as well, where the numbers and scope are so much larger."

"And if so?"

"Then we need access to it. And to someone who knows how to work it. It's the only way to find our safecracker—and your ledger—in the little time we have left."

Höss stood at the window, looking out at his camp. He tapped a pen idly against his front teeth. Finally, he put the pen down and nodded. "You assume correctly. There are such machines. They used to be centralized in Berlin, along with the few experts who knew how to work them. This centralized process worked with your ghetto and others like it. But our operation is so vast and complicated that the machine is housed here in its own room in the Farben factory with a full staff of eight Germans and one American to keep it up and running."

He motioned Fritzsch over to the window. Fritzsch listened for a moment before responding in angry hushed whispers. Höss heard him out, then held up his hand. When that didn't quell Fritzsch's objections, he sliced the air with the same hand.

"Spare me the dramatics, Fritzsch. We're running out of time here. Give them access." He turned to Graf. "But you will be present anytime the machine is accessed." He took in all of them with his stare. "And let this be the last 'request' I receive from any of you. The next time I see you, you will have answers, not more requests."

The investigators separated the next morning. Graf and Perla were escorted by one of Höss's lieutenants to the basement of one of the office buildings, where a female SS officer was waiting for them. The rest of the morning was spent in a two-hour training session on the Hollerith, including its capabilities and limitations. The SS officer gave them a pad of paper with columns on it and let them run a series of sample exercises. The two filled out the sample forms and stood back in amazement as the punch-hole cards flashed down a type of assembly line, the majority plowing ahead at amazing speed and a slim minority sliding off into nooks.

Once the training was complete, they set to work—with no success. Perturbed by their unsuccessful attempt to get it to do what they wanted, they eventually took a break.

"This is frustrating," Perla said. "It feels like the answer is there, but I'll be damned if I know how to get to it."

"We need to remember what our trainer told us at the start," Graf replied. "We need to think like the machine. It won't think for us. It will only answer yes and no questions. We can't ask it find all safecrackers. We have to ask if a specific person is a safecracker. Still, it's an amazing machine, isn't it?"

"Not if you've been on the receiving end of its power," Perla snapped, "like we were in the ghetto." She looked over and saw his face. "I'm sorry, Herr Graf. You're right. If you can take a detached view of it, it's an amazing tool. In the right hands. I hope to God the Allies are using this tool as well as you Germans have. After all, it's their machine."

Graf was affronted at the sudden turn in the conversation. "We didn't ask for this war, Frau."

"Please, Herr Graf. It's only the two of us. You Germans didn't just ask for this war, you demanded it. Lebensraum. It's Hitler's justification for Austria, Czechoslovakia, Poland—everything."

"You're ignoring the fact that Germany was punished after The Great War and pushed into very restrictive borders."

"We can relive history all you like, sir, but you know the rules. You lose a war, you live with the consequences. And the consequences for *this* war—once the Allies discover these camps—are going to be far greater than after The Great War. Unless your generals turn this war around, Herr Graf, 'Germany' and 'Germans' are going to be swear words for the next century."

When Graf didn't respond, Perla pressed on. "Tell me one thing, Herr Graf. I've wanted to ask this question since the day your troops marched into Warsaw, but I never had the opportunity." Her eyes grew hard and fixed on him. "The truth. Do you really believe you are biologically superior to me? Honestly."

There was a long and awkward pause. Perla kept her eyes on Graf, refusing to look away until she gained an answer. "No, I don't," Graf said quietly. "But you *are* my enemy, Frau Divko, both as a Pole and as a Jew. That much I *do* know." He nodded at the Hollerith. "Let's get back to work."

For his part, Divko returned to the administration building and the wall that housed the coal chute. He spent a few moments in conversation with the sight-impaired gardener, reviewing the old man's schedule and obligations. Once it was established that the gardener hadn't been back to the building in question since his conversation with the investigators, Divko thanked him and headed over to the chute. He walked slowly around the structure, his feet moving in a shuffle that ruffled the grass and disturbed the soil abutting the wall. On the far side of the chute wall, he found a stepladder folded and neatly placed against the wall and took it to the chute. When he mounted the ladder, he found that his shoulders were even with the bottom of the chute, and he was able to open the chute and hoist himself into it easily. He traversed the length of the chute and dropped into the boiler room, which he noticed had been cleaned of all traces of blood.

He hoisted himself back into the chute and elbowed himself back to the exit. Once there, he peered out and looked down at the top of the stepladder, which was now out of reach. He thought for a moment, then he grabbed the top of the chute's metal door and pushed out. The door swung open, bringing him with it. He pulled his knees up to his chest until he was fully out of the chute. Then he lowered his legs until his foot hit the top step of the ladder.

Continuing his search, Divko expanded it from the administrative building and its chute to the nearby administrative and barracks buildings. He tracked the traffic patterns, making notes of the time of day and foot traffic. The gardener had been right. There were three or four different shortcuts, two of which passed by the chute. He returned to the old prisoner and borrowed a hoe so he could continue his surveillance without drawing attention to himself. Using the hoe gently, he circled the area, stopping at the corners of the buildings that yielded a view of the chute. At his fourth stop his hoe moved through the longish grass and uncovered a cigarette butt and then two more as he cleared the area with his hands. He closed his hand gently around them and headed back to the warehouse to await the return of Perla and Graf.

They came back around five that afternoon, their shoulders rounded, their faces long. Divko poured them each a glass of water and waited for them to sit down. "So is it a miracle machine? By your faces, I'm assuming no."

"It can be," Perla replied. "But only if you know how it works. All we learned today is that if you don't ask it the right questions in just the right way, you get nothing."

"But the potential is there," Graf said, looking over at Perla, who nodded back.

"And how was your day of detecting, dear?" she asked.

"Productive, I think. Or I hope. The safecracker needed no help to access or leave the chute. Initially, I thought someone would have to be there to help him exit, as Herr Graf did with me yesterday, since you have to go in face-first and it's two-plus meters from the chute to the ground. But you can swing out, using the door to pull you out, and then either drop or use a stepladder."

"Anything else?"

He nodded and smiled. "The gardener was right about it being a shortcut. And since there was quite a bit of traffic there, our safecracker couldn't just walk up with a stepladder and hoist himself up into a chute without raising questions. Which meant he would have to do the same thing I did: surveille the scene and look for his optimal moment."

"And?"

Divko nodded at the table, where he had placed the cigarette butts. "I believe he smoked while he waited. Trying to look like he was on a break."

"Which means our first stop tomorrow is the canteen," Graf said. "Good work, Shimon."

# Thirty-two

THE NEXT MORNING, the clerk in the camp canteen passed the crumpled tobacco knowingly under his nose. "Definitely Turkish," he said. "Sultanas. Special order. This is a Davidoff camp. Almost everyone here prefers them. But a couple of the officers got in the habit of Sultanas at a previous camp, and a couple of enlisted men have picked it up as well."

"So how many Turkish aficionados are we talking about?" Graf asked.

"Less than a dozen, I'm sure." He nodded to a small metal box. "I have a list of all the special orders here."

Graf looked at the Divkos and raised his eyebrows. The clerk looked once through the box and frowned. "They were here. I'm sure of it." He went back through the cards again and this time separated two cards stuck together. "Here they are."

Perla took out her notebook and began to copy the names.

Back at the Hollerith machine, they met with the operator and showed her the list. As she punched in the names, Graf turned to Divko. "This lets us reverse our process. Yesterday we were putting in broad categories, like criminal pasts, and hoping. Today we'll try to match names with their backgrounds and skills."

"Which in this case would be what?"

Perla joined the conversation. "We'll start with the obvious: any criminal past or known criminal associations." She looked questioningly at the operator, who bent over a card, punched in a number of holes, inserted the card, and then nodded her readiness. She pressed the button and the machine swung into action, processing the cards in a second. But all the cards went straight ahead with nothing veering off into a side chute. The operator looked up questioningly.

"Okay, not a known criminal," Graf said. "That was too much to expect anyway." He looked at Perla. "What next?"

"Profession," Perla said. "Let's see if any of them worked with safes."

"Too narrow," Divko said. "How about safes and locks?"

Graf nodded to the operator, who repeated the process, again with the same results. The three of them sat dejectedly, looking at the neat stack of cards.

"Damn," Divko said. "I thought that would get us there."

"Maybe it wasn't his profession," Graf said. "Just his skill set."

"What do you mean?"

Graf turned to the operator. "Keep the same categories but add 'father's profession.'" He looked over at the Divkos. "We gathered that info during the last census."

The operator made the adjustment to the card and pushed the button. All the cards slid quickly down to their regular destination, save one, which slid out into a separate slot.

Divko reached for it. "Oskar Schmidt. Father was a locksmith. Good call, Graf."

⁓m⁓

"Before I begin my report, Oberaufseherin Brandt," Perla said, "may I express my thanks for the gift of last night. My husband asked me to thank you as well."

"No thanks required. You earned it. I trust that you and your husband had an enjoyable evening?"

"We did. It was nice to have such a . . . human moment." She switched gears. "I have news. We believe we have our safecracker. An Oskar Schmidt. We'll break him tomorrow, with the Kommandant's assistance, if needed, and see if he leads us to his employer."

"And the person who employed Schmidt is our murderer?"

"Unless he used a partner, yes. And given that a partner would just complicate life from our murderer's perspective, that is an unlikely scenario. So it looks like we're closing in."

"Your safecracker. Do you know if he's connected to our Herr Fritzsch or Frankel? Or to your Pervitin operation?"

"All we have currently is a name. Tomorrow will tell us far more."

"That's excellent progress, Frau Divko." In what was becoming a ritual during these briefings, Brandt lit two cigarettes and handed one to Perla, who acknowledged it with a terse nod. "Speaking of the motor pool, I've requested that a small transit truck be kept ready to be only at the Kommandant's disposal and no one else's."

"Aren't you afraid of someone having suspicions and asking questions?"

Brandt smiled. "Ask questions of whom? This is the Third Reich, my dear. Asking questions or harboring suspicions about one's superiors is not only verboten but often fatal. The answer is no, I'm not worried. The truck is under a tarp, and I have the only keys. I've secured and stored maps of Poland and the Baltics in the locked glove compartment. As for the other items, we will have your Latvian uniforms tomorrow. Again, good work, Frau Divko. If this project should prove necessary, I'm confident that all four of us will survive this war. And who knows, perhaps even thrive."

Perla smiled back at her. "*Fun dayn moyl in gots oyern.*" At Gisela's bemused smile, she translated it for her. That's Yiddish for 'From your mouth to God's ear.'" Perla finished her cigarette and looked through the thin smoke at Brandt. "May I ask a question, Fraülein? It's related to the escape plan, but it's also a matter of curiosity."

"Ask away. We're partners, after all. At least for the foreseeable future."

"If we have to activate the escape plan, doesn't it mean that the Allies have prevailed?" Not waiting for acknowledgement, she continued. "I have to believe that both the Russians and Americans are going to be in vindictive moods. Which means that once this war is over, there will be massive searches for not just the Nazi hierarchy, but their lieutenants as well. Won't the Kommandant be at the top of many lists?"

"Or put another way, why am I putting myself at such risk by staying with Rudolf when I stand a better chance of escaping on my own?"

"I wouldn't have put it that way, but since you have . . ."

"First off, I have to confess that I have a real fondness for Rudolf. But I'm also a realist, and I know that I'm senior enough here that the Allies will see me as an accomplice. So the key is for us to have gone underground and into the network before news of the camps becomes public."

"Network?" Perla asked.

Gisela sat back, as if considering whether to continue the conversation. Then she nodded to herself and smiled "I'll let you in on a secret, Perla. Because it won't be a secret once the war is over. Most of the Nazi leadership—I'm not speaking of fanatics like Goebbels or Göring but the next level down—aren't fanatics who will go down with the ship. We're pragmatic, especially when it comes to our own survival."

She stubbed her cigarette out and reached for the pack. "The moment that Rudolf and some of his peers saw the Russian invasion stall and then saw America join the war, they took it upon themselves to fund and develop an impressive escape network. All Rudolf and I have to do is get to Switzerland, at which point we'll receive cosmetic surgery, get new identities and passports, and travel to countries without extradition—most of them in South America."

Perla nodded appreciatively. "Impressive. And all of it funded by . . ." She nodded toward Kanada.

Gisela nodded. "For the two of us, most certainly. Each would-be escapee has contributed in his own way. Captured art, repossessed houses. Our gold and diamonds are the major source of funding, which puts Rudolf and me at the front of the queue, should it come to that."

"Who runs the network, if you don't mind my asking?"

Gisela smiled broadly. "It's run by the most unlikely of partners: the Catholics."

"How can that be? The Reich hates the Catholics. And they hate you."

Another nod. "But there's one thing we both hate more than each other: Communists. So when we approached the Church with our plan—and with millions in 'donations'—they agreed and put their local clergy and facilities at our disposal." Her smile broadened. "So if you and I should both survive this war and chance to meet in the future, I will probably be a dark-haired senorita living peacefully with my five children and Rudolf on a farm in Argentina."

# Thirty-three

"AS YOU REQUESTED, my Jew, it's just the two of us. I hope that Fritzsch's search wasn't too painful."

"I'm getting used to his familiarity, Kommandant. And it's a small price for both of us to pay to keep this conversation private."

Höss cocked his head and observed Divko with one eye closed. The prior deference in tone was missing, replaced by a new, confident voice. A small frown crept over the Kommandant's face. "And by your presence, as well as your attitude, am I to assume you've solved the case? And if so, where are my ledger and murderer, in that order?"

"I expect to deliver both to you by end of day tomorrow, murderer and ledger in hand."

"Then why are you here tonight? Not another request, my Jew. You're far past your quota."

"If 'request' bothers you, let's just call it a 'demand.'"

Höss gave way to a bitter smile. "I admire your balls, Jew. How they fit in your pants, I don't know. Let's hear your demand."

"Let's start with a basic assumption. We established that you—to give it a kind term—'rotate' your gas chamber Kapos every three weeks and the prisoners working your gold operation every two months."

"Correct on both counts."

"Which tells me that the moment we hand over your murderer and ledger, we'll be rotated as well."

Höss kept his smile and started to speak in smooth, reassuring tones. "You're very observant, Prisoner Divko. And in a normal situation, yes, you would be a liability. But I understand from Oberaufseherin Brandt that you and your wife may be of assistance at a later date, so I believe you're safe. For now." He raised his chin at Divko. "Does that change your . . . demand?"

"Herr Kommandant," Divko began, his tone pacifying. "Please excuse my pretense at arrogance. I just wanted to get your attention."

"Well, you have it. So out with it."

"As I'm sure you'll remember, sir, I initially refused to help with this investigation. I was willing to die in one of those imaginative fashions that you showed me."

"I remember. Why this latest stroll down memory lane?"

"I want you to know why I changed my mind. You played it beautifully, threatening Perla like that."

"Well, I knew, after your evening with Fritzsch, that I wasn't getting anywhere threatening you." He raised his late-night glass of Scotch in a salute but made no move to pour one for Divko.

"Well, you were correct in your assessment. And nothing has changed. Throughout this investigation, the driving force for me has stayed the same: Perla's survival. And I'm determined, as much as it is within my control, to ensure that she survives."

When Höss continued to stare at him over the cut crystal, Divko swallowed hard and leaned forward. "I appreciate our short-term alliance, sir, and the benefits it has brought with it. But I'm also mindful that we are long-term enemies. And I've seen what happens to your enemies. Which is why, since the moment I accepted this assignment, I've documented—with Perla's help—every step of this investigation. As well as your and Herr Fritzsch's operations. And hidden all of these findings, as life insurance for Perla and me."

The air between the two men seemed to shiver. Höss kept his face blank, but the clench of his jaw and the veins in his neck and temple took on a new pulse.

"You're bluffing, Jew."

"I'm not, sir, and you know it." He gestured out the Kommandant's window. "Think what we've had access to these past seven days. What we've been able to see. More importantly, what Perla, a first-rate researcher, has been able to document. The only question was whether we would be able to find an ally— someone we could both corrupt and motivate—to ensure the release of this information should anything happen to us." He stopped himself. "And before you think that it's Unterscharführer Graf, let me assure you that not only would he be too obvious a choice, he's also too loyal to you and the Reich."

He returned to his narrative. "Luckily, our investigation pro- vided us with the currency we needed to recruit our ally. You'd be amazed—or perhaps not—at what a diamond can buy. Especially when backed by the promise of one of your gold ingots upon the release of the information, should something happen to us." His eyes tightened on the Kommandant. "Do you still think I'm bluffing?"

When Höss didn't respond, Divko continued. "I'm not here to threaten but to present a proposal. Here it is: You allow Perla and Graf to return to the Warsaw ghetto ruins. The cover story, and it has the benefit of being true, is that Perla knows where the ghetto leaders hid the ghetto's collected wealth. Graf returns with the valuables, and you increase your value to the Reich."

"And what of Frau Divko?"

"Herr Graf will report that she was shot trying to escape."

"And you?"

"I am your hostage. In perpetuity. You can gas me at any time, but as I believe Fraülein Brandt would attest, in terms of your evacuation plans, I'm more valuable to you alive than dead."

Höss sat back in his chair and regarded Divko with a perplexed smile, letting the silence build for over five minutes while Divko sat patiently under the Kommandant's stare, showing neither defiance nor fear. Finally, Höss pushed back from his desk, the smile a bit more relaxed.

"I feel like Dr. Frankenstein admiring his monster. Stay where you are, my monster." He left the room and returned a moment later with Fritzsch in tow. "You have your partner in crime and I have mine" he said, nodding at Fritzsch.

Fritzsch took up a position on the far wall behind Divko, who kept his eyes on the Kommandant.

"So that Fritzsch and I are both clear, since it's our operations you're threatening to expose, in return for my acquiescence to your demand regarding Frau Divko, you'll be my eyes and ears for as long as I need them."

Divko sat back, relaxing slightly. "For as long as you need them."

"It's a generous offer, I'll give you that. And I'll accept it. But with one caveat." The Kommandant nodded slightly to Fritzsch, who stepped quickly to Divko. Brandishing a straight razor, he grabbed Divko's left ear and severed it with a single swipe. He then placed it on the table in front of Divko, whose face went white but whose eyes never left the Kommandant.

"You see, Jew, I only need one of your ears." He paused. "The question is, do I need both your eyes?"

Fritzsch grasped Divko's head and tilted it back. He looked questioningly at Höss, who seemed to weigh the option, then shook his head. "You've given me a lot to think about, Jew. And hopefully, I've done the same for you. The next time I see you, you'll have both my ledger and my murderer in tow. Now get out of my sight."

The guard opened the door and pushed a dazed and bleeding Divko into the room. Perla and Graf, who had been at the blackboard, rushed over to support him. Graf hoisted Divko's limp arm over his shoulder and guided him to a chair. Perla grabbed a towel from the bathroom and pressed it to his ear, the blood from which was flowing freely.

"Keep the towel hard against the flow," Graf said. "I'll go get supplies."

Perla pressed on the towel and drew Divko's head to her chest for extra pressure. "Shimon, Shimon," she said in a soft voice. "What did the bastards do to you?" But her question was met with silence.

A few minutes later, Graf returned with bandages and a tube of antiseptic cream. In his other hand was a bottle of whiskey. He handed the medical supplies to Perla and grabbed an empty glass. "Here, Shimon," he said, pouring the whiskey where Divko could see it. "Drink this."

Divko stared dully at the glass, not moving. He winced as Perla applied the cream, then he allowed her to begin wrapping the wound. "Drink it, honey," she said to him. "It'll help." She picked up the glass and handed it to him.

He looked at the glass for a moment and seemed to get his bearings. He downed the whiskey and placed the empty glass in front of Graf, who poured him a second shot, which he also downed.

Divko's wound bled through the initial bandages that Perla applied, so she unwrapped them and applied more pressure with the towel. Divko stayed silent the entire time, though his eyes were now clear. Perla checked the towel and the wound and saw that the bleeding had slowed. She took a new set of bandages out and began wrapping again.

Divko spoke up as she was finishing. "By God, that Fritzsch is a quick bastard with a razor."

"What did you say that angered him so much?" Graf asked.

Divko gathered his thoughts. "Fritzsch? Nothing? He was just doing the Kommandant's bidding. I think Höss is starting to panic and wanted to motivate us. I was just the messenger."

Graf poured all three of them shots of whiskey, which they each threw back in one swallow. "I can think of other ways he could have done it," Graf said, "but he definitely got my attention."

Divko tried a smile and gestured at the papers on the table. "Where are we?"

"I checked on Schmidt's schedule. We'll interrogate him tomorrow after roll call."

"Let's agree on this," Divko said, his voice now steady. "If we can't break Schmidt by noon, we enlist the Kommandant. He seems to have more methods of persuasion than we do."

# Thirty-four

"GUESS WHO DIDN'T SHOW UP for roll call this morning?" Graf said the next morning as he walked into the investigation room. Perla and Divko were back in front of the blackboard and the guard who had fetched them after roll car had remained in the room until Graf made his appearance.

"Our Herr Schmidt?" Perla asked.

He nodded. "I've recruited people I trust to conduct a discreet search for him. They'll find him, if anyone can."

"Did they say whether he was sick or sleeping one off?" Divko asked.

"They just said he hadn't shown."

Perla stood up suddenly and moved toward the door. "Come on. I think I know where we can find our Herr Schmidt."

When they got to the morgue, they found a man in a striped uniform on one of the metal tables. But the uniform was the only thing that indicated he was a prisoner. The body was too complete and fit and the hair was nicely cut. This contradiction and the accompanying paperwork had translated into the morgue doctor willingly and quickly ceding his authority to the investigators and exiting the room as quickly as he could.

"Good call, Perla," Divko said, looking down at Schmidt's body. "We wouldn't have found him today. Not dressed like this."

Graf looked at what was written on a clipboard. "He went into the wire last night after curfew. They found him at first light."

"So either he was afraid of what lay ahead—torture and either an execution or court martial—or he was pushed," Perla said. "My money's on the latter." As she talked she removed his socks and shoes. Then she spread Schmidt's toes. The blood was not completely dried, smearing at her touch. "God, I hate being played," Perla said, her voice raised.

"Played how?" Graf asked.

"The Pervitin has been meant to distract us the whole time. The three men are no more addicts than the three of us."

"But the drugs we discovered—"

"I'm sure the drug is popular here, based on what the Kommandant said, and that addiction is a problem. And I'm sure that, given the time, we could trace the drug operation back to Elster and Frankel. But at that point we'd realize we were chasing our tails. Elster, Frankel, and now Schmidt all needed to die to cover up the gold theft. But the postmortem stab wounds and injections were created to distract and mislead us." She looked down at Schmidt. "And it worked. So far, at least."

She looked at Divko. "Last night. With the Kommandant. Did you tell him about Schmidt? Specifically, did you tell him Schmidt's name?"

"I was going to, but we never got that far." He motioned at his bandage. "We got distracted."

"Our murderer has been ahead of us at each step of this entire investigation. Maybe more than one step at times." She paused. "I'm not sure of the 'why,' but the 'how' is starting to become clearer. But to be sure, Herr Graf, I'm going to need your assistance."

Perla quickly explained what she had just come to realize.

"If you're right," Divko said, "then she's played us all. Starting with the Kommandant."

"You're being kind, honey," Perla said, "but I'm the one who updated her every night, who fed her critical information that she needed to stay ahead of us by sending us in a new direction. I thought I was manipulating her when it was the other way around." She shook her head. "What a damn fool I've been."

"But why would she betray the Kommandant like this?" Graf asked. "It's common knowledge that she and the Kommandant are—"

"More than friends. But what if she has the same relationship with someone higher than the Kommandant?"

"Higher than the Kommandant? That's a very small list. And all Berlin-based." Graf looked at the blackboard. "I'm having a hard time believing this. The evidence seems a bit thin, don't you think?"

"Which is why we need to test it. Which is where you come in. I need two pieces of information to test my theory. Can you go to records and see when Fraülein Brandt's last vacation was? And can you see what numbers she's been calling from the outside exchange? And can you do it now?" Graf nodded and headed for the door.

"How sure are you it's her?" Divko asked once Graf had left.

"If I had to give it a number, eighty percent. But if I'm right, Graf is going to come back with the news that her last vacation was in May, the same month as Himmler's Bavarian holiday. And that her outgoing phone calls have been to the Reichsführer's office in Berlin."

"So her relationship with Himmler is . . ."

"Either the same as with Höss or she's been planted here as a spy."

"And the Pervitin connection?"

"That was brilliant. On the chance that an investigator with any skill would be assigned to the case, she injected Elster after she killed him. Then she did the same with Frankel, except that she increased the odds by planting the Pervitin in his closet."

"But we were the ones who discovered the injections and made the links to the Pervitin. She was betting a lot on our detecting skills, wasn't she?"

"Perhaps. But if we hadn't discovered the Pervitin operation, I believe she'd either have found a way to point us there or she had yet another misdirection at the ready. Bottom line, Shimon, is we have been struggling to determine our next move while she's been thinking three moves ahead."

Divko nodded his agreement. "She's got one other thing going for her: the Kommandant's libido. She doesn't need to cover her tracks until Himmler arrives. Just another day or so. If we go to the Kommandant with our suspicions and very little in the way of hard evidence, she'll play him like a fiddle, protesting her innocence and reminding him of their future together. By that time, Himmler will have arrived, and she'll deliver the ledger to him, wash her hands of Höss and Auschwitz, and return to Berlin with Himmler."

"And we go to the gas to take care of any loose ends."

Their conversation was interrupted by Graf's reentry. He started to speak, but Perla held up her hand. "Let me guess. The first week of May?" Graf looked at her and nodded. "And Berlin? The Reichsführer's office?" Another nod. Graf sat down, his disillusionment clear.

Divko joined in. "Which means we need to break Fraülein Brandt. Today. Before she can get to the Kommandant and muddy the water. And we need to do it without shaming him."

"I might have a way," Graf said. "I need to call the crew I used to search for Schmidt."

As the outer door to Gisela Brandt's office opened abruptly, the workers in the outer room lifted their heads quickly. Graf entered, yanking a resisting Perla in his wake and addressing the room in general. "Where is Oberaufseherin Brandt?" He pointed to the clerk nearest him. "You. Where is she?"

The woman leapt to her feet. "Conducting a roll call, sir. Shall I go fetch her?"

"I'll go myself," Graf said. He started to drag Perla with him but stopped. "This is urgent business, from the Kommandant. He nodded at Perla. This one will only slow me down." He looked at the door to Gisela's inner office, opened it, and pushed Perla in. Then he turned and faced the room. "She is not to leave this room, upon penalty of death. Hers and yours. Am I clear?" Every head nodded.

As the door clicked behind her, Perla set to work. She started with the desk first, searching the drawers closely, then the undersides of the drawers. She got down on her hands and knees and looked at the underside of the desk, touching each joint and latch without success. Next, she moved to the closet, starting with the shelves and then the hanging clothing. She shifted to the bookshelves, moving quickly but not frantically, taking books down at random and fanning the pages. Finding nothing, she leaned back against Brandt's desk and surveyed the room anew.

Then she walked over to the bulletin board, looked at the notes and postcards tacked up there, and smiled.

# Thirty-five

GISELA BRANDT STRODE QUICKLY past her clerical staff without acknowledging any of them, entered her office, and came out again within a minute. "Which of you was in my office? My papers have been disturbed."

"It was none of us," the head clerk answered. "Just Prisoner Divko. At the orders of the Kommandant's man."

"Hauptsturmführer Fritzsch was here?"

"No. The investigator. He locked Prisoner Divko in your office while he searched for you. Urgent business from the Kommandant, he said."

The woman started to say more, but Brandt was already out the door.

Five minutes later, she entered the barracks in Building 142. The room was completely empty and the tiered sleeping platform dark. She went back into the adjoining office and rummaged through the desk until she found the ledger of bunk assignments and Perla's bunk in it. She went back into the barracks and climbed the ladder to the second tier, looked around, and lifted the bedding. Feeling along the boards near the head of the bed, she came to an uneven area, lifted a slightly dislodged board, and looked in the hole. She extracted papers and notebooks, read through them quickly, pocketed them, and headed back down the ladder.

Brandt was back at her desk, reading through Perla's notes, when her door swung open without any knock or announcement. Three SS men entered. One took up a post blocking the door, the second took a seat and brought out a notebook, and the third stopped in front of the desk and looked down at Brandt.

"I have a message from your uncle in Berlin."

"I have no uncle, in Berlin or otherwise."

"Your uncle will be pained to hear that you've forgotten him so quickly, especially when he opened his home in Berchtesgaden to you."

Brandt nodded carefully. Exhibiting no emotion, she looked up at the man. "And if I were to suddenly remember this uncle, what would the message be?"

"That his visit in two days will be, to quote the Reichsführer, decisive. There will be no room for argument and no room for escape. Which means your uncle will be in possession of the ledger in time for his accountant to compare and prepare. You are to turn over to me the ledger in question, and I will return with it to Berlin on this evening's flight. You will stay here to ensure that your target does nothing to alter his fate, then you will return to Berlin with your uncle once issues are resolved to his satisfaction."

"You are misinformed. I do not have the ledger."

"The Reichsführer is never wrong, Oberaufseherin Brandt. Perhaps he is just premature in his knowledge. I've been told to tell you that either that ledger returns with me to Berlin or you do. And it won't be for a repeat of Berchtesgaden. Do I make myself clear?"

Gisela stood up and took an aggressive stance. "Perfectly. I can secure it, and I will present it to you by 16:00."

Ten minutes later, the three SS officers, now back in regular military police uniforms, stood in front of the warehouse table facing Graf and Divko. Graf gave each man a watch and two pieces of jewelry. "How did she seem?" he asked the men.

"Nervous," the first man said, "but cooperative in the end."

"And you, gentlemen?" Divko said to the others. "Your read?"

The man who had barred the door said, "Her reputation has reached us in Birkenau, so we expected someone cool and in control. She didn't disappoint."

Divko and Graf turned their attention to the third man, who nodded. "She's a tough read, even for police like us. But she had a confidence I wasn't expecting. I wouldn't be surprised if she's a no-show at 16:00."

Divko and Graf looked at each other and then stood up.

—⁂—

Gisela Brandt was exiting her quarters, a small suitcase in one hand and her briefcase in the other, when the two investigators approached. As the men neared, her posture straightened and she pulled herself up to full height. Recognizing the arrogance conveyed by her posture, she relaxed it and tried a slight smile.

"The Kommandant has asked me to go to Berlin to prepare the Reichsführer for the audit, perhaps to distract or confuse him enough that he delays his visit." She tried to move around them. "They're holding the plane for me."

"Odd," Graf said. "We just left him, and he didn't mention it all." He moved to take her bag. "But I'm sure we can clear this up quickly. He's still in his office."

Her face started to shift to rage, but as she looked at the two men and their certain faces, she adopted a face and voice of reason. "Let's cut to the chase. What do you want and what do I get if I provide it?"

"Ideally, we want the murderer and the ledger," Graf said. But of the two, the ledger is far more important, as you know. We could bring that to the Kommandant while we continue our search for the killer—a search that might very well prove fruitless or at least give the murderer time to make his escape." He smiled slightly. "Or her escape."

"And why would you let me escape? More importantly, why should I trust you?"

"Because our best chance for survival is to keep this as uncomplicated as possible," Divko said. "Our primary objective is the ledger, which, as the Kommandant has said many times, is his primary interest. We can explain that we are still trying to tie the ledger to a suspect."

She looked from Divko to Graf and back again. "And you would allow me to escape because?"

"Because we're not fools," Divko replied. "You're an unknown factor in this equation. We know the affection the Kommandant holds for you. Finding out that you are the murderer—and perhaps worse, in his mind, the thief—will make him feel foolish, a mood that you could exploit, causing him to either discount our findings or at least muddying the waters until Herr Himmler has arrived."

Gisela's face softened and she gave a girlish laugh. "He *is* smitten with me, isn't he?" She looked at Graf's surprised frown. "Come on, Graf. Don't play the upright Nazi with me. You've been hanging around these Jews long enough to know the real world when you see it." She looked from one man to the other. "Your friend Divko is right. My relationship with Rudy is strong enough to buy me at least the benefit of doubt. Which is all I need."

"We'll see what the Kommandant says when we give him the ledger," Graf replied brusquely.

She almost barked her laugh. "Now I *know* you're bluffing."

The three of them stood in the hallway in an awkward standoff. Graf looked for guidance from Divko, but Shimon's eyes were on Brandt, measuring her.

It was Brandt who broke the silence, looking more at Graf than at Divko. "What if I shared some of my gold with you?"

"*Your* gold?" Graf said. "I believe the Reichsführer is expecting to take full custody."

"And he will. But do you two really think that the Kommandant and Fritzsch are the only ones who deducted their share from this operation?" She unzipped her travel bag and took out two bars of gold. "This is just my travel gold, in case I need to bribe anyone along the way. I have three boxes of the same waiting for me in Berlin. Some of which could be yours." As Graf looked at her, she laughed sharply. "I wish Frau Divko were here to enlighten her two partners on what it's like to be a woman in a man's world." She looked from one man to the other. "I'm not going to spend my post-war years looking in a mirror, wondering when my chin will start to sag or my tits will begin to droop. I will be my own woman, either in a post-war Germany or in Argentina, and this gold is my ticket to independence."

She looked at Divko. "You called me an unknown factor just now. As such, I hope I surprise you with my next move. It concerns your beloved Perla." She smiled in satisfaction as Divko leaned forward, took out Perla's notes, and waved the notes in front of him.

"Documenting our operation is a treasonous offense, one punishable by death," she said. "Which is why, as we waste our time bluffing each other in this hallway, Frau Divko is being taken into custody and held in my office. And her jailer is under these instructions: If he doesn't hear from me within the next four hours, she goes to the gas with tonight's transport. So let's go see the Kommandant right now. By the time he hears your flimsy evidence and my counterarguments, your precious Perla will be nothing but—"

Her last word was choked off by Divko's hands around her throat. Her face held steady for a moment, calm and in control. Then her eyes bulged and her face reddened as Divko continued to squeeze. Graf grabbed Divko's arm with both of his hands and shouted his name, but his voice couldn't penetrate Divko's fury. Divko's wrist and fingers squeezed harder and dug deeper. Finally, as he pounded Divko's shoulders, Graf shouted Perla's name, and Divko raised his head. Graf held Divko's eyes and shouted that they needed Brandt alive if they were to free Perla.

Divko seemed to come back to the moment. His hands came off Brandt's neck as if scalded. She collapsed in the hallway, choking hoarsely and glaring up at Divko with a mixture of fear and hatred. As she tried to rise to her feet, he stepped back toward her. Slipping behind her, he wrapped her throat between his two forearms and choked her into unconsciousness.

Graf searched her pocket and found the key to her quarters. The two men dragged her inside. Once the door was shut behind them, Divko slumped to the floor next to Brandt. "I just ruined everything. But the way she was talking about Perla and the gas, and that smug look on her face . . ."

"She wasn't going to tell us anything anyway. Did you see her face when I told her we had the ledger? She was so sure of herself." He looked at the fallen figure. "At least now we can search for it in peace."

They searched her apartment thoroughly but came up empty.

"Let's try her office," Divko said.

Graf shook his head. "Perla was there earlier today. If it was there, she would have found it."

Divko knelt down next to her. "She was leaving, Graf. So she was either on her way to get the ledger or it's on her."

They searched her jacket and blouse. Finally, Divko reached into her underwear and came out with the ledger.

"We need to secure her and get this to the Kommandant. Then I need you to get Perla. But before we do any of that, I need to tell you about the deal I worked out with him."

# Thirty-six

DIVKO AND GRAF stood awkwardly before Höss and Fritzsch
as the Kommandant kept them waiting while he and Fritzsch
went over a series of documents. Finally, Divko stepped forward
and placed a manila envelope atop the papers the Kommandant
was working on. "It's all there. The ledger as well as the supporting evidence."

Höss grabbed at the envelope with eager hands, opened it,
and examined the ledger. A wide smile filled his face. He looked
up at Fritzsch and nodded to him to approach. The two men
looked at the ledger, not bothering to hide their excitement.

"Herr Kommandant," Divko said, waiting until their eyes
were on him before continuing. "It's your decision, of course,
but the supporting evidence is for your eyes only—especially the
correspondence with her overseer."

Höss's head jerked. "Her?" He put down the ledger and
immediately started to thumb through the stack of papers. Then
he looked up impatiently.

Graf coughed drily and straightened. "The murderer—and
thief—is Oberaufseherin Gisela Brandt."

Höss said nothing as he stared blankly at the papers in front
of him. Fritzsch looked at Divko in astonishment before planting

his eyes firmly on the floor, turning slightly away from the Kommandant. "That's not possible," Höss said finally in an almost strangled voice. "She's been my . . ."

"Whatever her role or activities here in Auschwitz has been," Divko said, "that role was superseded by her relationship with Reichsführer Himmler."

"The full nature of that relationship," Graf added, "its history and its extent, we can extract from her tomorrow. But we wanted to get you the ledger immediately."

Höss slammed the ledger down on the desk, scattering the papers he had been working on. "Impossible! She would have . . . You're telling me that all this time—"

"Herr Kommandant," Divko said, his voice firm but respectful, "Fraülein Brandt played us all for fools. All of us. She has one and only one allegiance: to herself."

Höss looked up at Fritzsch in disbelief. "My God, has it come to this? I'm getting sympathy from a Jew." His gaze shifted to Graf. "And you agree with this theory?"

"It's more than theory, sir, as those papers will attest. Please, sir. Just examine the evidence. It speaks for itself."

Höss glared icily at Graf. "Then bring her to me. I have to hear this for myself, not from some Jews and their talking dog."

Divko looked sideways at Fritzsch and then stepped forward slightly. "Herr Kommandant." He waited until Höss raised his head. "Before we bring Fraülein Brandt here, can we finalize the other business?"

"What other business?" He raised the ledger. "According to your evidence, our business is concluded." He dripped the last word out.

"Our deal involving Herr Graf and Perla. There's a truck leaving this evening and—"

Höss laughed bitterly. "Our *deal?* Where did you ever get the idea that a Reich official and an *Untermensch* are on the same plane?"

"So I was wrong to trust your honor?"

Fritzsch's step forward was halted by Höss's raised hand. "Honor is between men. Not men and lice." He turned to Graf. "Take this one and his wife to prison. Then you and I will work through this evidence on our own."

Divko was enraged. "You need us, Herr Kommandant. If the war keeps going the way it is, you'll need someone who—"

"You're right. I'll need *someone.* But that someone won't be you. I needed your ideas, and now I have them. There are plenty of Jews who know Poland as well or better than you. And whose smug faces and pity I no longer need to tolerate."

He turned his attention to Graf. "What are you waiting for? Take him and his bride to prison and come back here immediately. With Gisela Brandt in tow."

Graf grabbed Divko roughly by the arm and turned him toward the door. But Divko slipped the grip and lunged at Höss, knocking the table over and scattering the papers. Before Fritzsch could react, Graf balled his fists and brought them down at the base of Divko's neck, stunning him and knocking him to the floor.

Höss gathered himself and issued a tense smile and slight laugh. "I've changed my mind, Graf. I want this piece of shit and his wife to join this evening's transport in the gas chamber. See to it." He turned to Fritzsch. "This is one gassing I want to witness for myself."

He waved his hand, dismissing Graf and Divko. "Oh, and Graf." He waited for Graf to turn back. "You had better be right. Because tomorrow, one of you—either you or Fraülein Brandt—will be following the Divkos into the gas chamber."

As they drove off, Divko rubbed idly at the base of his neck. Graf looked over. "Did I hit you too hard?"

"No. Just right. And with just enough force to make it look real."

"How did you know he wouldn't keep his word?"

"That was the one part of the investigation I was certain of from the start. In the end, we are who we are. He's a Nazi and I'm a Jew."

Graf looked forward, his hands tense on the steering wheel. He drove cautiously, slowly, as if delaying the inevitable. "Blood and honor is our code. It's what we're raised on. But what are we without our honor? What are we shedding our blood for?"

"Then you'll do it?"

"I know my fate here. The Kommandant's eyes made that clear just now." He looked over at Divko. "I'll do it."

"You've got the uniforms?" Graf nodded. "And the pills? It won't work without them both."

Graf nodded. "I've got them. Are you sure Perla will go for this?"

"She's a stubborn woman. But if she hears it from both of us, if she sees the inevitability of it all, I think so." -

As they drove past the gas chamber, the first of the transports arrived. "We'll need to hurry." He nodded at Graf's dagger. "Give me your knife. It'll go quicker." Graf nodded and handed it over.

Höss donned his long leather coat and checked himself out in the mirror, nodding to himself. There was a brisk knock on the door. Fritzsch entered. "The car is here. The gassing will begin in ten minutes."

"Once we've seen our detectives off, if Graf hasn't brought me Gisela Brandt within the hour, go fetch them. Both of them. Kicking and screaming, if necessary. We will resolve this tonight and be ready for Himmler tomorrow."

Fritzsch saluted, a gesture that caught them both by surprise, and exited. Höss took one last look in the mirror, straightened his tie slightly, and turned to the door. His hand on the doorknob, he paused and looked back at his desk. Then he went back over to the desk and picked up the manila envelope. He started to open the envelope but looked at his watch, put it inside his jacket, and left the room.

# Thirty-seven

THE TIP OF THE SMOKESTACK glowed an angry orange going to red as it sent ash into the air and onto the courtyard where inmates continuously raked it into piles and carted it off. The bored Sonderkommandos sat on benches, their brooms and rakes at their feet, watching the assembled group of naked prisoners being addressed by the SS guard in Polish and then in German.

"It's been a long journey for you, we know. And we apologize for the crowded conditions on the train, but as you know, most of our trains are at the front. And the sooner we win this war, the sooner we can return you to your homes." He smiled. "But you are here now and are part of helping us win that war. This will be your home until the war is over and the Reich is triumphant."

He motioned at their discarded clothes. "Because the ghetto was full of disease and vermin, we have confiscated your clothes. You will be receiving new clothes once you have showered and been treated with disinfectant. When I blow this whistle, please move in an orderly fashion into the shower hall. I will greet you on the other side with the uniforms and tools you will need for the remainder of your stay at Auschwitz." He stepped away and motioned for the Kapos to begin prodding the line.

Ten minutes later, Graf's vehicle pulled up at the gas chamber. The line of prisoners, which had stretched out over two hundred yards, was now down to a dismal few. Graf killed the engine and leapt out. Grabbing his two charges, each by an arm, he pulled them roughly from the back seat and toward the platform. Divko, the steadier of the two, put out a sheltering, consoling arm and guided them both into the line under Graf's constant urging.

An SS officer walked over and surveyed the new arrivals. The man was trying to be brave, consoling the woman, who was burrowing her head into his shoulder, denying and refusing to view the line and the destination ahead. He'd seen this kind of reaction before from the more experienced and worldly prisoners who knew their real fate. "What's with these two? Why aren't they undressed like the others?" he demanded of Graf.

"A last-minute order from the Kommandant. The Sonderkommandos can strip them afterward."

"And what's with the tape over her mouth?"

"She's not a new arrival. She knows what's to come. We don't want her spooking the others."

The SS officer took out his Luger. "Then let's just take the two of them around back and put a bullet in them. A stampede is the last thing we need tonight. Makes it more difficult to untangle the bodies afterward."

Graf looked up the line, which was moving slowly but steadily through the large doors. "Look, I'm sympathetic. That's why I put the tape on. But as I said, these two are by special request of the Kommandant, who is on his way to watch. If gas is what he wants for them, gas is what they'll get." He dismissed the SS with a nod toward the front of the line and pushed the Divkos back in line.

The Kommandant's car pulled up on the far side of the gas chamber. Divko nodded at the Mercedes to get Graf's attention.

They both looked over as Fritzsch exited the front passenger's seat, opened the back door, and helped Höss out. The two Nazis looked down the line until their eyes stopped at the three figures at the end. Fritzsch said something to the Kommandant and pointed at the line.

"Hit me," Divko said. "Quick, while they're watching." Graf frowned, but Divko fixed him with a stern gaze. "Hard. They can't have any doubts about your loyalty."

Graf nodded, pulled his fist back and buried it in Divko's solar plexus. Divko gave a loud grunt, stayed bent over, and spoke, keeping his face turned from the Kommandant. "Good job. And Graf—"

"Helmut."

"Helmut. You've turned into a fine detective."

Graf pulled Divko roughly to an upright position and looked him in the eye. "Stand by the vent. It's quicker." And he walked away.

As Graf neared his vehicle, he heard Fritzsch call his name. Turning, he saw the aide walking briskly over to him. Graf moved just as aggressively toward Fritzsch, meeting him halfway, a peeved look on his face.

"What is it, Hauptsturmführer?"

"Where do you think you're going?"

"To get Fraülein Brandt, as the Kommandant requested."

Fritzsch looked at Graf, then at the line, and frowned. "Tell me where she's being held. I'll send a—"

"Fritzsch. They're closing the doors," the Kommandant barked.

He turned back to Graf. "Stay here. When this is done, we'll get her together." Graf nodded and returned to his car. The moment Fritzsch disappeared into the gas chamber's observation area, Graf got into the car and started the engine.

Divko's feet were steady and his consoling grip strong as the Kapo shoved them roughly into the gas chamber. There was the solid sound of the door clicking shut, then a slight whisper as the outer and inner seals connected and the harsh clack of the bolts settling into their locking mechanisms.

In the observation room, the Kommandant shrugged off the leather coat draped over his shoulders. A junior SS officer caught it and arranged it over the empty chair. He motioned Höss and Fritzsch to two chairs that had been set up in front of a heavy glass oval. Taking a seat, Höss looked at Fritzsch. "Clean it," he said, gesturing at the window. "I want a good view of our detectives' last moments."

Another soldier stepped forward with a pitcher of water and a towel. Fritzsch dampened the towel and scrubbed the thick glass vigorously. He stepped back as the Kommandant leaned forward, cupping his hands to seal out the viewing room's harsh light. Less than ten feet away stood Divko, still playing the consoler. Höss fixed his eyes on Divko, willing him to look up, but Divko's eyes were fixed on Perla.

Footsteps from overhead indicated that the soldiers were bringing the Zyklon up to the roof. Then came the slight scraping sound as the vents were opened. The soldier with the Kommandant's coat looked inquiringly at Fritzsch, who nodded back. The soldier said two words to his partner, who opened the door and called up to the roof. He kept the door open, allowing the sound of the Zyklon pellets being poured into the roof grates to trickle down into the observation room. Then came the sound of the vents being closed.

Even through the heavy glass, the cries of the assembled prisoners were audible to the viewers. Höss leaned further forward, his eyes fixed on Divko. As the gas began to settle in the room, Divko finally looked up. Höss knuckled the heavy glass to get Divko's attention. As their eyes met, Höss gave Divko a mock salute.

Divko nodded back, his face oddly calm. Then he turned to his companion and whispered something to her. Abandoning his consoling posture, he unwound the tape from her mouth and turned her so she faced the window.

Höss's eyes widened in disbelief as Gisela Brandt came into view. She choked once, her knees buckling, and shouted, "Rudolf! Help me!"

Höss turned to Fritzsch and the soldiers. "Stop the gas!"

"It's too late, Kommandant," the soldier next to the door said. "The door can't open for at least five minutes. A safety precaution. It's on a timer and can't be overridden."

Höss threw open the door and ran down the corridor. As he ran, his mind flashed a series of images: Divko and Graf taking Gisela somewhere private, like her quarters, where they drugged and stripped her, then hacked off her hair and put her in prison garb before gagging her and putting her into the vehicle. And Divko making a show of comforting his 'wife,' all the time hiding her in plain sight, first in the line and finally in the chamber. And if Divko and Gisela were behind that door, where were Perla and Graf?

He reached the gas chamber door and pulled at it, but it didn't yield. Calming himself, he took stock of the situation. In a commanding voice, he called for something to pry the hinges. As two soldiers scurried off, the SS officer from the observation room approached him. "The hinges aren't the issue, sir. It's the bolts. And they're time-controlled. I'm sorry, Kommandant. There's nothing we can do."

Höss returned to the observation room window and cupped his hands over his eyebrows. Inside the chamber, only a few prisoners were still standing, Divko and Gisela among them. Divko released Brandt and stood back. She directed one last panicked look at the window and then collapsed.

Divko coughed once heavily, bending over as he did so. He staggered for a moment, then straightened up. Returning the Kommandant's stare, he brought his hand up, returned the mock salute, and collapsed.

Inside the observation room, there was complete silence. Höss leaned his forehead on the observation window ledge, and Fritzsch stood by the door with the soldier. Then the phone rang. The soldier picked it up, listened wordlessly, and handed the phone to Fritzsch, who listened for a moment and hung up.

"That was the airfield, Kommandant. The Reichsführer's plane just landed."

"Now? He's not due until tomorrow."

"The tower says your investigator called him and told him to move his schedule up a day, that you had great results to share with him."

Höss sat up suddenly. Reaching into his coat, he took out the ledger and opened it. He looked at it, his eyes skittering across the pages, then held up the book to Fritzsch, revealing a child's drawings and scrawls.

"That goddamn Jew switched it on us when he attacked me in my office! Find Graf! It's our only chance. Alert all the gates. Tell them he's with a woman in an SS uniform. They are to be stopped and detained. Shot if they resist. But stopped at any cost."

# Thirty-eight

PERLA AND GRAF rode silently as they put distance between themselves and the Birkenau killing center. They were traversing the outer camps, Graf pushing the vehicle to its limits, trying to reach the final gates before the alert signal went out.

"We've got enough fuel to get to Ostrava," he said. "We overnight there and head for Germany the next day. That gives us two days to figure out a plan for getting us, the gold, and the evidence across the Swiss border."

Perla didn't react to anything he said. She sat rigidly in her Nazi uniform and cap, the wisps of white-blonde hair peeking out. Her eyes were dry, but her lips were moving slightly, as if in prayer. Behind her eyes, theatre-like, her final moments with Divko played out, starting when Graf halted the vehicle before the final turn in the road that led to the gas chamber and her husband had stepped down from his seat and looked at her with such sad eyes

*"What's going on? Where is Graf going?"*

*"He's giving us privacy. So that we can say good-bye."*

*She stood back. "Good-bye? The three of us are taking the transport, along with the papers." She motioned at the gagged Gisela. "And we've got a hostage, should we need one."*

He nodded. "There's been a change in the plans. I can't go with you."

"Don't joke around, Shimon. This is too important. And we don't have much time."

"We don't have any time, my love. The Kommandant will be at tonight's gassing. In ten minutes, he's expecting to see the two of us breathe our last. If we don't show up, he'll initiate a search. We won't even get to the main gate."

"Then we go to the gas together, like we discussed. We're a team, Divko."

"Then we die romantically, but in vain. And the world never learns about this place. I can't die with that on my soul. And neither can you."

Graf returned cautiously, still avoiding Perla's eyes. "It's time." Finally, he looked at her. "I'm sorry, Perla."

Divko held up one finger. Graf nodded and stepped back away. Divko wrapped his arms around Perla. She resisted for a moment, softly pounding his chest with her fists. Then she returned the embrace.

She leaned back to look at him. "This is not how we're supposed to end, Shimon."

He smiled crookedly. "You think I like it?"

"Our first day here, we promised each other we'd survive this place."

"And this is the only way to do that." His grip on her tightened. "If you escape, then part of me survives with you. You need to know that because it's true. You need to carry that in your heart. Always."

She held on to him, refusing to cry. "What will I do without you?"

"You fight. Always. For both of us. And trust me, I'll be watching, so don't screw it up." He tilted her head up, and their eyes grabbed at each other, tears starting to form. "Let me do this," he said in a hoarse voice. "For both of us."

Perla took his face in her hands. As she studied his face, her nose started to drip. She dried her nose on his chest, then looked back up at him and smiled. "Aren't we the romantics?" As he smiled back, she pulled his face to hers and kissed him hard. "Okay," she said in a strong, steady voice. And then she let him go.

"Do you have the ledger?" Graf asked. When Perla continued to stare out of the windshield, Graf leaned over and touched her shoulder. "Perla. The ledger. Do you have it?"

Moving robotically, she picked up a manila envelope from the floorboard and shook its contents into her lap. She placed the ledger to the side and put the rest of the papers back in the envelope, glancing at each one as she did. Along with her notes, which she had rescued from Brandt's office, were three leather-bound books from Incoming, a detailed history of four weeks of transports and gassings. She thumbed through one of the books. The sleeve of her jacket rode up slightly, revealing the last two numbers of her tattoo.

"Numbers," she muttered, as she adjusted her sleeve. "It all comes down to numbers."

The final gate came into view, guarded by two sentries. One was inside the gate house, his body lit by the gatehouse light. The sentry outside was carrying a machine gun. "Perla, the ledger. Now!"

She blinked her eyes and looked over at him. Depositing the rest of the evidence in the envelope, she sealed it and placed it back on the floorboard. She handed the ledger to Graf as they pulled up to the gate. The armed guard placed himself in front of their car, his gun resting on the metal gate arm that barred their progress.

Graf looked through the windshield and motioned the guard to come around to his window. The soldier approached, lowering his machine gun as he came. As he reached the window, Graf took on a stern face and nodded, then motioned toward his partner, who was inside the glass-walled structure and on the phone, listening intently.

Graf held up the ledger. "This document is of the utmost importance. It is critical that it get to Reichsführer Himmler, who has just landed at the airport and is on his way here." He looked at the man and hesitated. "What I'm about to give you requires a witness, so fetch your partner."

"He just received an urgent call, so if you could just—"

"More urgent than the Reichsführer?" He put the ledger back in his lap. "Then let us through and I'll try to get to him before he leaves the airport. But he won't be happy if I miss him."

The soldier stepped back. "One moment, Herr Unterscharführer." He strode quickly into the structure and put a hand on his partner's arm. The other soldier shook off the arm and gestured at the phone.

Graf looked over at Perla. "We may need to make a run for it if that phone call is what I think it is. Be prepared to get down on the floorboard."

They watched as the soldier with the machine gun took the pen from his partner's hand and wrote quickly on the pad of paper. The other soldier looked at the pad, then out at Graf and his transport. He spoke into the phone, hung up, and walked outside with his armed partner. The two of them stopped and stood at attention next to Graf's window.

Graf kept his face stiff and stern. "The two of you are to have an honor I hoped to have for myself. But my assistant and I have to drive all night to reach our destination." He paused, as if reconsidering the situation, then shook his head. "Maybe we should wait here and give it to the Reichsführer ourselves." He looked over at Perla. "What do you think?"

Perla considered the question, then just tapped her wristwatch and motioned impatiently at the road ahead.

"You're right," Graf said to her. "We need to get going. Looks like the honor—and the Reichsführer's thanks—will have to go to these two." He looked at them closely, his hand still tight on the ledger. He nodded at the book. "Can I entrust you two to make the delivery?"

The two men straightened. "Absolutely," the armed guard said.

Graf handed over the ledger to the soldier who had been on the phone. "Then the honor is yours."

He nodded with his head at the metal arm that barred their progress. The soldier with the gun scurried over and pressed down on the end, lifting the arm and motioning them forward. Graf kept his foot light on the gas until the transport cleared the cone of light from the station. Then he pressed the pedal to the floor.

As they picked up speed, a parade of lights came from the opposite direction. In the lead were two motorcycles, followed by a large staff car and a transport full of soldiers bringing up the rear. Graf pulled over, and as the oncoming lights illuminated the transport cab, he saluted. Perla mimicked the salute. Inside the staff car sat a narrow-faced bespectacled figure. If Himmler saw Graf and Perla, he gave no indication. The car hurried past, but as Graf watched in his rearview mirror, it slowed as the guard at the gate waved it down.

Graf and Perla watched as Himmler's motorcade came to a stop. One of the guards leaned into the driver-side window of the staff car and said something to the driver. A moment later a hand came out of the back passenger window, palm up. The guard placed the ledger on the palm, stepped back, and joined his partner in a rigid salute. The hand and ledger disappeared into the car and the entourage shot forward.

Graf looked at Perla and let out a sigh, his shoulders relaxing. Perla regarded him for a long moment, her face a mask of grief. Then her eyes took on a determined look and she nodded at the windshield and the beckoning night. "Let's get the hell out of here."

# Acknowledgments

THIS IS THE NICEST PART of writing a book: thanking everyone who has been a part of it in some way.

First, thanks to the folks who read *The Devil's Breath* in its earlier forms and made such valuable suggestions: Jenny Overstreet, Elaine Cummings, Jim Decker, Larry Loper, and Amanda Iles.

Once the book was what I regarded as "finished," I submitted it to Melanie Mulhall, editor extraordinaire, who used her considerable talents to greatly improve what's in your hands or on your screen.

Thanks to my marketing team, which has coordinated everything from social media to publication to publicity: Amber Gray, Annika Kalac, and Rene Bordelon of Trusty Oak and Cheryl Callighan, who guided me through all the processes and pitfalls of bringing a book to market.

Also, thanks to the gang at Pinthouse for their hospitality and vast range of IPAs.

Finally, you're a fortunate man if you have one special woman in your life. I've been fortunate and grateful beyond words to have five: my mom, Peggy Hogan (102 and still a force of nature); my business partner and great friend, Carol Broadbent; my daughters, Rachel and Maya (who also designed the book cover); and my best pal and best gal (as we say in Texas), my wife, Pamela Pearson.

# About the Author

TOM HOGAN is the author of *Left for Alive*, a novel, and coauthor of *The Ultimate Startup Guide*. He is the cofounder of Crowded Ocean, a Silicon Valley-based marketing agency that helped launch over fifty startups, including many current market leaders. Prior to his time in Silicon Valley, Tom was a lecturer in Holocaust and Genocide studies at Santa Clara University and University of California, Santa Cruz. Married and the father of two daughters, he recently retired to Austin, Texas, where he now writes full-time. His third novel, *The Confessional*, is due out in early 2022.

# Connect with the Author

THANKS FOR READING. If you enjoyed this book, please consider leaving an honest review on your favorite store.

Connect with me on:
WEBSITE: https://tom-hogan.com/
BLOG: https://tom-hogan.com/blog/
FACEBOOK: https://www.facebook.com/tomhoganauthor
TWITTER: https://twitter.com/hogcom
GOODREADS: https://www.goodreads.com/author/show/15211235.Tom_Hogan

Sign up for my newsletter and learn about upcoming/future books. https://tom-hogan.com/books/

One-third of remaining Holocaust survivors in the US have to choose between food and heat, medicine or rent. Half of all profits from *The Devil's Breath* will go to KAVOD, a mission-based organization that provides emergency aid to Holocaust Survivors in need to ensure they live their remaining years with dignity and honor. https://kavodensuringdignity.com/